CRIES IN THE NIGHT

Denver After Dark Series, Book #2

by

Kathy Clark

License Notes

This ebook is licensed for your personal enjoyment only. This ebook may not be re-sold or given away to other people. If you would like to share this book with another person, please purchase an additional copy for each person. If you're reading this book and did not purchase it, or it was not purchased for your use only, then please return to Amazon.com and purchase your own copy. Thank you for respecting the hard work of this author.

This is a work of fiction. Any resemblance to any place or person, living or dead, is purely coincidental.

TABLE OF CONTENTS

BOOKS BY KATHY CLARK & BOB KAT

NEW ADULT
Life's What Happens (written under pen name of Bob Kat)
Baby Daddy (Book #1 of Scandals Series) scheduled
November, 2013

YOUNG ADULT
OMG Oh My God! (written under pen name of Bob Kat)
(#1 CUL8R Series)
*WINNER OF BEST INDIE YOUNG ADULT BOOK
OF 2013*
BRB Be Right Back (written under pen name of Bob Kat)
(#2 CUL8R Series) April, 2013
READER'S FAVORITE 2013
BION Believe It Or Not (written under pen name of Bob
Kat) (#3 CUL8R Series) July, 2013
RIP Rest In Peace (written under pen name of Bob Kat) (#4
CUL8R Series) scheduled January, 2014

SUSPENSE
After Midnight (#1 Denver After Dark Series)
*WINNER OF BEST INDIE SUSPENSE BOOK OF
2013*
READER'S FAVORITE 2013
Cries in the Night (#2 Denver After Dark Series)
Graveyard Shift (#3 Denver After Dark Series) scheduled
for fall, 2014

ROMANCE & CONTEMPORARY WOMEN'S
FICTION
Angel of Mercy (#3 Angel Series)

Another Sunny Day
Born to be Wild
Cody's Last Stand
Cold Feet, Warm Heart
Count Your Blessings
Golden Days (sequel to Another Sunny Day)
Goodbye Desperado
Hearts Against the Wind (Crystal Creek Series)
Kissed By an Angel (#1 Angel Series)
No Satisfaction
Passion and Possession
Phantom Angel (#2 Angel Series)
A Private Affair
Risky Business
Sight Unseen
Stand by Your Man (Crystal Creek Series)
Starry Nights
Starting Over
Stroke of Midnight
Sweet Anticipation
Teacher's Pet
Tempting Fate

DEDICATION

My father was a firefighter with the Houston FD, and some of my best childhood memories were of the times I visited him at the firehouse or listened to his incredible stories. I've never known anyone who loved his job more than my dad. Just like the proverbial Dalmatian, whenever he saw smoke when he was off duty, we would jump into the car and track down the fire. He was the kindest, gentlest, strongest man I've ever known. This book is for my dad . . . my hero.

Thanks to all those amazing men and women who risk their lives every day to rush into burning buildings while trying to get everyone else out alive. Forget sports and movie stars . . . the real heroes wear clunky rubber boots, fifty pounds of equipment and fire helmets, drive big bad-ass fire trucks and know how to save the day while looking gorgeous and cooking great meals in the firehouse.

A special thanks to the firefighters at DFD Station 26, especially Captain Steve Barker (who helped me with the details and is also a brilliant editor!) and Scott Cruz (who modeled the uniforms for me). Their information on day-to-day operations was invaluable. And also to South Metro Fire Rescue, especially Becky O'Guin. I was lucky enough to attend their Citizens Academy which I would highly recommend to everyone. It's a fun and an eye-opening experience. I hope I didn't screw things up too badly and that I did you proud.

CRIES IN THE NIGHT

CHAPTER ONE

The back door slammed with such force that the small house shuddered. In the spare bedroom the woman froze in front of the ironing board, the iron paused in mid-air. Steam poured out of the holes with a hiss, but she didn't notice. Instead, her gaze raced across the room and met the wide eyes of her son who had been playing with a boxful of Matchbox cars.

He dropped the tiny red Ferrari he had been holding and scuttled backward, disappearing under the bed. No words had been spoken, but he knew the drill. This wasn't his first rodeo. He had learned early that out of sight also meant out of the line of fire.

The woman wasn't so lucky.

Heavy, quick footsteps signaled the man's approach down the hallway. Her heart pounded in her chest, and she realized she hadn't taken a breath since he had entered the house. She exhaled slowly, trying to calm her nerves and steel herself for the battle ahead. Even before she saw his face, she knew he was angry . . . at her, at his son, at his boss, at his life. It didn't really matter. He always came home to share his dissatisfaction with her.

"Where the hell is he?" The man wasn't large, but when he was in one of his moods, he seemed to expand in size until his presence filled the doorway.

"Who?" she managed to ask, struggling to keep her expression under control. For some reason, it made him angrier if she showed fear even though her legs were visibly trembling.

He threw his car keys at her. She tried to dodge, but the unexpected movement and her own swollen bulk slowed her. The keys smashed into her left cheek, then fell to the floor with a clatter.

"You know who. That piece of shit kid. He left his goddamn sled in the driveway and I ran over it. Twenty bucks. Trashed. I work hard and get paid shit. And he just throws his toys around like they were nothing."

"He's usually really careful . . ."

He cut her off. "Didn't he go to school today?"

"They had a teacher's workday."

"Then he has no excuse for not bringing in the garbage cans."

"It was snowing too hard."

"Not too hard for him to play." He kicked the basket of laundry against the wall. "You fuckin' baby him too much."

"He's only six." She knew that arguing only made him angrier, but her motherly instinct was to defend her young.

The man's dark gaze raked the room before focusing on the abandoned Matchbox cars. His nostrils flared and he moved toward the bed, knowing it was the most likely hiding place.

"No!" the woman cried. "Leave him alone." She reached out to grab him, but he swung his arm to fend her off as if he was swatting away an annoying insect. She reacted by striking back. Unfortunately, the iron was still clenched in her hand. The hot surface landed flat against his forearm and the back of his hand. Steam oozed out of the holes as the skin sizzled.

With a guttural roar, he jerked back as quickly as possible and looked down at the arced-shaped blisters that had already bubbled up. Like an enraged bull in the ring distracted by the matador's cape, he turned his attention back to her.

"What the fuck?" He knocked the iron out of her hand, grabbed the front of her sweater in his meaty fist and pulled her forward, over the ironing board which clattered to the floor. Her feet scrambled to keep upright as he dragged her over the metal legs.

"I . . . I'm . . . sorry, Carlos. I didn't mean to . . ."

He silenced her with a punch in the jaw so hard that her teeth rattled. Momentarily dazed, she didn't struggle as he slammed her back against the door frame. Her head cracked against the wood and she could feel the sharp edges biting into her shoulders. She didn't fight back as he hit her again and again. She knew she deserved this. If she hadn't hit him with the iron, he wouldn't have come at her like this. The skin over her eye slit under his knuckles, and she could feel the warm flow of blood pour down her face. As bad as it hurt, she knew it was nothing like the pain he was feeling from the burn. So she let him take it out on her. She owed him that.

It wasn't until his blows moved lower that her defense mechanism got its second wind. His fist buried into her breast. Swollen from the imminent birth of her baby, the pain shot through her like a lightning bolt. He drew back and would have landed a blow in her expanded abdomen, but she collapsed, trying in the only way she knew how to defend her unborn baby. He released his hold on her sweater, but instead of stepping away, he kicked her.

She curled her body in a protective shell, putting all the flesh and bone she could between his steel-toed boot and her stomach. He kicked her again and again, cursing her with words that burned her soul as much as her ears. Finally, she blacked out.

A child's scream woke her. She struggled to open her eyes, but one was swollen shut.

"Mama, mama!" the little boy cried.

Her hands slid in the puddles of blood on the floor as she struggled to push into a sitting position. Her blood. She could see it staining the white yarn of her sweater. In the back of her mind came the random thought that that was her favorite sweater, and now it was probably ruined. She had so few clothes that still fit.

Her son's small hands wrapped around her wrist and she stifled a scream as he pulled. Pains shot up and down her arm telling her it was probably either broken or badly bruised. Her brain struggled through the fog as she tried to remember where she was and why she was bleeding and aching all over.

Carlos! She straightened and tried to look around. Was he hurting Danny? Her son seemed to sense her fears and with a maturity well beyond his years, he comforted her.

"He's gone. But he hurt you," Danny told her.

"I'm okay," she lied, trying, as always, to protect him from the truth. But this was worse than the last time which had been worse than the time before that which had been worse than the time before. She could remember them all. In a twisted measure of days, months and years, each marked a new ending and a new beginning of sorts. She had never doubted that she had done something wrong to deserve his anger, and she had never doubted she would survive. This time, she wasn't so sure.

A searing pain, much deeper than all the others pierced through her, starting deep in her stomach and radiating out. She heard another scream and was surprised that it had come from her mouth.

"Mama . . .?" Danny's voice was terrified.

The room began to swirl around her, and her vision blurred. Another pain doubled her over and she slid back to the floor.

Julie's cell phone began ringing as she juggled a bag of groceries in one arm and inserted the key into her back door lock.

"Hold on, hold on, hold on . . .," she chanted as she hurried inside, dropped the bag on the table and pulled her phone out of her purse.

"This is Julie," she spoke into the small receiver.

"*We've got a domestic and fire at 238 W. Maple Ave.,*" the voice recited crisply.

"I heard it on my scanner." As she spoke, Julie held the phone against her ear with her shoulder and jotted down the address on a piece of unopened mail. "I'm on my way."

"*I'll notify the officers on-scene. What's your ETA?*"

"I'm pretty close. I'll be there in ten."

The line clicked off and Julie let the phone slide off her shoulder and into her hand. She grabbed the perishable items out of the bag and tossed them into the refrigerator and left the rest of the items to be put away later. She picked up her keys, checked to make sure her thin billfold was still in her pocket and left without bothering to take the address with her. She knew it by heart. She had been there before.

Less than ten minutes later, she found a parking space. It had been snowing off and on all day, and it had picked up again just before she arrived. Julie looped her scarf around her neck, buttoned her coat up, pulled on her gloves and got out of her car. A white ladder truck and an engine with the familiar DFD logo painted on it were parked directly in front of the house, their hoses snaked across the snow. The generators rumbled, spotlights focused their harsh beams on the action, radios crackled with sporadic chatter and firefighters shouted back and forth to each other as they focused a steady stream of water on the blaze that had gobbled up the left side of the house.

Julie quickened her pace as much as she dared on the icy sidewalk made worse by the steady flow of water that was draining from the house. An ambulance was at the end of the driveway. The back doors were open and the stretcher was out.

"Hey Julie. Sorry to get you out on a night like this," one of the cops said as he approached her. He flipped his little spiral notebook closed and tucked it into the breast pocket of his jacket.

"Is she alive?" Julie held her breath, afraid of the answer.

"Barely. He beat the shit out of her . . . again."

"No surprise there. Why can't you guys put him away for good?"

The cop shrugged. "She always bails him out and won't testify against him."

"I thought she had a restraining order against him."

"She does. But an RO is only paper. It doesn't stop fists."

Two paramedics pushed the stretcher down the driveway from the house. A thin blanket covered the woman's prone body. Her young son walked beside it, his hand on his mom's arm, a gesture that was probably reassuring for both of them. It wasn't until she got closer that Julie noticed the rounded mound showing the woman was pregnant.

"Oh my God," Julie cried and hurried over to the stretcher.

The woman looked up at her . . . or tried to. Her swollen and battered eyes clearly hampered her vision, but she was able to recognize Julie. An expression flashed across her face, one that was part embarrassment and part happiness to see someone she knew. "Julie . . . I know what you're thinking . . . don't be mad at me," she said in a voice that shook with pain.

"Gloria, you don't have to apologize to me . . . or to him," Julie rushed to calm her. She gently took the woman's hand and walked next to the stretcher as the two paramedics struggled pushing it through several inches of unshoveled snow and over the shattered remains of a sled.

"He didn't mean to hurt me," the woman told her.

Like hell he didn't, Julie thought, but aloud she said, "How do you feel?"

Gloria lifted her other hand that already had an IV attached and rubbed her belly. "Not so good. I'm worried about my baby."

Julie looked up at one of the paramedics and he shrugged. "They're going to do everything they can to help you both," she told the woman.

"I burned him with the iron. That's why he got so mad," Gloria continued, anxious that Julie know why the event had happened.

"You need to focus on yourself and your baby," Julie spoke soothingly. "I'll stay with Danny until someone comes. Have you called your mother?"

Gloria turned her head as if afraid of being overheard. "No, would you do that for me? Her number is in my phone . . . you know, the one you gave me. It's hidden in the laundry room. Danny will show you." She tried to give her son a smile, but she could manage only a stiff grimace.

The little boy looked at Julie and nodded shyly.

"We've got to go," the female paramedic said as the stretcher reached the ambulance. She and her partner prepared the stretcher for loading and Julie reached out for Danny's hand.

"Only *my* mother," Gloria pleaded, twisting around and leaning toward Julie. "Don't let him go with anyone else. Promise me."

"Don't worry about him. I promise I won't leave him until your mother comes for him," Julie assured her, and Gloria relaxed back against the cushion. The two women weren't long-time friends or even acquaintances. Their relationship had started almost two years ago when Julie had responded to a domestic call. That one hadn't resulted in hospitalization. But it had been the first in several similar events that had created a trust great enough that Gloria knew she could leave Danny in Julie's care.

Danny trembled but didn't pull his hand away as he watched his mother being loaded into the ambulance. The red and blue lights bounced off the surrounding trees and houses, magnified by the stark whiteness of the snow and turning the still-falling snowflakes into confetti. Julie looked down at the little boy whose gaze followed the twinkling lights as they disappeared down the street. Looking down she realized he wasn't wearing a coat. She unbuttoned her own, took it off and knelt down in front of Danny. Even though it was much too large and drug on the ground, he burrowed gratefully into the warmth of the wool. Shivers of cold and lingering fear shook his tiny body. "They're going to take good care of your mama. But right now we need to call your grandma. Can you tell me your mom's secret hiding place?"

"It's in the house," he told her, then lowered his voice to a conspiratorial whisper. "In the smelly things."

Smelly things? Her mind scrambled for what that might mean. "Dirty clothes?" she asked.

"No, the good smelly things. You know, the ones with the little bear on the box," he whispered back.

"Dryer sheets?"

He nodded.

Good choice. Men like Carlos never did laundry, so it would be unlikely he would stumble on it there. Julie looked around. Apparently the fire was out. Smoke no longer billowed from the roof, and the firefighters were straightening out the hoses in preparation of rolling them back up. One of the firefighters walked out of the house with an axe swung over his shoulder. She lifted her hand and waved at him. She recognized him from several other fires she had been called out to.

He noticed and walked toward them. He was tall, well over six feet. Dressed in full firefighting uniform, he looked big and menacing, sort of like an urban alien. Steam radiated from his long black coat with its yellow reflective stripe and the top of his black helmet. He had an air canister strapped on his back, but he had unfastened his respirator and it hung off to one side. His face was smudged with a layer of carbon, marked with paths where sweat and water had streaked down. After giving Julie a crooked grin, he swung the axe to the ground and knelt in front of Danny, as if he knew what an imposing sight he must be.

"You must be Daniel," he said to him. "I saw some amazing drawings on the refrigerator. I was hoping I would get to meet the artist. Were those yours?"

Danny nodded solemnly, but Julie could see that he was flattered.

"And that must have been your room with the race car posters."

Again Danny nodded. "Did my room burn up?"

"No, we were able to stop the fire before it got to your room. But I'm afraid some of your things got a little wet and are going to smell like smoke."

"How about my baseball cap? The doctor people made me and my mom leave so fast I didn't get it."

The firefighter said, "Oh yeah, I remember seeing a couple caps in there. They'll be fine." He took off his helmet and held it out to Danny. "Maybe you'd like to wear *my* hat."

Danny's brown eyes stretched wide. "Oh yes, sir."

The man set the hat on the boy's much smaller head and it settled down to cover his ears and face all the way down to his nose. Instead of taking it off, Danny lifted his chin and looked out from underneath it. But most noticeable was the twitch of a smile that had softened his tense lips.

The firefighter stood and turned his attention to Julie. He pushed the heavy cloth hood off his head, revealing rumpled dark brown hair. As he looked at her, she was struck by the clarity of his bright blue eyes.

"You're Julie, aren't you?" he asked.

She was a little surprised that he knew her name because they had never actually spoken. Not that she was a stranger to any of the public responders because Julie or one of her volunteers showed up at all of the more serious crime, fire or accident scenes. "Yes, I am. And you're . . .?"

"Rusty," he answered and pointed toward his last name that was printed on his jacket as he added, "Wilson. I'm sure you know my younger brothers."

"Oh, so you're *that* Wilson," Julie teased. She was very well acquainted with his brothers. Sam was a Denver cop who she worked with often, and Chris, the youngest, was a paramedic out of Denver Health. He wasn't one of the ones on scene tonight, but their paths had crossed often in the course of their jobs.

Rusty held up his hands. "Whoa, you can't believe everything you hear about me."

"Why do you assume it's all bad?" she asked.

"Because some of it is true. I'm the first to admit that I enjoy life. But my brothers like to exaggerate my . . .," he grinned, ". . . transgressions."

Julie shrugged. This was not a point she wanted to debate in the middle of a snowy night when she was without a coat. "I was just wondering if someone could take me inside for a minute. I need to get Danny's things and . . . well, something else."

"Sure, I'll take you in, but he needs to stay out here." Rusty called over one of the other firefighters. "Jackson, would you hang with my friend Daniel for a few minutes?"

Jackson, a middle-aged black firefighter who had just finished shutting off the hydrant and screwing the cap back on, nodded and knelt down next to Danny. "Hey buddy. My name is Jackson. Do you mind keeping me company while they go get some of your clothes?"

Danny nodded, solemn again. He stayed, but his gaze moved back to Julie.

"Don't let anyone take him away, okay?" she asked Jackson.

"Gotcha," Jackson confirmed.

After giving Danny a reassuring pat on the head, she turned to follow Rusty.

"Don't forget my cap," Danny called after her.

"I won't," she called back.

"Watch your step," Rusty cautioned. He had taken a flashlight out of his utility belt and turned it on, illuminating a wide arc of destruction.

Apparently, the electricity was off and the spotlights didn't penetrate past the front door. The dark house took on a sinister spook-house sort of feeling as they stepped over the threshold and into the smoldering interior.

"The fire didn't make it to this part of the house, but the back two bedrooms are pretty much gone," he added as they made their way around pieces of furniture that had been knocked over or tossed out of the way.

"Any idea what caused it?" She followed directly behind him, keeping her hand on his back because nothing could be seen outside the beam of his light.

"Looks like an iron on the carpet. But the investigators will find out for sure."

They picked their way along the soggy carpet of the hallway. Even though the flames hadn't made it into the hallway, the sheetrock was damp and there was a heavy, acrid smell that burned her lungs. When they arrived at Danny's room, she hurried to collect his jacket and a few items of clothing, including his Little League baseball cap that was sitting on his chest of drawers. She also scooped up the stuffed monkey that held an obvious position of importance on his pillow and stuffed it all into his Cars backpack.

"We need to get out of here," Rusty reminded her.

"I have one more thing," she told him. "Did you happen to notice a laundry room?"

"Not in this part of the house. Maybe off the kitchen?" He led the way back down the hall and across the small living room to the kitchen. Sure enough, in the mud room that led outside was a small stackable washer and dryer that had probably been one of Gloria's prized possessions. But Julie had eyes only for the box of Snuggle dryer sheets on the shelf next to it.

"Really?" Rusty asked when he saw her pick it up.

She didn't answer, but pulled out the sheets until she reached the bottom of the box. Nestled there, just as Danny had told her was the emergency cell phone she had given Gloria the last time Julie had been called out to this house. It was something she often gave to victims of domestic abuse because their controlling spouse or partner often refused to let them have any contact with the outside world. She was glad to see that Gloria had listened to her recommendation to hide the phone in a safe place where Carlos wouldn't find it because Gloria clearly hadn't paid any attention to Julie's other advice to not let him back in her life. Julie held up the phone so Rusty could see it, then followed him out the back door and to the driveway.

Once back outside, she took deep, cleansing breathes of the crisp cold air. "I don't know how you guys do it," she admitted to Rusty.

He flashed her a grin, his teeth looking incredibly white against his soot-blackened face. "Are you kidding? I'd do this even if they didn't pay me. But don't tell anyone."

Julie flipped open the phone, turned it on and watched as it booted up. "Hey thanks," she told him.

"No problem." His expression sobered. "You do good work, you know. They need someone like you to help them after all this." He motioned around them at the devastation. Yes, they had saved most of the house, but the smoke and the water had ruined much of what the flames hadn't consumed. These people had lost a lot, if not everything, and they would need all the help they could get.

"Hey Wilson. We're ready to roll," the captain called and gave Julie a wave of acknowledgment.

They walked back to where Danny and Jackson waited. Rusty reached down and lifted his heavy helmet off of the boy's head. "Thank you for taking care of my helmet for me. It looks good on you, but I'm going to need it in case I have to go to another fire tonight."

"Sure," Danny said with pride at having accomplished something so apparently important.

"Maybe you can get your mom to bring you by the fire station sometime when she feels better," Rusty suggested. "I'll give you a tour and let you sit in a fire truck."

"Really? Wow, okay," Danny agreed.

Rusty looked back at Julie. "And I'll see *you* around."

"Yeah, we seem to hang out at the same places." She smiled. "Thanks again." She nodded her head toward Danny, indicating that his kindness toward the little boy hadn't gone unnoticed.

Rusty dismissed it with a shrug, but he gave her another grin as he put his helmet back on and headed toward the waiting fire truck.

"Julie, we're finished, too," the police officer who had been standing nearby talking to the captain told her.

"We can sit in my car and wait for his grandmother," she suggested, but the officer shook his head.

"I can't leave you here. It's still a hot scene."

Julie glanced around, suddenly nervous. "You mean he's not in custody?" she asked while being careful to keep the conversation as neutral as possible.

"He was gone when we arrived, but you can bet he'll come back."

She shivered, not just because of the cold that was penetrating her heavy sweater. She had never actually met Carlos, but she had seen his handiwork on at least three occasions. "Let me make a quick call to Danny's grandmother so she can be on her way." She went to the Contacts' list. There were only two numbers in it. Gloria's mother and Julie's cell phone. Even though she had encouraged Gloria to call her if Carlos came back, it was now clear that that hadn't happened. She clicked on the word *"Mom"* and put the phone to her ear.

It rang five times before a sleepy voice answered, *"Hello."*

Julie turned away so Danny couldn't hear the conversation as she gave Gloria's mother a quick summary of the evening's events. "I'm taking Danny to the police station. We'll wait for you there." She gave the woman the address, and after getting her confirmation, Julie hung up.

"Okay, Danny, we're going to get to ride in a police car. Have you ever done that before?"

He shook his head, but there was a spark of excitement in his eyes.

"First, I'm going to trade you coats," she told him. She released his parka from his backpack where she had clipped it and handed it to him. He took off her coat, and they exchanged. She welcomed the warmth as she slipped her arms into the sleeves and buttoned it up. Danny had a little trouble with his zipper, so she helped him get it started, then reached into the backpack and pulled out his cap. The first genuine smile of the night spread across his face as he put it on and tugged it into position. She didn't even need a voiced "thanks" because his expression said it all.

The police officer unlocked the doors of his cruiser and opened the back door for them. Julie glanced back at her white Kia that was parked down the street. She knew it was city policy that she couldn't carry civilians in her personal vehicle and she had promised not to leave Danny's side until his grandmother arrived. That left her no choice but to ride with him in the patrol car to the station. She would worry about getting a ride back to pick it up later. Since Danny's grandmother lived in Fort Collins, it would take her several hours to get dressed and drive to the station.

The spotlights that had illuminated the scene switched off as the fire trucks prepared to leave. With only the red and blue emergency lights still flashing, the night seemed darker and the shadows deeper. Julie glanced around. She had the uncomfortable feeling that Carlos was there, out of sight, but watching as she took his son away from him, hopefully forever. She shivered again and silently urged Danny to hurry up. She wanted to be inside the safety of the cruiser.

As soon as he was inside, she climbed in after him and tried not to notice the telltale smell of urine and vomit that usually clung in the air of the back seats of all the patrol cars. It had been a long day and was turning out to be a long night. But she, like Rusty, loved her job and would rather be here than any place she'd ever been. Only she knew how desperate she was to never go back.

CHAPTER TWO

By the time Danny's grandmother arrived, it was almost seven a.m. Julie carried the sleeping child to the grandmother's car and settled him in the backseat. He was so exhausted, he didn't wake even when she buckled him into the car seat and tucked a blanket around him. She handed the grandmother Danny's backpack and made sure his cap was zipped safely inside.

"I'm so sorry it took me so long," the grandmother said. "The roads are icy, and I didn't want to slide off into a ditch."

"I don't blame you for taking it slow. We stopped at McDonald's and Danny ate some chicken nuggets," Julie told her. "Then he conked out. I'm sure it was a traumatic day for him. Who knows when it all started."

His grandmother shook her head. "I've told Gloria to leave that worthless piece of shit, but she won't listen to her mother."

"Yeah, well, she didn't listen to me either."

Gloria's mother's anger faded as she asked, "Did she lose the baby?"

Julie shrugged. "I don't know. I haven't talked to anyone from the hospital since they took her away. I'm going to drop by to see her later today."

"It's Denver General, right?"

"Yes," Julie confirmed.

"I'll swing by there on my way home. Maybe they'll let me talk to her."

"She needs to have a safe place to go," Julie said gently. "I'm sure Carlos will come looking for her at your place, and you shouldn't try to confront him. He's going to be furious. And we both know he likes to hit women."

"I have to admit, I'm afraid of him."

"You should be. He's dangerous and he's desperate. That's a lethal combination. I wish I could tell you that a protection order would keep you safe, but you and I both know it won't. Do you have a friend or a relative that Carlos doesn't know where Gloria can hide out? At least until they can find and arrest him."

The grandmother nodded. "There is an aunt . . ."

Julie held up her hand. "No, don't tell me. Don't tell anyone. Just get her there and keep your mouth shut. And don't let her bail him out . . . again."

"I'll do everything in my power to keep her away from him." She gave Julie an awkward hug. "And thank you."

Julie smiled and shrugged off the gratitude. She watched until the grandmother's car turned out of the parking lot and headed toward Speer Blvd. Her shoulders drooped. She hoped this was the last time she had to rescue Gloria and Danny, but statistics weren't in her favor. Gloria could be the poster girl for someone caught in the abused wife syndrome. One minute he was beating her senseless and the next he was bringing her flowers and begging for forgiveness. Sadly, Gloria was more likely to take him back than she was to kick him out.

Julie had seen it all too often in the last five years. Ever since she had taken over as the head of the Victim's Advocate Department, she had seen so much tragedy. Her duties included showing up whenever there was a death or an accident or a domestic dispute. Any kind of an incident that left someone vulnerable and needing a friendly face and a calm, logical voice. Emotions were always high. The police were there to deal with the actual event, not to offer comfort. Julie or one of her volunteers were there to help the victim ease to the next step in their acceptance and healing process, as well as tell them where to find legal advice when necessary.

She wasn't there to see the victims recover and heal. She was there only when things were at their worst. Julie rarely saw happy endings.

That didn't bother her as much as being called out to the same address again and again, especially for a domestic or child abuse case. That meant she had failed in her earlier attempt to help the victims escape from their dangerous situation. It was almost a sign of success when she didn't hear from them again.

Julie shivered and pulled her coat tighter around her. She turned to go back inside and see if she could talk one of the cops into taking her back to her car. A horn honked behind her, and she jumped.

"Hey, need a lift?" a cheerful voice called out.

She whirled around and saw Rusty, smiling at her out the open window of his red Explorer. "What are you doing here?"

"Just got off work and figured I'd swing by and give you a ride back to your car."

"How did you know I was still here?" she asked, then waved her hand to stop his answer. "Never mind. It's the brotherhood thing, isn't it?" Cops and firefighters were notorious for how quickly news spread. "I'm sure I can get a ride from someone . . ."

"What am I, chopped liver? I'm here and the heater is already warmed up."

"*Your* heater or the car's?" she was compelled to ask.

"It's eight o'clock in the morning, and I just finished a hard night's work. Right now, all I'm offering is vehicle heat. Maybe next time . . .?"

"You are doing nothing to mitigate your reputation."

His handsome face creased into a crooked grin. "Good. Wouldn't want to change something that's taken me years to build." He leaned over the seat and opened the passenger door. "I'm letting all this wonderful heat escape."

As tired as she was, she had to smile. It was pretty ridiculous to be standing in a snowstorm discussing something as unimportant as whether or not he was a player. "Give me a minute to log out."

He nodded and pulled the door closed to keep the warmth inside. She could feel his gaze on her as she ran back into the building. It actually took a couple of minutes to log out and lock up her office, but soon she was back in the parking lot and climbing into the Explorer. As promised the blowing heat on her chapped skin felt wonderful. She took off her gloves and rubbed her hands in front of the vent.

"Thank goodness it's Saturday and I can sleep in," she said.

"Lucky you're off on the weekends."

"Yeah, lucky me. But I'm not really off. I usually take the night shifts on weekends because it's so difficult to get the volunteers to commit."

"On call or in the office?"

"On call." The warmth swirled around her like a caress and she realized how very tired and hungry she was. It had been well over eighteen hours since she had grabbed a bag of Doritos and a Diet Coke out of the machines in the break room. Her stomach growled in protest. She pressed her hand against it and slid a look over at Rusty, hoping he hadn't heard it.

Of course he had.

"Tom's is right on the way. Why don't we swing by there for breakfast?" he offered, almost successfully hiding his smile.

She was tempted, more for the food than the companionship. Breakfast sounded heavenly, but Tom's was a well-known cop hangout, and the last thing she wanted was to be seen there . . . with a firefighter. At this time of night, or rather morning, she could only guess what assumptions would be made. She had gone five years without accepting a date or even a casual dinner from any of the cops and firefighters she worked with, and she wasn't going to open that door now.

"No, all I want right now is a long, hot bath and some sleep." She kept her gaze focused out the windshield as if the flurry of snowflakes was mesmerizing.

"Some other time, then," he offered vaguely.

The rest of the drive along the almost deserted streets of Denver was in silence. Surprisingly, it wasn't uncomfortable as neither felt compelled to keep the conversation going.

Gloria's house was a dark hulk in the otherwise well-lit street. Rusty pulled up next to Julie's Sportage and stopped. She gave him a grateful smile and opened the door. The acrid smell of burned lumber, plastic and chemicals hung in the air, overwhelming the clean, crisp scent of fresh snow.

"I'll follow you home."

She shook her head. "I'll be fine."

Rusty reached out and grabbed her wrist. "He still hasn't been arrested."

He didn't have to go on. Julie knew all too well that if Carlos was out there and saw her, he would be probably be angry and possibly want revenge. She would be the easiest target. He couldn't go after the police or the firefighters, but the woman who was advising his wife to take his kid and leave him was a person who deserved to be punished. Victim's advocates often became the recipient of transferred emotions because the abusers didn't like losing control. Instead of accepting blame, they held the advocates responsible for the loss of their families.

She shrugged and nodded her acceptance. He let her go and watched as she got into her car, started it and pulled out. He stayed behind her, his headlights providing a comforting glow in her mirrors as they traveled through the dark roads of sleeping neighborhoods until they reached her small two bedroom bungalow on Grape St. He followed her into the driveway and waited while her garage door opened, and she drove inside.

The garage was not attached to the house, so she had to cross a short covered breezeway to get to the back door of her house. She had left in such a hurry that she hadn't turned on the back porch light, so she was actually grateful for the illumination of his SUV's headlights. The garage door eased closed behind her as she turned the key in the lock and opened her back door. She reached inside and flipped on her lights, then leaned back out and waved at Rusty.

The headlights blinded her, but he gave her a quick flash of his high beams before backing out of her driveway. She was about to close the door when a flash of gray rushed out of the darkness and pushed its way inside, then began winding its way around her ankles.

Julie smiled as she closed the door and snapped the locks into place. "Bet you were about to give up on me tonight, weren't you?" She leaned down and stroked the tiger-striped cat's cold back. The loud hum of his purring welcomed her home. She hadn't chosen to have a pet, but he had chosen her. The old tomcat had showed up on her doorstep a couple of years ago and she had shared her tuna fish sandwich with him. He had stayed, sleeping indoors during the day and running outside to roam the neighborhood at night. On cold nights, he often finished his travels early and appreciated his warm perch on the ottoman in front of the floor vent.

She snapped the top off a can of cat food and dumped it in his bowl before she opened the refrigerator and stared inside. After deciding it was too much of an effort to even microwave a frozen dinner, Julie finally settled on string cheese and an apple. It was too late and she was too exhausted for anything more complicated. She poured a glass of wine, turned out the lights and took her picnic to her bathroom where she ate it as she relaxed in the tub. A shower would have been quicker, but she preferred a hot bubble bath after a cold, stressful night. Besides, it wasn't easy to enjoy a glass of wine in a shower.

Her mind drifted back to Gloria. Danny was already a veteran in the war between his parents. Now there was going to be a new victim. That is, *if* the baby survived.

Julie had been shocked that Gloria was pregnant . . . shocked and horrified. It was bad enough that Gloria chose to put herself and Danny in constant danger. The poor unborn infant had no idea it was about to be born into a hostile world where its father was likely, sooner or later, to kill its mother.

Babies are so fragile. No one knew that better than Julie.

She finished the apple and tossed the core into the trash can in the corner, then took another sip of the wine. The water felt wonderful and she slid lower until the back of her head rested on the porcelain rim. Her eyes drifted closed, but against the darkness of her lids, Rusty's face intruded. She was genuinely grateful for his kindness, but equally bewildered by why he had come back for her. It was probably because of her association with the police department. Not only did she work as an advocate for crime victims and other citizens, but she was always there to support the families of all the cops and their families, as well as the other emergency responders. Just last year, she had visited Rusty's brother Sam when he was in the hospital after being shot during a routine traffic stop that had gone horribly wrong.

Julie smiled. That had actually turned out okay because the incident had caused Sam to meet Kate, an actress-wannabe who had gotten caught up in a scam that almost cost her her life. Now they were so cute together, it was almost sickening, but Julie couldn't help but like them both.

In some ways, Julie envied what they had. For the most part, she was comfortable being alone. She had had her chance at happily-ever-after, but that had turned out badly. So badly that she didn't think she would ever totally trust a man in that way again.

She drained her glass, then hurried to finish her bath. Coming back from a particularly brutal domestic beating always made her melancholy. Right now she just wanted to brush her teeth and fall into bed and hope that by the time she woke up the next day Carlos would be safely in jail, Gloria and the baby would be on their way to recovery and Julie would be rested and ready to move on to the next case.

Once in bed though, sleep eluded her. Her body was relaxed, but her mind wasn't ready to shut down yet. The glow in Danny's eyes when she rescued his favorite baseball cap reminded her how utterly devastating a fire could be. Gloria was actually lucky that the entire structure hadn't burned. She would be able to salvage a lot of her kitchen items and maybe even a few personal things although the worst damage had been done to the master bedroom and the spare bedroom next to it. Danny's had escaped the worst of it because it had been across the hall and next to the bathroom whose contents weren't as flammable which had worked to retard the spread of the flames. It was unlikely they would be able to move back into the house any time soon, especially since it was a rental and who knew whether or not the landlord had insurance. Julie would be willing to bet that Gloria didn't.

Julie snuggled deeper under her comforter. She loved her little house and knew how upset she would be if something catastrophic happened to it. It was over a hundred years old and had been in sad shape when she had bought it three years ago. Nestled in an area of Denver called Park Hill, she had been able to look past the holes in the floor and the water stains on the ceiling to see the potential. Julie had immediately felt a kinship with the structure. She and it had good bones and just needed a little love and attention.

In the case of the house, it also needed a lot of time and money. Luckily, she had been able to purchase it for practically nothing because it had taken a generous portion of her savings to pay for the repairs. She had hired out the new roof because she wasn't sure she was ready to risk her life learning how to install shingles. Not that she knew how to do any of the work on the inside. But she had the internet and a friendly staff at the local Lowe's. It had taken almost a year and a lot of bruises and smashed thumbs. Somehow she had managed to fix the holes in the floors and walls, update the old cabinets with paint and new hardware, repaint everything inside and out and even update her plumbing fixtures. She had figured out how to install tile and refinish the wood floors. All that was left were now new countertops, but that would take a few months of saving since she really wanted granite or one of those stone composites.

She had gradually collected pieces of furniture for her bedroom, the living room and breakfast/dining area that overlooked a shady backyard. There was no immediate need for furnishing the extra bedroom, so that was put low on the list. But finally she was able to sit back and look around her with a sense of pride and accomplishment. This was the first home that was truly hers, and she loved every inch of it. It was her hideaway, her retreat from all the pain and disappointment of the world outside.

Julie hadn't actually met many of the neighbors. The neighborhood had been declining for many years, but it was coming back and had become a highly desirable location, especially for young professionals and families. Since Julie had little in common with either group and her schedule was kind of unpredictable, she wasn't particularly motivated to mingle with them. Other than a friendly wave in passing or a greeting when they happened to go to their mailboxes at the same time, she hadn't even spoken to any of them. Which probably made her a bad neighbor, but without kids to play in the yard or dogs to walk, she simply didn't bump into any of them. Instead, she hurried home to her cozy bungalow and spent most evenings with a good book and occasionally the cat if he chose to stay in.

Slowly her eyes drifted closed. Inside these walls, surrounded by all her unknown but reputable neighbors, she felt safe.

On the street outside her house, a vehicle's engine idled. The windows were fogged from the heat inside fighting the cold outside. A man's gloved hand wiped a moist circle on the glass. Julie wasn't as safe as she thought.

CHAPTER THREE

Grocery shopping was one of her least favorite activities, especially on the weekend. Every aisle was filled with oversized baskets and people as anxious to be done with the chore as she was. Whining kids added their shrill voices to the chaos, making standing in the long lines to check out almost unbearable.

Julie spent most of her time in the produce area stocking up on fresh fruit and vegetables, then migrated to the frozen food section where she selected enough packaged meals to make it through the week. Some cheese, bread, milk, Greek yogurt and a last minute calorie splurge of a package of cream horns, and she joined the masses in line.

"Only a crazy person would shop on Saturday."

Julie turned to see who was speaking and recognized Kate standing behind her. "Said the crazy woman in line behind me," she answered with a smile. "How's the acting going?" She had heard that Kate was keeping busy in local theater and an occasional TV commercial.

Kate's beautiful face became sad. "Not so good. Heritage Square Music Hall is closing down at the end of this year, so I'll be out of a job."

"Closing for good? That's awful. I've been to only a couple of their shows, but I really enjoyed them."

"They're the most talented group of people I've ever met, but the economy has hurt their attendance."

"I'm sorry to hear that," Julie told her. "But I'm sure you'll find another job quickly."

"I have an audition for a film that will be shooting in Denver in the spring."

"Are you still hoping to get something in L.A.?" Julie had heard that Kate's original goal had been to build her resume in Denver, then move to California or New York where the opportunities were more plentiful.

Julie's expression softened. "I have to admit that I'm not as motivated as I was. Now that Sam is back to work, I've realized how much I would miss him if I was away too long. If I can keep busy here, I'm happy."

"Sam is definitely one of the good guys," Julie agreed.

Kate nodded. "I know. Hey, we're having a barbecue at Rusty's apartment tomorrow to watch the game. Why don't you come over and join us?"

"No, I'm on-call tonight," Julie answered quickly. "My weekends are usually a little unpredictable."

"We'd love to have you. There'll be plenty of food, and you probably know almost everyone who'll be there."

"Maybe next time." Julie moved up in line and was relieved to be distracted by unloading her groceries onto the conveyor belt.

"I'll hold you to that," Kate promised.

Julie paid for her purchases and called a last farewell to Kate. It wasn't that she didn't like Kate or Sam or any of the others. They were as close to friends as she had, but that was close enough. Julie kept to herself, spending long hours at work and enjoying her handiwork at home the rest of the time.

She had once been much more outgoing and had been very popular in high school and college. That had all changed when she fell in love her junior year at University of

Connecticut. Julie pushed those thoughts from her mind. The bad memories outweighed the good. She had found it was easier to be happy in an environment she could control.

"What's wrong with you people?" The pretty petite brunette shivered and wrapped her scarf around her neck. "It's December, for God's sake. Time to take the party indoors."

"The Wilson brothers have pure adrenalin instead of blood running through their veins," Kate snuggled against Sam's warm body, and he obligingly wrapped an arm around her shoulders and pulled her even closer. She didn't seem to mind the brisk air as long as she was with him.

The temperature on the outside patio of Rusty's condo was a balmy thirty-five degrees. It had stopped snowing Saturday morning, but it hadn't warmed up enough for it to start melting. Denver's weather was one of the great urban myths of all times. People who didn't live there thought that it snowed all winter and there were mounds of the white stuff on the ground constantly. The truth was that Denver's climate was dry and mild. It didn't usually snow much in the winter with most of the average fifty-five inches coming in two or three big storms, often in the spring. Regardless of the amount, it usually melted quickly and rarely stuck around long. The Chamber of Commerce was proud to boast that Denver got more than three hundred days a year of sunshine, more than almost any other place in the U.S.

And it was that sunshine that had moved the Wilson boys and their dates and friends out to the patio in spite of the chill. Besides, with the French doors swung open, there was a clear view of the big screen TV on which the Broncos were challenging the San Diego Chargers at Mile High

Stadium. There weren't quite enough chairs for everyone, so Chris, the youngest Wilson, was sitting on the ice chest and Rusty was manning the grill.

If it had anything to do with flames, he was the expert. Ever since he'd been a kid, he had been fascinated by fire. By his teens, he had become the king of the barbecue pit, and no one had ever been able to dethrone him. He had the timing down perfect on when to turn the steaks and where to put the corn-on-the-cob so it didn't burn.

"Toss me a Corona," Rusty called out and wiped his hand on the stained white apron that had *Come on Baby, Light My Fire* printed across the front. Chris stood up long enough to dig a cold bottle out of the ice in the chest. He tossed it to Rusty, then sat back down.

"Hey, don't get too comfortable. We need a couple over here." Sam didn't even try to hide his smile at his younger brother's groan.

Chris stood again and opened the ice chest. "Anyone else?"

Sara, a petite blond with huge blue eyes held out her hand. "Sure. But make mine a Bud Light Lime."

"Don't tell me you're watching your calories," Kate told her. "I feel like an Amazon around you two ladies."

Sara flexed her arm into an impressive muscle. "I'm stronger than I look."

Chris snorted. "You should see her hoist people onto the stretchers. Trying to keep up with her is why I work out every day."

Sara flashed him a surprised look. Hearing a compliment from her long-time friend and ambulance partner was a rare event. She had grown up with all of the Wilson boys and had shared their ambition to go into some area of public service. Her interest in medicine had led to her applying to be a paramedic. With an ultimate goal of becoming a doctor, she worked as many classes as she could in between her crazy hours. That left little time for romance, but for now, that suited her just fine.

When Chris had completed multiple tours as a Marine medic in Afghanistan, she had encouraged him to hire on with her unit. Their long-time friendship had moved easily to a working relationship. They even shared a two-bedroom rent-controlled apartment in downtown Denver. So far, neither had been tempted to take it any further, but it insured Sara a place at all the family gatherings.

Chris handed a couple of bottles to Sam and Kate, then glanced over at Heather who shivered again as if the very thought of a cold beverage made her more miserable and shook her head. "I'm going to sit inside."

Everyone watched her go and although nothing was said, everyone knew that would be the last time they would be seeing Heather. She clearly didn't have what it took to hang out with the Wilsons, and Rusty would quickly move on to someone new.

Sam had never been much of a player, and almost as soon as he met Kate, he had known he'd found his soul mate. They had settled into a comfortable relationship and were planning an intimate wedding in the spring. Chris was still adjusting back to civilian life and the crazy schedule of being a paramedic and taking classes at the University of Colorado. He dated occasionally, but so far he hadn't met anyone he enjoyed hanging out with as much as he did with Sara. She was very serious about advancing her career in medicine, and even though he was two years behind her in school, they were able to study together. He wasn't aware of the pool Rusty and Sam were running behind his back about how long it would take Chris to realize Sara was a beautiful young woman and not just a drinking buddy.

Then there was Rusty who, as the oldest brother, was determined not to be the first one to marry. In fact, he was quite happy to be single and playing the field. All three brothers were in careers that attracted groupies, but firefighters seemed to be the biggest target. Maybe because they were always the heroes and never the bad guys like cops. Or maybe it was because they saved people and puppies and houses. They were perceived to be strong and brave and physically fit, willing to run into a burning building when everyone else was running out.

Rusty was all that, and at thirty years of age, he felt he was at the prime of his life. And he made no excuses about enjoying his freedom to its fullest.

"So why didn't you work the game today?" he asked Chris.

"And miss a free meal cooked by the master? Not likely," Chris answered. "Besides, I've got finals in a week, and I'm going to spend this evening studying."

Rusty glanced over at Sam. "I don't even have to ask you why you're not working today."

"Are you kidding?" Sam scoffed. "Let's see, would I rather be sitting here with a beautiful woman rubbing against me or standing out in the cold, directing traffic and dealing with drunk fans . . . ?" He pretended to be considering the choice, then shook his head. "No contest."

"There are plenty of beautiful women at Mile High who'd be glad to rub up against you to keep you warm," Rusty pointed out.

"I'll leave that to you," Sam responded. "I've got the girl I want. And you'd better stop trying to make trouble. She's got a mean right arm and her bottle's almost empty."

Rusty gave Kate a measuring look and pretended to be concerned.

"Don't worry," she assured him. "I wouldn't throw anything at you. However, . . ." she paused for effect, "I'm going to do everything I can to find a woman who'll wrap you around her little finger. And then we'll see if you can keep that firewall up around your heart."

"Ha!" Rusty's laugh was hearty and genuine. "You might as well hit me with the bottle because there's no chance of that happening any time soon."

From the living room where she'd been listening, Heather gave them a startled look. Apparently, she had been completely unaware that she had no chance at all. Rusty noticed her expression, but didn't feel any regret. He'd made her no promises. In fact, he'd invited her only at the last minute to keep the numbers even. He knew there would be a little drama when he took her home as soon as possible after the meal. His ego wasn't so big that he believed it was because she had any real feelings for him. After all, they'd met just a couple of days ago at the car dealer where he'd gotten his Explorer serviced. He recognized a girl who was caught up in the firefighters' myth and wanted to add him to her scorecard. He was a player, but he didn't keep a scorecard. Yes, he liked to date lots of women, but he was completely honest with all of them. Most of them were out for a good time as much as he was. But sometimes the groupies got burned. It was an occupational hazard that he didn't lose sleep over.

"Steaks are done. Is anyone hungry?" he asked rhetorically. Everyone grabbed their drinks and reluctantly moved inside where they could eat at the table.

Julie had a leisurely Sunday. After her trip to the grocery store on Saturday, she had stopped by the hospital to visit Gloria and her new daughter. Other than the obvious cuts and bruises, a broken arm and several broken ribs, the new mother was already on her way to recovery. Battered women usually had an amazing ability to recover . . . that is, if they survived.

Saturday night had brought only three calls, all minor incidents that consisted more of offering suggestions for places where they could get financial assistance, counseling or legal advice. Julie had been home and in bed by two a.m. which was unusually early. But she knew Sunday would probably make up for it.

She slept late, had time to read the entire *Denver Post*, clean her house and even cook one of her favorite meals, chicken and rice, from scratch. She called the hospital to check on Gloria and found out that her mother had already come by and picked her up. Hopefully, the mother would do as she had promised and hide Gloria, Danny and the baby far from Denver and her abusive husband. Julie knew there was always the chance that Gloria would go back to Carlos even though next time, she might be going away in a hearse instead of an ambulance.

As Julie did her chores, the Broncos game was on TV in the background. She liked football and had often spent Sundays watching games with her dad when she was young. Now she cared who won for an entirely different reason than hometown pride. A Broncos' loss guaranteed a flood of abuse calls.

Football, basketball and even NASCAR races brought out the worst in people. When a favorite team suffered a loss, the sports fan often took out his or her disappointment on whoever was closest. A friend, a spouse, a child, a pet . . . all were potential victims at the hands of an angry fan. Of course, liberal alcohol use added fuel to the fire, and a long day in front of the TV with unlimited beer or hanging out at a bar with each score being celebrated with one or more shots magnified everyone's emotional investment in the outcome.

It came down to the last two minutes, and when Peyton Manning threw a touchdown pass that sealed the win, Julie heaved a sigh of relief. At least the Broncos fans would be happy.

But there were other teams, losing teams who had unhappy fans. Her phone starting ringing at ten-thirty. The first call was a possible child abuse. Julie tucked her small billfold into the pocket of her slacks, picked up her keys and hurried out. As soon as she opened the door, the cat streaked out, anxious to get started on his nightly rounds. He had shared her lazy day, sprawled out in his favorite spot near the heating vent. Julie had no idea how old he was, but his graying muzzle and his increased time indoors told her that he was a little past his prime and heading toward his senior years. He paused long enough to rub against her legs and give a loud meow before bounding into the night. Now that he was a regular houseguest, maybe it was time to actually name him. It had been a long time since she had had a pet, and she was actually enjoying having him around.

Locking the door behind her she pressed the garage door opener that she always carried with her. She had heard it was dangerous to leave it in your car because anyone who broke in would not only have your name and address on the car's registration, but they would also have access to the garage. The last thing she wanted was to have someone surprise her in her own garage.

Thankfully, only her car was inside, and soon she was on her way to her first call.

It was an address she hadn't been to before, which made her both happy and sad. Happy because it wasn't a person who was in a bad pattern of victimization and sad because someone else had found a way to hurt another person.

Or in this case, it was a television set.

"Hey Julie. The kids are in the back bedroom," the cop on duty told her.

"What's going on, Don?" she asked as she looked around the living room, surveying the damage. An empty bottle of Crown Royal rested on its side on the end table and a dozen or so crushed Coors cans littered the floor around a well-worn leather recliner. Other than that, the house was pretty nice, if you could look past the clutter. Sitting on the couch, probably because he wasn't sober enough to stand, was a man with his hands cuffed behind him. His eyes were bloodshot and his hair tousled, but even in his present condition, he had the poise of an executive used to giving orders, not taking them.

"This is all a misunderstanding," he said, slurring it together as if they were all one long multi-syllabic word. "I have a permit for the gun."

"It's illegal to shoot in the city unless you're at a range," the police officer reminded him as he continued to take photos of the scene.

"I'm in my own goddamn home, and that's my own goddamn television. I can shoot it if I want."

"Not in your living room with your kids just ten feet away. If those bullets had penetrated the wall, you could be looking at homicide instead of an illegal discharge of a weapon." The officer's voice was stern and businesslike, but his expression showed his disgust.

"Wasn't my fault. Fuckin' Raiders." The man slumped sideways, about to slip into unconsciousness, but the officer unceremoniously jerked him to his feet. With a nod of greeting toward Julie, he half-dragged, half-marched the guy to the front door.

"Nice role model," Julie muttered.

"Yeah, I'm just glad he didn't miss the TV. A few inches above or to either side, and . . ." Don's voice trailed off. It wasn't necessary to finish the sentence, because they both knew the possible consequences. "The kids are pretty upset."

"I'll take care of them. Does their mother live here?"

"Nope. Divorce. Just another fun weekend with Dad," he told her.

"Has she been notified?"

Again he shook his head and smiled. "We save the fun stuff for you."

"Thanks." She walked down the hall and into the bedroom, glad that she was going to be talking with live children and not consoling a mother grieving over her dead ones.

The two young boys were sitting on the floor in the corner, huddled in each other's arms.

"Hi, my name is Julie, and I'm going to stay with you until your mother gets here." She knelt down next to them. "Do either of you know your mother's phone number?"

The oldest boy nodded.

"Good. I knew you would. You're what . . . eight?"

"I'll be nine in January," he said proudly.

She pulled her phone out of her jacket pocket. "Okay, let's call your mother and see if she can pick you up early."

He told her the number and she punched it in. To the boys she said, "I'll be right back. Are you two okay for a minute?"

They both nodded solemnly, and she walked back into the hallway so she could talk to the mother out of their ear shot. The mother was understandably upset and promised to be there as soon as possible. Julie returned to the boys and squatted down next to them.

"She's on her way. Do you have anything you need to pack?"

Again they nodded. She stood and they followed suit. "What's your name?" she asked the youngest boy.

"Effan," he said.

The older brother immediately corrected him. "It's Ethan. He has trouble with his letters."

"Oh. That's probably because he's missing his two front teeth," Julie told him. "I'll bet once they grow back in, he'll be Ethan again. And what's your name?"

"Patrick," he told her. "I'm named after my daddy."

Julie found a small duffel bag in the corner and placed it on the bed. "Let's put your things in here."

They collected some clothes and their Gameboys and put them in the bag, working silently for several minutes. Finally, Patrick couldn't resist asking, "Did they arrest my daddy?"

"They took him to the police station," she told him.

"Will he be okay?"

"He'll be fine."

"He killed the TV, didn't he?" Ethan asked hesitantly.

Julie nodded. "I think it's pretty messed up."

"Daddy drank a lot of beers." Patrick looked down at his tennis shoes, as if he couldn't look at her as he admitted, "He yelled at Ethan."

Julie kept her voice neutral as she asked, "Did your dad hit you or Ethan?"

Patrick shook his head. "He got really mad at Ethan for spilling his milk, but he didn't hit us. We got scared and hid in our room."

She reached out and ruffled his hair. "That was a really smart thing to do. You took good care of your brother and kept him safe."

Patrick's shoulders lifted and he looked up. Before he could say anything else, there was the click of heels on the hall floor and a woman, obviously their mother, swept into the room.

The two boys dropped everything and ran into her arms. The woman looked over their heads at Julie and mouthed, "Thank you."

Julie nodded and smiled. Almost a happy ending. Likely the court would arrange a more protected environment for future visits with their father and, hopefully, she would never see any of them again. For her that was a success.

She went back into the living room where Don was finishing up.

"Looks like we're through here," he said.

"Yeah, I'm going to head home, but I'll probably see you again tonight." She pulled her jacket back on and zipped it up.

"Let's hope you're wrong. It's still wicked cold out there."

The mother and two boys came out of the bedroom. She had their duffle bag slung over one shoulder and was holding tightly to each boys' hands. Don held out a piece of paper, and she let go of Patrick's hand long enough to take it.

"Here's the information about your husband."

"Ex," she reminded him.

"Ex-husband. He'll be in detox overnight, and they'll set bail for him tomorrow."

Her finely arched brows lifted. She didn't say it aloud, but clearly her plans didn't include bailing him out. "Thank you both for taking care of my boys."

"No problem, ma'am."

Julie smiled at the boys. "You have two wonderful sons," she told the mother.

The mother seemed close to tears as she nodded. "I know." She led her boys out the front door and into the night.

Julie gave Don a little wave and followed them. They split at the sidewalk, and she walked alone to her car. The snow had stopped earlier in the day and the skies were clear. Her breath made frosty puffs in the crisp air, even inside her car. It was a short drive back to her house so her heater had barely started working when she arrived. She parked in the garage and hurried to her back door. Her gloved fingers fumbled with the key, but she finally fit it in and the deadbolt clicked open.

She paused in the doorway and looked around for the cat. "Kitty, kitty," she called softly, not wanting to bother the neighbors. She waited a few seconds and walked in, locking the door behind her. She dropped her purse and keys on the table and took a glass out of the cabinet. As she was filling it from the refrigerator water dispenser, she felt something brush against her legs. Startled, she looked down at the cat who was greeting her with his usual arched rub, twining back and forth until she bent down to pat him.

"How'd you get in, Mister?" she asked with a frown. She could have sworn he'd run out when she left, but then how . . .? He must have slipped inside when she opened the door, and she just hadn't noticed. Dismissing it with a shrug, she took a drink of her water, then poured some dry kibble into his dish.

"Maybe I should name you Houdini," she told him as she squatted down to stroke his striped back while he attacked his food as if it was his last meal. The ringing of her phone brought her back to her feet. She grabbed her clipboard where she kept her call sheets.

"This is Julie," she spoke into the phone.

No one answered.

"Hello," Julie spoke again and waited.

There was only silence on the other end of the line. Actually, it wasn't really a silence because she thought she could hear the soft whisper of breath as someone inhaled and exhaled, but it wasn't the heavy breathing of an obscene caller. Someone was clearly there; they just weren't talking.

"There must be something wrong with the connection," she said, not really expecting an answer . . . and not getting one.

She hung up, but stood there with the phone in her hand, waiting for it to ring again. If it was dispatch, they would definitely call right back. If it was someone else . . . She really didn't know how to finish that thought. It was too late for a sales call. She had no family and no friends who would call her at this time of night.

Slowly, she set the phone on the table and stared at it as the answer would flash on the screen. The window lit up and the phone rang again. This time she took time to read the caller ID before she picked it up.

Private. The phone kept ringing and she was torn between the ridiculous compulsion to always answer a ringing phone and the hesitation to hear that sinister silence again. Her fingers hung suspended in the air over the phone, almost touching the *Answer* button.

The phone stopped ringing as abruptly as it had started. The quiet that followed was almost worse. Suddenly, Julie had the feeling that someone was watching her and she slid her gaze around the room to all the windows.

Outside he watched. He could see her, scurrying from room to room, shutting all the blinds like a frightened mouse trying to hide from a prowling cat. He could still see her shadow moving around inside, so helpless, so alone.

He had her where he wanted her.

CHAPTER FOUR

Mondays were full of paperwork and schedules. As much as Julie loved her job, she'd much rather be in the field than in the office. Only the manager of the department received a salary, and she couldn't afford to support herself as a volunteer. Julie had never had any experience either working in an office or as a supervisor, but she had discovered she had a knack for it. However, depending on an all-volunteer workforce had its own complications.

Every month there was a meeting with a speaker, usually a member of the emergency response team, a medical or social services professional or a psychologist. It was also a time for everyone to select at least four twelve-hour shifts for the upcoming month. Most of her volunteers were either retired or unemployed and they usually offered to work more than their required four shifts. When someone had an illness or something unexpected came up, Julie would usually cover their shift if she didn't have time to find a replacement.

So when Janice called in with the flu, Julie decided it would be a good excuse to get away from the desk if a call came in. Always in the background, here and at home, she had a police scanner tuned to the frequencies Denver PD and FD used. After years of listening to it, she had grown accustomed to the alerts and dispatch chatter. She was in the middle of her weekly report when she heard the code for a Victim's Advocate. Only seconds later her telephone rang.

"This is Julie."

"We have an auto accident involving three children on the 1400 block of York St. VA has been requested to standby with them." The familiar voice recited the details over the phone.

"Got it. I'm on my way." Julie had jotted down the information on an incident sheet. They were color coded by event, but since she wasn't sure what this particular case would be, she used a white sheet temporarily. She grabbed her coat and purse and headed to the parking lot. York Street was only about ten blocks away, so she arrived as quickly as the traffic would allow. She parked close but out of the way of the fire truck and police cars that were already on-scene.

As she approached, she saw a car that was leaning on its side against a giant blue spruce. Several firefighters were using the hydraulic cutters, better known as the Jaws of Life to cut the mangled door off. Julie knew she couldn't help until the occupants were out. She walked over to a cop who was also standing by, waiting for the fire department to rescue the victims.

"Do we know who's inside?" she asked him.

"Three juveniles. I'm not sure of the ages, but they looked young."

"Were they skipping school?"

"From the amount of beer cans in the car and the pot cloud inside when we arrived, I'd say this is leftover from a late night joyride."

Julie still had lots of questions, but clearly the cop didn't have any more answers than she did. They stood together and watched while the firefighters stabilized the car to keep it from rolling over or falling back, then pealed back the roof and dismantled the door. The paramedics rushed forward and leaned into the car to check on the kids' condition and stabilize them, if needed. The firefighters continued to foam the ground where gas had spilled while holding the metal back so the paramedics could get to everyone.

Julie and the cop watched and waited as the paramedics disappeared inside the car. Several minutes later, they climbed back out . . . without the boys. Julie knew what that meant even before the lead paramedic called out, "Call the ME. There's nothing we can do." He handed the cop the car's registration. "This is probably one of their parents."

The cop looked at the piece of paper and shook his head. Without saying a word, he walked away, dialing the medical examiner as he went. One of the firefighters set the hydraulic cutter he had been holding on the ground and took off his helmet and face shield, and she saw that it was Rusty. He looked up and saw Julie, still standing off to the side and headed toward her. He stopped directly in front of her with his back to the car.

"Hey, sorry I got them to call you out for this." He dragged his fingers through his hair, darkened by sweat to almost black. Streaks of grease marked his forehead and, in spite of the cool air, water beaded on his face. "I saw it was kids, and I thought . . ." His shoulders drooped. There was no sign of the cheerful, teasing man she had been with on Friday night.

Impulsively, she reached out and rested her hand on his arm. "I don't mind. I was hoping I would be staying with them until their parents arrived."

He glanced back at the car, then returned his gaze to her. "They were probably out joyriding. They shouldn't die just because they did something stupid. Hell, I'd have been dead a long time ago."

Julie was profoundly touched by the grief written on his haggard face. "It's tragic, especially when they're so young. I'm sure there was nothing you could have done to save them."

"Maybe if we'd gotten here faster or we'd gotten into the car sooner . . ."

She squeezed his arm. "Don't. It was likely already too late. It doesn't look like they were wearing seat belts, and few people survive banging around in a car like that." She had seen the bloody marks on the broken windshield that had indicated both of the front seat occupants' heads had crashed into it. "Looks like it rolled a couple times."

He nodded. "At least twice. The airbags deployed but after the initial hit, they didn't help much." He sighed. "Kids think they're invincible."

Her eyes searched out his. "Sort of like firefighters, huh?"

One corner of his mouth lifted. He couldn't disagree.

"I know it's a cliché," she continued, "but you can't save them all."

"Doesn't mean I don't try."

"So do I. But you have a much better percentage of success than I do." Her dark eyes reflected her disappointment in herself, especially when it came to helping abused partners get away and stay away from their abusers.

He reached over and covered her hand with his much larger one. He was about to say something else when the ME's van arrived, along with three hearses. The empty ambulances had already left. It was standard policy that they transported only living patients. The city was responsible for transporting bodies to the morgue.

"I'd better get back to it," Rusty said. "He's going to want us to extricate the bodies for him."

"I'll check with the cops and see if the parents have been notified or if they want me to go with them to notify." Julie moved her hand away, and for a split second, he didn't let it go.

His eyes continued to stare into hers for a moment longer, then he stepped back and walked toward the car.

Julie watched him, a little shaken by the intimacy in that last lingering look. Her first impression of him had been that he was an emotional lightweight. But he had clearly been upset by the accident which showed her a whole new side of him. She suspected it was not a side he let many people see. It gave them a strange connection, one that she wasn't sure she welcomed.

Rusty didn't want to be alone. He picked up his cell phone and flipped through his Contacts list. *Amanda, Ava, Becki, Carly, Denise, Emily, Fiona, Ginger, Heather, Kim, Pam, Rachel, Stacy, Tamara, Tawny.* None of them stirred anything in him. Nothing.

It had been a tough shift. The day had started with the car accident. He had barely gotten back and cleaned up when there was a fire on the third floor of an office building downtown. Papers, furniture and the typical chemicals generally found in an office had provided enough fuel to turn that one into a roaring inferno, but everyone had safely evacuated. It had taken several hours to completely extinguish the fire and make sure it hadn't spread. Luckily it had been a quiet night after they returned from that one. But the shift had been exhausting, both physically and emotionally.

He'd gotten a few hours of sleep at the station. His, and all his fellow firefighters, worked a 24/48 schedule which meant he worked twenty-four hours, from 7:30 a.m.

to 7:30 a.m., then was off forty-eight hours. Unless he was out all night on a fire, he preferred to not go to bed as soon as he got home in the morning, but to try to keep to a regular nightly sleeping schedule.

That narrowed down who he could spend his days off with because most non-fellow emergency responders worked normal eight-to-five hours. He didn't really want to spend time with his brothers either. Besides, they probably had other plans.

He popped the top on a can of beer and plopped down on his recliner. He selected an episode of a popular TV drama that he had recorded on his DVR. For several minutes he stared at the screen, the plot not capturing his attention. Instead, for some reason, his thoughts wandered to Julie.

The deaths of the three teenage boys had shaken him to his core. It was awful when an adult didn't survive, but it was always worse when there were kids involved. They hadn't had time to really experience life and love or to make their mark on their futures. No one would ever know if they would have discovered a cure for cancer or some other remarkable invention. So much potential lost.

And Julie had understood. As they stood together at the accident scene yesterday morning, she had comforted him with more than words. He had felt her empathy. Every day she walked in his shoes and saw the same tragedies he did and shared the anguish of loss or the thrill of success. Like him, she went on calls without knowing what to expect on the other end. Like him, she dealt with it on a daily basis.

What he didn't know was what sort of support system she had at home.

He'd heard rumors. She wasn't married. Or she was married, but no one had ever met her husband. Or she was gay . . . or straight. No one knew for sure.

Julie was sort of an enigma in the department. The only things that were known by all were that she didn't have any kids, she worked hard, but didn't socialize with her co-workers . . . and she didn't date cops. But what was her policy on firefighters?

Rusty smiled. Where did that thought come from? There were enough women to choose from. He, too, had a personal policy of not dating people he worked with. Now that women in the firehouse were common, it just wasn't good for long-term relationships to get involved with any of them sexually. Workplace romances were ripe for disaster.

Julie didn't fall far outside that circle.

He took a drink and rested his head on the back of the chair. Why was that thought so depressing? He sighed. It had been a rough day. Maybe tomorrow he would drive into the mountains for a little skiing. Yeah, that's what he needed . . . some R&R. Maybe a hot snow bunny would lift his spirits. Maybe lift more than his spirits.

And yet, as his eyes drifted closed, an image of Julie, her black hair pulled back into a severe ponytail and her chocolate brown eyes warm with compassion hovered behind his lids. She wasn't beautiful, in a classic sense, but it wasn't her looks that made her memorable. It was something far less common and tangible. She had an understanding and generous heart. Definitely not assets that were usually on his list.

CHAPTER FIVE

The week was going well, or as well as any week could go. There were the usual numbers of rapes, wrecks and abusive situations. But everyone on her staff was working their scheduled shifts, and Julie was able to catch up on her paperwork and the follow-ups. She liked to call as many of the victims as possible, even those where she hadn't been the first contact. It wasn't a step required by the department, but one that Julie felt was important. Her hope was that that one extra point of contact would be the final brick in the wall of someone's commitment to make the changes needed to move them out of danger. Or it could simply be a kind voice at a time when someone's spirits were low. Hers was not a position of power, but it could offer support and a path to positive change.

Gloria was not one of the people she had been able to talk to because her mother had followed through with relocating her out of state. Her husband Carlos was still in the wind, and Julie hoped that didn't mean that he had found his wife. She knew that this transgression might be the one that Carlos couldn't forgive.

She believed what she did in the office was necessary and important, but she missed being out in the field. These people needed someone to help them, whether it was to get a list of funeral homes or lawyers or counselors or addiction support, or just to have someone's shoulder to cry on, a stranger who could share their load, at least for a moment.

Julie loved to help and to feel like she was making a difference.

But she had a good staff who received regular training. It simply wasn't practical or even possible for one person to handle it all. Almost every event was emotional, and a single person couldn't absorb the constant drain. Soon they would have nothing left to give.

So Julie looked on these days in the office as her way of recharging her batteries so she could handle the busy weekend evenings. She completed her current batch of reports, scanned them and forwarded them to the chief of police who would review them, then forward them to the City of Denver. She had no idea what they did with them, but she kept the paper moving on her end of the chain.

As usual, the scanner was on in the background taking the place of the typical office Muzak. Julie turned her attention to the pile of call sheets for her follow-up calls and had the receiver in her hand, ready to dial when she heard the alert tone.

The dispatcher calmly gave out the address of a fire at a neighborhood nearby. Julie listened, but there was no request for a VA. Her gaze wandered to the calendar on her desk. It was Friday, so Rusty was probably on his way to the fire. She didn't stop to question why she should have remembered his 24/48 schedule or even why his name had popped into her mind. He was just one firefighter out of many she worked with. Just another colleague. Just another civil servant doing his job while she did hers.

Julie dialed in the number on the call report and listened while the phone rang on the other end.

"*Hello*," a soft voice answered.

"Hello. This is Julie Lawrence with the Denver Police Department Victim's Advocate department. Is this Sandy Johnson?" Julie asked. She knew Sandy's husband had been killed in a car accident and that the funeral had been last week. If Sandy's experience was like most, she had been surrounded by family and friends from the time of the accident until the day after the funeral. Once relatives returned to their homes and friends resumed their busy lives, Sandy would be left with the vacuum left by her husband's death. Her life would never return to the normal it had been before. And the quiet could be deafening.

"*Yes, it is.*"

"Mrs. Johnson, I was just calling to see how you're doing."

"*I'm fine,*" the woman replied.

Julie could tell that the answer had been repeated so often, it was automatic . . . and probably not truthful. "Is your daughter still staying with you?"

"*Oh no. She had to go back to Omaha. She has a very important job, you know.*"

Julie didn't know, but she said, "I'm sure she does. Maybe it would be a good idea for you to go stay with her for a while. I'm sure your grandkids would love to have their grandmother there for Christmas."

"*That would be nice, but I have to stay here. Who would take care of the mail and the bills . . . ?*" Her voice trailed off. "*Frank used to do all that.*" Her voice caught.

"Mrs. Johnson, may I call you Sandy?"

"*Yes, of course you may, dearie.*"

"Sandy, I'm sure all those things can be taken care of long distance. Why don't I drop by this evening and see if I can help you get organized."

Sandy sniffled. "*That would be really nice of you. But you don't have to.*"

"I'll be leaving here around five. Would five-thirty be good for you?"

"*Yes, that would be perfect.*" Already there was a little lift in her tone. "*I'll make us some cookies. Do you like chocolate chip?*"

"Of course. Who doesn't like chocolate chip?" Julie assured her. "I'll see you soon."

"*I'm looking forward to it. Goodbye.*"

"Goodbye, Sandy."

Julie hung up the receiver and jotted notes on the bottom of the call sheet. She'd do what she could to help Sandy make sure her bills were paid on time and, depending on the circumstances, see if a trip could be arranged. From the notes on the call sheet, Sandy and Frank had been married almost forty years. Being all alone for the first time in that many years would take a big adjustment. There was nothing like a few weeks with the grandkids to welcome a little peace and quiet back home.

Later that evening as she was driving home after her visit with Mrs. Johnson, Julie was smiling. She hadn't expected to stay but a half hour or so, but her visit had stretched to over three hours. She had been able to help Sandy set up a schedule and automatic bill pay for most of her bills and showed her how to forward the rest of her bills to her daughter's house. But mostly, she had listened to Sandy's stories about what a wonderful husband and father Frank had been. There had been a tour of the photo wall and descriptions of who everyone was and what they had been doing at the split second the shutter snapped. There had been tears and laughter and hugs when she was leaving. Sandy promised to consider taking the trip to Omaha and Julie told her she would stop by early next week just to see if Sandy needed anything else.

The garage door shut behind her as she inserted her key into the lock. Cat twined around her ankles, anxious to get inside and have dinner. Julie wasn't really hungry. The chocolate chip cookies had been good, and she even let Sandy warm up some leftovers for them to eat because Julie knew how often someone recovering from the loss of a loved one didn't care about eating . . . alone. At least she knew Sandy had eaten one good meal that day.

After hanging up her coat, she opened a can of cat food and dumped it in Cat's bowl. It looked and smelled disgusting, so she got a fork and separated the gelatinous fish into chunks, making it look a little more appealing. Cat didn't care one way or the other and dug in with his usual appetite as soon as she placed the bowl on the floor. Julie got a glass of ice water and went into the living room, making sure all the curtains were closed as she went. She picked up the remote and clicked on the TV.

"We're live at the scene. We don't have anything new to report, but if you're just joining us, two firefighters have been taken hostage and are being held inside the house behind me."

Julie whirled around and stared at the familiar blond reporter as she stood across the street from a small brown house that was bathed in spotlights. Police cars, fire trucks, ambulances and armored vehicles filled the rest of the screen. The woman continued, *"SWAT is on standby, but the resident has said if anyone approaches the house, he has booby-trapped all of the entrances and has several bombs he will set off. The police are waiting for the hostage negotiation team to arrive. The names of the firefighters have not been released. We'll pass on any more information as soon as we get it. And now back to your regular programming."*

Rusty.

They hadn't mentioned his name, but Julie just knew he was one of them. She stared at her cell phone as if challenging it to ring. She wanted to be there, even though she knew there was absolutely nothing she could do.

Apparently, there was nothing anyone could do. Except wait.

Julie's gaze flickered around the room. There was no way she would be able to sit and pretend to watch some silly sitcom when there were lives at risk. Not just any lives, but two firefighters who had gone there to put out a fire, not be taken captive by a psycho.

She needed to know more, and she couldn't wait for that ditsy reporter to come back and toss pieces of information out between commercials. Julie went into the bedroom and hurriedly changed into jeans, heavy socks and a thick sweater. She pulled on her coat and checked the pockets for gloves, then added a scarf and a wool stocking cap. Without bothering to turn off the TV or the lights, she locked the back door and waited impatiently for the garage door to open. Within minutes, she had parked several blocks from the hostage house, behind the dozens of emergency vehicles and local news vans.

A group of cops stood off to one side, and she made her way through the crowd of reporters and onlookers to reach them. She saw that Sam was one of them, which didn't necessarily mean Rusty was one of the hostages. He could be here just because he was on-shift.

"Hey Julie," Don greeted her. "Did they call you already?"

"No, I just heard it on TV. What happened?"

Don shook his head. "No one knows what's going on inside, but apparently, this guy called in a fire report and when the truck arrived, he let them in, then . . . well, it gets sort of hazy from there. We just know that he's holding them and threatening to blow up the whole neighborhood. We've evacuated all the houses in a three block radius just in case that nutcase really does have a bomb."

"So who went in?"

"Oh, you mean the hostages?" When she nodded, he continued, "Some rookie named Jason Lewis and Sam's brother Rusty."

Rusty. She sighed. Oh, and Jason, she quickly added. She had met him on a job a couple of weeks ago, and he had impressed her with his enthusiasm. But she couldn't keep from thinking it was a good thing that Rusty, a seasoned veteran, was there with Jason. She didn't know Rusty all that well, but she sensed that if anyone could talk his way out of a bad situation, it would be him.

Rusty hadn't seen it coming. As usual, he had entered the house in full gear and carrying a hatchet. The man had been standing on the front porch, looking nervous and upset, all perfectly normal reactions from a person whose house is on fire. Once in the living room, Rusty had stopped so quickly that Jason, only a couple of steps behind had run into his back. "Sir, please stay outside while we go through the house. Did you see flames or smell gas?

"Nope." The man, who had followed them inside, shut the door and calmly slid the bolts on a half dozen locks.

"What the fuck?" Rusty asked, his gaze falling on a dozen two liter bottles of clear liquid placed around the room. He couldn't tell exactly what they were, but each had a timer and a separate compartment with another liquid in it. Also taped to the bottles were tin cans. Rusty couldn't see inside them, but he guessed they were filled with nails, screws, ball bearings or something else that would rip through flesh and walls and anything in its path. Rusty was certainly no expert, but he knew he was looking at enough homemade bombs to blow the entire block off the map.

He had taken a few classes on bombs, but more along the lines of how to put out the fires they caused or minimize the damage and not how to keep them from going off. The thing that had made the biggest impression on him from the class was that most bombs weren't stable or predictable, and definitely not something he wanted to be sharing a space with.

"So there's no fire?" Jason asked, not quite comprehending the situation.

"Not yet," the man said. "But there'll be an epic blast if you guys don't help me."

"Help you how?" Rusty asked, focusing on the man while covertly trying to survey the room and assess the situation. The more he saw, the more concerned he became. This was no spontaneous idea. All the windows had been boarded up from the inside and the doors blocked by furniture. Like a spider with a web, the man had been waiting for his victims to be lured to his web. But why?

"Call your captain and tell him to keep everyone back," the man instructed.

Rusty again eyed the bombs as he keyed in his radio, then spoke into it. *"No fire, just a shitload of bombs. Clear the area and stay back."*

The captain quickly answered, *"What's the plan?"*

"Not sure. We're okay for now."

"10-4."

Rusty looked back at man who nodded.

"They'll listen to me now," the man said with a satisfied smile. "I just had to get their attention."

"Who?"

"The government. Obama. Congress. All of those fuckers that are screwing up this country. I'm sick of them sticking their noses in my life. I've worked hard all my life. I've paid money into my retirement. And now it's all gone. I lost my job and nobody's hiring. My 401K is drained. My unemployment has run out. I'm losing my house. My whole life's gone to shit."

"Things have been bad for everyone," Rusty tried to find a point of agreement from which they could build.

"Not you," the man challenged. "You've got a job. And health care. And retirement. And probably a hot wife waiting for you at home."

"Actually, no wife . . ."

"Shut the fuck up," the man yelled. "I know how women are about firefighters. Hell, my wife ran off with one."

Rusty couldn't really counter that one.

The man started pacing, his voice getting more agitated with every step. "I've got nothing. You've got everything. It's not fair . . . but I'm making it right."

A piercing alarm went off and the man pressed his hands against his ears and whirled around. "What the hell is that?"

Rusty and Jason both wiggled their asses and the alarm quieted. "If we don't move for thirty seconds, it goes off so we can be found if we're trapped or unconscious."

"Don't let it go off again," the man screamed.

Since they were difficult to reach, especially when they were in full uniform, Rusty moved behind Jason and turned off the personal alarm security system unit that was attached to his air tank, then let Jason do the same for him.

The man picked up a package of long tie wraps and tossed it to Jason.

"Kid, use this on your partner's hands," the man ordered.

"Why don't you just let us walk out of here before anyone gets hurt? You know they 're going to surround this place," Rusty pointed out, hoping his voice sounded calmer than he felt.

"I'm counting on that," the man said calmly. He waved his hands as if beckoning for everyone to come forward.

The plan was chilling. Timing was going to be critical. If Rusty jumped him now, the man could trigger the bombs and dozens, possibly hundreds of people could be injured or killed. There were innocent people in houses all around this one, sitting down to dinner or homework or watching TV. Outside on the lawn the fire crews and paramedics were waiting for him to report back. They were likely close enough to be killed immediately.

As much as Rusty was tempted to just take his chances at disarming the man, he couldn't risk all his friends, co-workers and unsuspecting citizens. If the situation was handled as he knew it would be, within an hour after his captain knew what was going on inside the house the entire area would be evacuated. Of course, by then the police, SWAT team and the ATF would be involved. A later detonation would likely take out many of them . . . emergency responders like himself who were just doing their jobs and trying to protect the public, but at least the citizens should be out of harm's way.

"What's your end game plan?" Rusty asked the man, both stalling and trying to distract him from tying them up.

"Talk less, listen more. Put your hands together," the man's comment was more of a command than a suggestion.

"It's pretty hot in here. Can we take off our coats and air packs?" Rusty asked.

"Suffer." The man was clearly not sympathetic.

Jason looked at the tie wraps in his hand, then up at Rusty, silently asking what he should do. The man noticed and pulled a remote control out of his pocket.

"We can end this right now if you want," the man offered. "But I'd rather wait until everyone gets here. I want to take out as many of you government shits as possible."

Rusty decided it was better to buy some time and hope someone smarter than he was came up with a plan on how to get everyone out without blowing the roof off. He nodded and put his hands together.

"Behind your back," the man ordered.

Rusty reluctantly complied, his movements stiff in the heavy black jacket. Jason took out a tie wrap and tightened it around Rusty's hands. The man jerked the tie wraps out of Jason's hands and signaled for him to turn around. He threaded the heavy plastic through the holes and yanked it, then pulled the end of Rusty's to tighten it another couple of notches.

"Have a seat, *gentlemen*," he said sarcastically. "We're going to be here awhile."

Rusty dropped down on the couch and Jason followed. They exchanged a worried look, then turned back to their host.

A phone rang, causing all three of them to jump. The man took a small black cellphone out of his pocket and answered.

"Yes." He listened for a few seconds, then answered, "They're right here. No, they're not hurt. We've just been talking a little politics." He listened for a few more seconds. "No, I'm not going to shoot them . . . yet. I should warn you that I've had a lot of spare time on my hands for the last six months. A man can put together a shitload of explosives in that amount of time. I wouldn't recommend anyone trying to breach the premises or . . . kaboom! Yeah, it'll be ugly." He listened again. "We don't have enough time to list all the things I want, but we can start with giving me my fucking life back. Hell, I'm realistic. Staying in Denver doesn't sound like a good idea for my future health and well-being. I could probably put all this behind me with a couple million in unmarked bills and a free pass to Mexico." Again the voice on the other end spoke, causing the man to glance back at the two firefighters. "You know what, asshole? I've got nothing more to lose. Do you?"

CHAPTER SIX

Julie was unabashedly eavesdropping as the cops and firefighters discussed their options. They were at a stalemate in the negotiations. SWAT was still off to the side, trying to formulate a plan, but with the windows boarded up and the doors rigged, there weren't a lot of ways to get into the house. They were looking into the possibility of breaching the premises through the basement or even the attic, but so far nothing conclusive had been decided.

Rusty's and Jason's families had arrived several hours ago and were trying to arrange the ransom, but a million dollars each was a lot of money for middle class families to raise in the middle of the night. They were ignoring the city policies for not giving in to kidnappers or terrorists and scrambling to try to find a way to meet the man's demands.

Julie hesitated to butt into the family's unit, but Sam and Chris were busy talking to the cops and the father was tagging along with his sons. A middle-aged woman stood all alone. Worry lines were etched across her forehead and her lips were pressed together tightly. Sam had hugged the woman when she arrived, so Julie guessed she was his, Sam and Rusty's mom. If ever there was a victim, that woman was one.

Julie switched into advocate mode and walked over to her. She held out her hand. "Mrs. Wilson?"

The older, but still attractive woman took Julie's hand in a firm grip and didn't release it, as if she were holding on in hope of getting more information. "Yes . . . yes, I am. Do you have any news about Rusty?"

"No, not yet," Julie told her. "But I know they're still in contact with the man inside. As long as they keep him talking, it gives them time to plan."

The woman looked into Julie's eyes. "I go through this every day, worrying about whether or not my boys will come home at night. I was out of town when Sam got hurt this summer, and they kept it from me until Jack and I got home. He's lucky he survived or I would have killed him." She gave a short little laugh that was more hysterical than humorous. "My name is Pat."

"I'm Julie Lawrence. I work for DPD as a Victim's Advocate, but I'm here tonight as a friend. In the course of my job I run into one of your son's at least every day."

"I know they love their jobs, but it sure is hard on their parents."

"I'll bet it is," Julie agreed.

"So why is this psycho doing this?"

"The cops are running a background check on him, but I haven't heard if they've found out anything."

Pat brushed a tear off her cheek. "I always worried that Rusty would get hurt in a fire. Never something like this."

With the windows blocked and the only clocks visible being the timers set on the bombs, Rusty had no idea what time it was or how long they had been tied up. Periodically, the phone would ring and the man would have a brief conversation. Other than that, he didn't talk much. He paced a lot, the remote never leaving his hand. In spite of the room being relatively cool, beads of sweat glistened on his high forehead. His cheeks were flushed and his hands shook constantly. Rusty was a little concerned the man was going to have a heart attack and collapse, falling on the remote. Even an accidental detonation would be a disaster.

The house had once been very nice. The draperies had flouncy treatments on top and delicate sheers blocking the sheets of plywood that covered the windows. The drapes were not something a man would buy and the plywood was a recent addition. The furniture wasn't fancy, but it was of good quality. There were colorful throw pillows on the couch and chairs and a drooping silk flower arrangement on the mantle. Everything was dusty and the carpet had not been vacuumed for months . . . or longer. But it was clearly a house that had been decorated and loved at one time by a woman. The missing wife, no doubt.

Photographs were everywhere, hanging on the walls, arranged on the mantle and sitting on the furniture. Most of them were of a smiling dark-haired woman who wasn't beautiful, but there was a twinkle in her eyes that made her appealing. The man was with her in several of the photos, holding her hand or giving her a kiss. They appeared to be a happy couple in love. Rusty could see why the man was so upset that he had lost that connection.

Odd that he hadn't taken down all her photos and stuck them in a drawer or a box in the back of the closet. That's what most broken-hearted lovers did when the romance was over. Rusty wondered how long she had been gone. Maybe the police would be able to track her down and get her to talk her husband out of blowing them off the face of the earth. Rusty was sure that his brother, Sam, would be following every lead he could find. Actually, if one of them had to be in here and one out there, it was better that it was Sam on the outside. He would know how to handle the situation. Rusty was just the crazy brother who ran into burning buildings.

All the lights were on in the house, probably so the man could keep an eye on things while preparing to blow up half of Denver. He had a TV turned on and was enjoying his fifteen minutes of fame. It was also providing him with a constant update on what was going on outside. If he got out of this alive, Rusty vowed to talk to the local TV stations about their very detailed reporting and how it provided too much information to the bad guys while the crime was in progress.

The TV was angled away from the two firefighters, so they couldn't get a good view, but they could see that quite a crowd had gathered. Rusty's heart ached when he saw his mother's pale, drawn face, but he felt surprisingly better when he saw Julie standing next to her with an arm around his mother's shoulders. He also saw his brother Sam in a circle of other cops as they stood in front of the huge RV-like vehicle that was the Mobile Command Unit in situations such as this. He knew they were going through all the scenarios and would choose the one they thought was best. Soon, he hoped.

Even though the temperature in the room was cool, Rusty and Jason were sweltering inside their heavy gear. All the things that provided protection against the flames were acting like a portable sauna. They would both probably be pounds lighter when . . . or if . . . they walked away from this. The man was growing more restless and probably more unstable by the moment.

The FD provided continuing education and Rusty remembered one on conflict negotiation. He wished now he'd paid a little more attention, but he had honestly never thought he'd have to use it. Everyone liked firefighters. They saved lives and rescued kittens from trees. Although, to be perfectly honest, he'd never actually retrieved a kitten from anything. He'd pulled a raccoon out of a gutter once, but he didn't think that would impress this guy much.

Befriend him. He remembered hearing that somewhere. It was certainly worth a try.

"I'm Rusty and this kid is Jason. Since we're all in this together, what should we call you?"

"We're not ever going to be drinking buds," the man snorted. He was silent for a moment as if considering how much information was safe to share. "But I guess if we're going to blow up together, you should know who's lighting the fuse."

"That's a colorful image that I could have lived without," Jason murmured and Rusty jabbed him with his elbow.

The man didn't seem to have noticed. "My name is Joe. Just Joe. That's all you need to know."

"So, Joe. What sort of work did you do?"

"Why? You gonna offer me a job?"

Rusty could see this was going down a dark path, so he changed the subject. "Why Mexico?"

"Because it never friggin' snows there," Joe responded, then shrugged. "I heard the fishing's good and a little bit of cash will go a really long way."

"I wouldn't miss the snow either," Rusty agreed. "Hot beaches and beautiful women . . . or was it the other way around?"

Joe's expression darkened as he studied his captives critically. He resumed his agitated pacing.

"It sucks that you lost your job, but sooner or later the economy is going to get better, and you'll find something."

"No, it'll never be the same. Shit, I'm forty-eight years old. Nobody will hire me. It's too late to start over."

Rusty couldn't argue against what was obviously true, but he tried to minimize it to make Joe feel better. "I know how much people are struggling. I see it every day."

"Then today's your lucky day because you're seeing it up close and personal." Joe glanced at his watch and shook his head. "I don't think they're going to save you."

Rusty exhaled slowly. As Joe had pointed out over and over, the economy was rotten. The City of Denver couldn't afford the money even if they were inclined to pay it. Of course, the city wouldn't pay the ransom or provide an escape to Mexico for Joe. It was their policy not to make that sort of deal with extortionists. And there was no way Rusty's parents could dig up that kind of cash. Nor would he want them to.

Rusty knew it wouldn't be in his best interests to pass any of that information on to Joe. He decided to try another track. "You don't strike me as a guy who really wants to die. There's still an easy option to get you out of this."

Joe snorted. "Yeah, being someone's bitch in prison."

"But you'd have free room and board . . . and health care," Jason pointed out.

Both Rusty and Joe turned to glare at the younger man who realized, a moment too late, that his comment wasn't exactly helpful. In fact, it only served to irritate Joe even more. His finger shook as it hovered over the buttons.

Julie eased closer to the command vehicle. The waiting was driving her crazy. She couldn't imagine what hell the Wilsons were going through.

Sam was leaning against the large truck. He looked exhausted . . . and beaten. She paused. She didn't want to bother him, but he would have the most up-to-date information.

"Sam," she said softly. If he didn't respond, she would respect his privacy and walk away. But he looked up, his blue eyes, almost exactly the same shade as his older brother's. She knew that he was as much a victim in this as the two firefighters trapped in the house. Maybe it would help him to talk it out. "How are the negotiations going?"

"They're not. He says he wants cash and a way out of the U.S., but I think there's something else going on. I just can't put my finger on what." Same leaned his head against the cool metal of the vehicle.

"What have you found out about him so far?" Julie asked.

"Just another poor schmuck who lost his job and his house is in foreclosure. Used to be a chemist out at the Suncor plant. Now he's a terrorist."

A familiar CNN reporter approached Sam, and he quickly ducked around the back of the command center. Julie, too, turned away, but since she didn't appear to be *somebody*, the reporter walked right past her. Which was just fine with her. The last thing she wanted to do was be on camera.

The aggressive reporter managed to corner the fire chief, and she spoke into her microphone. "I'm standing here with Fire Chief Bill Taylor on the scene of the hostage situation in Denver. Chief Taylor, who is the man holding your firefighters and what is he asking for in exchange?" She shoved the microphone in front of the chief.

"Obviously, we can't tell you anything that might compromise our negotiations. We're not clear about his motivations or why he chose to kidnap firefighters, but I can say that we think the suspect's name is Joe O'Neil. We're still checking on his background."

The interview continued, but Julie didn't hear anything after the man's name. She recognized it. He had been one of her first victims five years ago when she was starting out. But most importantly, she had kept in touch with him through the years, although it had been a few months since they'd last spoke. They'd always had a good relationship. Maybe he would talk to her now, and she could convince him to give himself up.

Julie whirled around and headed directly for the entrance of the command vehicle. She knocked on the door, gingerly at first, then more forcefully. Sam opened the door slightly and peered out the crack. Seeing it was Julie and not the reporter, he opened the door all the way. His eyes widened in surprise as she brushed past him and went inside. No one except official personnel was allowed in during a crisis such as this.

Most of the RV was set up as a large meeting/planning room. TVs lined the walls, all tuned to different channels but with the volumes off. A long wooden conference table was in the center of the room and there were plat maps and house plans spread out on it. Members of SWAT, ATF, DPD and DFD were leaning over them, talking and pointing at specific points. Another SWAT member was drawing on one of the half dozen white boards that were mounted on the walls. As she entered, everyone froze and all eyes lifted to focus on her. Since most of the men and women in the room had never worked with her, they were shocked at this blatant breach of protocol.

They had no idea that this was very much outside her own character. Julie had never been the one to make waves or draw attention to herself. If she wasn't so convinced she could help Rusty and the other firefighter, she would never have put herself out there like this. Now all she had to do was convince them that she wasn't as crazy as they probably were thinking she was.

"I'm sorry to intrude," she began as she stopped at the table and met their wary gazes. "I'm Julie Lawrence, and for those of you who don't know me, I work with the DPD as the head of the Victim's Advocate department."

"I'm sure we'll need your services at some point, but as you can see, we're pretty busy right now," the ATF agent reprimanded her. "We'll call you . . ."

"Wait, I have something important to tell you," she interrupted him. The other men in the room rocked back on their heels, startled that she had challenged someone who was clearly accustomed to being in charge. The only other woman, a DPD liaison turned her head away, but Julie thought she saw a hint of a smile.

"I know Joe McNeil," Julie continued. "I helped him get through the death of his wife five years ago."

"That's not possible," the police chief said. "He told us that she left him for a firefighter."

Julie was momentarily taken aback. Could she be mistaken? Her gaze shifted to a photo that was stuck to one of the magnetic boards. It was definitely the man she had been communicating with, and she knew he did not have but the one wife. "With all due respect, sir, that information isn't correct."

There must have been something in her tone that made them believe her, or perhaps the ATF agent decided that if he just let her finish, the more quickly she would leave. "Exactly why would you question our intel?"

"Joe's wife . . . his *only* wife . . . ran a red light and was hit by a fire truck almost five years ago. She died at the scene. I accompanied Officer Don Vincent when he notified Joe about her death."

"And how can you be so certain there wasn't a second Mrs. O'Neil?"

Julie was a little reluctant to tell him because it wasn't exactly in her job description that she should continue to contact victims for years after the incident. "Well, sir I feel that part of my job is to follow-up to see if the people we've visited have been helped. In Joe's case, he was particularly devastated by the loss of his wife and I've kept in touch with him longer than most."

"In a romantic way?" the ATF agent asked.

"Absolutely not!" Julie exclaimed, shocked at the suggestion. "I called Mr. O'Neil every few months because he needed help. I tried to get social services involved, but he wasn't deemed to be any danger to himself or others, so they refused."

"Obviously, a bad decision," the police chief muttered.

"I've helped him through several rough spots," Julie told them. "Maybe I could reason with him and he would listen."

"That's all very interesting, Miss Lawrence," the ATF agent dismissed her. "But we can handle this."

"Sir, I think we should let her try," Sam said as he stepped forward. "Our negotiators aren't getting anywhere. What do we have to lose?"

"Two firefighters," the ATF agent replied stiffly.

The room was quiet for a moment as the men exchanged questioning glances. Finally, the police chief spoke up. "Why not? It just might work."

The ATF agent seemed about to object, but then he shrugged. "There's the phone. Let's see what happens."

Sam pulled out a chair in front of a speaker phone and motioned for Julie to sit. Nervously, she settled on the cushion and stared at the phone. What if Joe refused to talk to her? What if her call ticked him off and he killed Rusty? What if she was totally wrong about him, and he'd been lying to her all along?

Flashes of their past conversations flickered through her brain. She remembered Joe's tears when she'd sat with him as he first heard the news from Don. He had been devastated, so much so that he had shut out the rest of the world. She had found him a month later, wallowing in his grief. Apparently, he hadn't been eating properly or taking care of himself or the house. And he hadn't been going to work.

Julie had brought over some groceries and cooked him a good meal. She had tidied up the house while she sent him to the shower. She had washed his clothes and encouraged him to call his boss and talk to him about his job. Ultimately, he had lost that job when the plant had lay-offs, and she believed it was partially due to that lapse into the dark side. She had tried to help him find a job, but there were much younger, better qualified candidates for every job and a high unemployment rate that quickly discouraged him.

She had known he was depressed, especially when his unemployment ran out. Then he had been suffering with a horrible toothache and couldn't afford to take care of it, so she had sent him to her own dentist and helped Joe pay for it. When the notices for foreclosure had started to arrive in his mailbox, she had tried to help him sell his house and recover some of the equity, but Denver's real estate market was stagnant, and he'd had no luck finding a buyer.

All the while, she had been trying to steer him toward professional counseling at the free clinic, but he refused. She couldn't force him, but she hadn't given up. She hoped that sooner or later she could get him there. Apparently, time had run out.

Julie picked up the receiver.

"It's on speaker, so you don't have to use the receiver. Just hit the redial button," the police chief told her.

She replaced it in the cradle, then punched the button as directed and listened to the melodic tones as it dialed.

"*You got the money ready?*" the voice on the phone answered.

"Hi Joe. It's Julie," she said.

There was dead silence on the phone, and for a moment she thought they had been disconnected.

"Joe, are you still there?"

"*Julie. Is this a friendly call or are you out there with the sycophants?*"

"Of course I'm calling you as a friend. But yes, I'm out here with Rusty's and Jason's families and friends." She hesitated, wishing she was sitting across from him rather than separated by phone lines. It was so much easier talking to people when she could look into their eyes and read their body language. "I'm worried about you."

"*Why would you be? I'm fine.*"

"Come on, Joe. We've always been honest with each other. What happened to make you do this?"

He was quiet for a few seconds. When he spoke again, there was a catch in his voice. "*I miss Amy so much.*"

"I know you do."

"*My life has fallen apart. I just can't go on like this.*"

"But the firefighters have nothing to do with your bad fortune."

"*They killed her.*"

"We've talked about this," Julie reminded him gently. "Amy was in a hurry to get home and she was tired because she'd worked a double shift at the hospital. It was an accident, a horrible, terrible, tragic accident. But it wasn't the fire department's fault. And it certainly had nothing to do with those two firefighters you have in your house."

"Maybe not these two, but they're wearing the same uniforms and driving the same truck."

"Joe, you know those other firefighters didn't hurt Amy on purpose. They were on their way to a fire. They were running with full lights and sirens. She simply didn't notice them."

"*It wasn't her fault*," he practically shouted.

"No, she was tired and in a hurry. But it wasn't the firefighter's fault either." Julie took a deep breath. "You and Amy had something really special. You and I both know how rare that is. But it's time you let her go and moved on with your life. It's what she would want you to do. She wouldn't like to see you in such pain."

"*I've lost it all.*"

"You have so much . . . skills, brains and experience. It's not too late for you to start over. But you need to let the firefighters go. Their hands are clean."

"*I want someone to pay.*"

"You can't put a price on Amy. She was the love of your life. I'm sorry I never got to meet her, but you've told me so much about her that I feel I knew her. I know she would never want you to hurt someone else."

There was another long, silent pause. "*Julie, you've been a good friend to me. You're the only person who stayed with me. I respect your opinion. But I have to think about this. I've got to go now.*"

"Joe, you're a good man. You can get through this. I'll do all I can," Julie promised.

"*Thank you, Julie, for all you've done . . . for me and for Amy.*" The phone line went dead.

Once again, everyone in the room was staring at Julie. But now their expressions were both amazed and impressed. In spite of that, her shoulders slumped and she collapsed against the back of the chair. She hadn't been able to help Rusty and Jason. And she hadn't been able to help Joe. She was drained and disappointed.

She felt a hand squeeze her shoulder and she looked up to see Sam. His smile told her he knew she had done all she could.

It just hadn't been enough.

Her feet dragged as she left the command vehicle and walked back toward the crowd. She gave a mental shake. She had to have her emotions under control by the time she reached Rusty's and Jason's parents. They needed hope. And right now, she had none.

The chatter of reporters came from all angles as they continued to circle the scene and interview everyone who looked remotely involved. Julie ducked her head and blended with the crowd.

She had almost reached Pat Wilson when there was some activity at the house. The front door swung open and Jason and Rusty walked out. Alone and free. A hush fell over the crowd as they watched, unsure of what they were seeing.

Rusty turned back and spoke to someone in the doorway, but his voice didn't reach the crowd. Jason continued forward as Rusty hung back. After a few seconds, it became clear he was trying to talk the man inside into doing something. He motioned with his hand for Joe to join them. The crowd watched, transfixed as the conversation continued for several minutes. Finally, Rusty smiled and continued across the front yard, away from the house.

The crowd surged against the yellow tape that marked the perimeter boundaries. Jason reached them and was immediately surrounded by his parents, sisters and girlfriend. Rusty had almost reached the street when there was a whoosh, followed by a thunderous explosion.

CHAPTER SEVEN

Rusty slowly lifted his head and spit out a mouthful of grass and dirt. The blast had knocked him to the ground. Luckily, he hadn't reached the street yet or he would probably be spitting out teeth. His heavy coat had protected him from the flying debris, but his ears were ringing from the pressure and his head was spinning. Damn, he'd left his helmet in the house and . . .

His head cleared enough for him to realize that Joe had gone through with his threat. Rusty pulled himself into a sitting position and turned to see a black, flaming hole where Joe . . . and his house had been.

The paramedics reached Rusty and started trying to examine him by checking his eyes and his pulse rate. They couldn't stop him from getting to his feet even though his knees almost buckled and he could feel himself swaying.

"Let us get a stretcher," one of the paramedics suggested.

"I'll be fine. Go see if there's someone else who's really hurt," Rusty replied.

"Ignore him. He needs to go to the hospital," a voice from the crowd spoke up. Chris finally managed to push his way through and joined the other paramedics. Sara followed close behind. Chris stepped in front of Rusty and forced him to meet his gaze. "Don't argue with me. You put out fires. I keep people alive. Right now, you need to get checked out."

"I'm okay . . ."

"You were knocked down by an explosion and nearly killed. You have no idea what kind of damage could have been done."

Rusty and Chris didn't butt heads often. The four years' difference in their ages had kept them from traveling in the same circles for most of their lives. All three brothers had strong type A personalities and didn't lose any battle with grace. It was proof that Rusty was more shaken up than he realized that he finally accepted his brother's diagnosis. But he insisted on walking to the ambulance under his own power.

The firefighters had immediately surged forward to take care of the fire. The force of the blast had destroyed part of the two houses on each side of Joe's, and they, too were on fire. The police were struggling to keep any non-emergency personnel from crossing the perimeter. Even Rusty's parents had to wait until he reached them. They wrapped him in a warm, protective hug that closed out everyone else, including the swarm of reporters that had surrounded them.

Rusty ignored the outstretched microphones, preferring the attention of his family. His mother climbed into the back of the ambulance with him. As soon as the doors slammed shut and the vehicle moved forward, Rusty's head began swimming and he reluctantly obeyed the paramedic's request to lie down.

He closed his eyes, but that didn't stop the images that tumbled through his brain. "Did Joe make it?" he asked his mom.

"Who's Joe?" she asked. "The man in the house?"

"Yes. Did he make it out?"

Pat and the paramedic exchanged worried looks. "Just you and Jason came out before the explosion," she said.

Rusty rolled his head away from his mother and faced the wall of the ambulance. He had spent several hours not knowing whether he was going to get out of that house alive. No one had been more surprised than he when Joe had hung up his phone, paced around the room a couple more times, then picked up a knife and approached the two firefighters.

"Stand up and turn around," Joe had commanded, and they had reluctantly obeyed. Rusty had felt a tug on his wrists and his hands had fallen free. Another jerk of the knife had freed Jason. "Now get out of here. Fast."

Jason looked at Rusty, silently asking him if this was a trick. Rusty jerked his head toward the door and Jason had bolted for it. He paused before opening it until Joe waved him on. "It's not wired." He held his hands up, showing that the remote controller wasn't there. Jason cautiously turned the handle and eased the door open. When nothing happened, he pushed the door wider and ran out.

Rusty had followed at a more measured pace. When he realized Joe wasn't coming with them, he had tried to convince him to walk out with him and give himself up. Joe had hesitated, as if he was considering the possibility. He had even said, "Go on. I'll be right behind you. I want to grab a photo." Rusty had hesitated a moment longer, not wanting to leave Joe open for the SWAT team. As wrong as Joe had been to take the two firefighters hostage, there was something so deeply sad about him and so relatable that Rusty had almost understood the message Joe was trying to get across to the world. Besides, Rusty was in the business of rescuing people, and Joe needed to be rescued.

He had thought Joe was with him, right behind him as promised. It wasn't until the bombs had gone off and the earth had shaken seconds before the force of the blast had hit him from behind that Rusty had known that Joe had changed his mind. Two lives had been saved, but one had been lost. For most people, that would be a success, but for Rusty, it was a crushing failure.

Julie watched the ambulance wind its way through the crowd, its blinding red and blue lights ricocheting wildly off the multitude of faces. The driver hit a couple of siren boops to get people's attention so they would move out of the way. He didn't turn the sirens on full blast until he was well past the blockage and heading out of the neighborhood.

A whoosh of air rushed out of her lungs, and she suddenly was overcome with a flood of emotions. Joy, sadness, disappointment, panic, all rushed through her as the hundreds of people pushed and shoved, trying to get a better view. Reporters were everywhere, jostling for position so that the flaming remains of the house would be behind them as the cameras rolled. To the east, the sky was lightening, showing the first signs that this nightmare night was truly almost over.

Every muscle felt strained and every nerve stretched to its limit as she wound her way through the crowd and away from the frenzy of activity. She climbed inside her car and just sat, wrapped in its silence and isolation for a few minutes before she summoned enough strength to start the engine and drive home.

The TV was still on as she walked into her house. She clicked it off, filled Cat's water dish, turned off the lights and, after a quick shower, she fell into bed. Today she would have to trust her crew to handle whatever incidences that occurred. She'd done enough for one shift . . . one painfully long shift.

It seemed like she'd just shut her eyes, but when she awoke it was daylight outside, but the milky gray light that settled on a cold winter evening, just after sunset. A glance at her clock confirmed that she had slept the day away. She couldn't remember the last time she had slept for almost twelve hours straight through. Her first impulse was to jump out of bed and check in with the dispatcher.

But she knew Janice was on shift tonight and she was solid. Instead, Julie settled back against the pillows and let her mind filter through the events of last night. She tried to tell herself it was just another night on the job, but it had been more than that. She always cared about her victims, but when it had been two firefighters, it had been particularly stressful. The panicky look in Jason's mother's eyes and the way Pat had leaned against her husband as if she couldn't support her own weight was burned into Julie's memory. These two women who probably had never met before they'd arrived on scene had shared an emotional experience that only a mother could imagine.

Julie understood that fierce protective instinct of motherhood. It was so deep and so strong that she knew a mother would do anything for her child.

That thought ventured into an area she didn't want to remember, so she forced herself to get out of bed. A quick trip to the bathroom where she brushed her teeth, dressed in a pair of faded jeans and a baggy Colorado Rockies sweatshirt made her feel a little more refreshed. There was no reason to put on any makeup or do anything with her hair, so she let it fall free around her shoulders.

Cat had been particularly polite to let her sleep. He must have sensed that she needed it, but now that she was up and moving around, he was making her aware of his discomfort. It was edging into his prime hunting time, and he was anxious to get outdoors.

Julie's stomach growled, reminding her that she hadn't had anything to eat in a really long time either. So with Cat leading the way, she walked through her quiet house to the back door. Her hand was on the knob when a knock reverberated through the door. It was so unexpected that she literally jumped back a step and gasped. The knock sounded again.

Her heart was still pounding as she pulled aside the frilly curtain and peered outside. Rusty's smiling, but slightly frantic face looked back at her. "Let me in. Please hurry," he shouted. His voice was muffled through the glass, but she didn't hesitate to open the door.

Cat streaked out and Rusty hurried in, carrying a large pizza box and a brown paper bag on top.

"What . . .?" she started to ask as he shut and locked the door and pulled the curtain back over the window.

"Have you looked outside lately?" he asked as he put the pizza on the kitchen table.

"No, why?"

He led the way to her living room. "Just look out your peep hole."

She had no clue what he was talking about, but she went to the front door and peeked outside. She was shocked to see two local TV station's remote trucks parked in front of her house. A small crowd of people, some holding microphones, others with steady-cams on their shoulders and still others she recognized as neighbors were clustered on the sidewalk. A young mother Julie had waved to in passing was giving an interview. Julie turned around slowly and leaned back against the door.

"Why are they here?"

"Apparently, the word got out that you talked Joe into letting us go," Rusty told her as he studied her face for a reaction. "You're a hero."

She shook her head. "I didn't do anything special. You guys were the heroes."

Her expression changed. "What are you doing here? I thought they took you to the hospital."

"They did, but I checked out this evening. The last thing I wanted was to spend another night there."

"Are you okay?" she asked, her gaze moving all the way down to his tennis shoes and back up, as if she could see through his clothes for cuts, bruises and broken bones. "You hit the ground pretty hard."

"I'm fine. For some reason not all the bombs went off or I'd be in baggies at the morgue." He shrugged. "Guess it just wasn't my time."

"All of you adrenalin junkies have that attitude. Then again, you probably wouldn't go into a burning house or rescue someone from a car that's about to blow up if you didn't."

"I'm not crazy, and I'm not careless. But usually, we don't have time to overthink the situation before we move. It's all instinct and training."

Julie was average height for a woman, but as she looked up at Rusty, she realized he towered over her. It made her aware of how much bigger and stronger he was than her, and she shivered. Involuntarily, she took a step backward. "I don't mean to sound rude, but why are you here?"

"That didn't sound rude at all," he teased.

She had the grace to blush, and he had the chivalry to ignore it.

"After hospital gruel, I wanted pizza, and I owed you a meal. I didn't know if you'd be home yet, but I thought I'd take a chance."

"I didn't go in today. It was almost seven when I got home, and I knew I didn't want to fall asleep at my desk."

"They ran tests on me all day. I knew I'd have to get out of there if I hoped to get any sleep tonight," he told her.

"I don't know . . ." Her hesitation was automatic. She wasn't accustomed to sharing her safe space, even temporarily. The smell of pepperoni made its way to her nostrils, and she gave in. After sharing last night's experience, how dangerous could sharing a pizza be? "I've got some beer in the fridge," she told him as she opened the cabinet and took down two plates.

He took two bottles of cold beer out, opened them and set them on the table while she tore off sheets of paper towels for napkins.

"I don't entertain much," she explained apologetically as she tried to make them fancier up by folding them and placing them on the plates.

"Hey, at least you have paper towels. I usually use the napkins that come in the fast food bag," he told her.

He was, in fact, the first male guest in her home, and although it should have made her uncomfortable, his casual acceptance of her amenities . . . or lack of . . . kept it from being awkward. They dug into the pizza with gusto, not talking until only one piece remained.

Rusty looked at it, then at Julie. "The last piece is yours."

She leaned back in her chair. "No, take it. I'm stuffed."

He didn't hesitate and picked it up. "I'm impressed. You ate your share. I like a woman who knows how to eat."

"Eating is one thing I do well," she said with a smile, "that is, when I have time." She stood up and went to the refrigerator. "Want another beer?"

"Do you have to ask?" Rusty finished off the piece of pizza and wiped his lips on the paper towel. She opened two more bottles, handed one to him and returned to her chair with hers. They each took a drink.

She could feel his gaze on her and she looked up.

"You're going to think I'm crazy," he said thoughtfully, "but I could have sworn you had brown eyes."

Julie immediately ducked her head, hiding her naturally blue eyes from his view. *Damn.* She'd forgotten that she wasn't wearing her brown contact lens. Her mind raced for a plausible explanation. She looked up again, but avoided his direct gaze.

"I prefer brown eyes, so I usually wear brown contacts. I just woke up about an hour before you got here, so I haven't put them in."

"Are you near or far-sighted?"

"Uh . . . neither, actually. I wear them just because I like the way they look."

He didn't appear to believe her explanation, but he didn't challenge it. Instead, he changed the subject back to one they had studiously been avoiding.

"So, how did you talk Joe into it?"

"I didn't think I had." She ran her fingers through her hair, flipping the long black strands over her shoulder. "When we ended the conversation, he didn't give any indication that he had changed his mind. I was afraid he would . . ." her voice trailed off.

"It's weird, but I kind of understand the whole Stockholm Syndrome thing after this. I had no idea whether or not he was going to trigger those bombs at any minute," Rusty told her. "Even though I really thought he was going to kill us, I couldn't help but feel sorry for him. No job, no insurance, no wife, about to lose his house. Everything he had worked for . . . gone. Poor guy. The more time I spent in that room, surrounded by all that stuff that was obviously exactly the same as it had been the day his wife left him . . ."

"His wife didn't leave him," Julie interrupted sharply.

"Yeah, she did. She ran off with a firefighter," Rusty insisted.

Julie shook her head. "No, she didn't. She was killed by a firefighter, well, sort of. She died in a collision with a fire truck. She was either distracted or fell asleep after a night shift at the hospital where she worked as a nurse. She ran a red light and probably never knew what hit her. I was with him when he was notified."

Rusty leaned back in the chair. His forehead creased in bewilderment. "I don't understand. Why would he tell us she had run off?"

Julie sighed. "I thought he was past all that."

"You knew he was delusional?"

"I knew he was having difficulty accepting that she was gone forever. He was in therapy for several years. The last time I talked with . . . before yesterday, of course . . . he was talking about redecorating the house and donating a lot of Amy's things to the Salvation Army."

"I thought the place looked like a memorial. It seemed odd that he hadn't put away any of her photos," Rusty commented. "But why would he rather think she had left him than that she had died? Isn't that more of a betrayal?"

"I'm not a psychologist, but I think it was that he just couldn't accept that she was dead and never coming back. Somehow, in his mind, he could still believe she might walk through the front door and everything would go back to normal if he made himself think she had run away."

"That's fucked up," Rusty muttered.

"Aren't we all?" she challenged.

Rusty was silent for several minutes as he digested that information. "I can't imagine loving someone that much," he finally spoke, his voice soft and almost wistful.

"Neither can I," Julie agreed. "Every day I see what happens when people love too much. It takes away their logic and their self-respect. They let themselves be beaten, cheated on and even killed."

Rusty shifted his gaze focused on her. "Wow, I've finally met someone who's even more cynical about love than I am."

"Show me a man and woman who are truly in love and don't want to hurt or cheat or control each other, and I'll show you a fiction novel or a Reese Witherspoon movie. It just isn't real life."

"My sentiments exactly." Rusty lifted his half-empty beer bottle and she raised hers and they clicked them together in a toast.

"So what's in the paper bag?" she asked, nodding toward the brown sack on the counter.

Rusty stood and retrieved it. "I almost forgot. I don't know about you, but whenever I eat Italian food, I like dessert." He pulled out two Styrofoam boxes and handed her one. "Pino's cheesecake is the best."

Julie got a couple of forks out of a drawer and handed him one. "I love cheesecake. I've never eaten at Pino's, but I heard it was good. The pizza was delicious." She opened her container and admired the generous slice of cheesecake topped by cherries in a thick sauce. Without further hesitation, she cut off a piece with her fork and took a bite. The thick, creamy filling melted on her tongue and the crunchy graham cracker crust was light and buttery. "Ummm, this is amazing. Is that crushed pecans in the crust?"

"Beats me," Rusty said, his mouth full. "I just know that I like it."

"I thought all firefighters were great cooks."

"I know my way around a grill, and I make the best barbecue sauce in the world. Other than that, I eat whatever shows up on my plate at the station or I grab some takeout," he admitted. "I didn't notice much in your refrigerator. What's your excuse?"

"Time and, well, I guess, motivation. It seems so pointless to spend an hour cooking a meal for one person. I get home late, and it's just easier to take out a Stouffer's or a Marie Calendar's meal. They're tasty and quick."

He gave her another long, measuring look. "You're young, you're attractive, you're intelligent . . . so why is there no Mr. Julie?"

"I don't need a man," she responded a little defensively.

"Maybe not. But aren't they good for . . . something else?" One corner of his mouth lifted in a teasing grin.

"Nothing I can't do for myself."

He laughed out loud. "God, you're a female me."

She couldn't resist smiling. "From the rumors I've heard about you, that might be an insult."

"They're probably all true. It's good to meet people's expectations. It saves me a lot of conversation on dates."

"Yeah, and it probably saves you a lot of second dates."

He nodded without any sign of remorse.

A loud knock startled both of them.

"Sounds like they finally gave up on you going outside," Rusty commented.

Julie felt a flutter of panic in the pit of her stomach. "I don't want to talk to them."

"Maybe a quick wave and a '*No Comment*' would satisfy them."

She shook her head emphatically. "No, I can't . . . uh, I don't want to be on the news. I didn't do anything. They have no reason to bother me."

His eyes narrowed as he studied her thoughtfully. "Then ignore them. I'm sure you can get the PR department to issue an official statement on Monday. Maybe by then, they'll be distracted by a new story."

She glanced at the front door, imagining that the person outside was waiting impatiently. Surely, they would give up and move on to something else if she didn't offer them anything to make into a story.

"How did you get in here without them following you?" she asked him, suddenly curious how he had managed to make it through the gauntlet.

"I parked a couple blocks down, ducked my head and just walked up the driveway. They thought I was the pizza guy."

One eyebrow arched accusingly as she said, "So now they think I'm involved with a pizza boy because you've been here way longer than a normal delivery."

"Maybe you're a good tipper."

"You're ruining my reputation." But her complaint was softened with a reluctant twinkle in her blue eyes.

"Yeah, well, that's *my* reputation."

She stood and started cleaning up. Instead of hanging back, he, too, got up and joined her, throwing away the trash and recycling their bottles. When the kitchen was back to normal, she wiped her hands on a towel. "Hey, thanks for the pizza. That was a nice thing for you to do."

"I'll admit that it wasn't all altruistic," he admitted. "I really wanted to talk about . . . well, everything. I'm sure they'll run me through psych next week, but I knew I could be totally honest with you. You were there. I saw you outside with my mom . . . and I wanted to thank you. You're really good at your job."

She shrugged off his compliments. "It helps just to have someone there, standing next to you when you're going through something traumatic. I didn't want her to be alone."

"Thanks for that. And for listening to me. I just can't figure out why he thought this would fix anything." He shook his head, baffled by Joe's story as much as by the man's twisted solution to his grief.

Julie hung the towel on a rack so it would dry. Her expression was bitter as she shrugged. "Yeah, well, it's just another way that love can kill you."

CHAPTER EIGHT

As Rusty predicted, the news crews were gone the next morning, thanks to a bi-polar Santa who had gone berserk at Cherry Creek Mall. Apparently, an old, wrinkled naked man with a long, flowing white beard, wearing only black boots and a red cap was more newsworthy than a woman making a phone call to a kidnapper. Julie made a mental note to send Santa a thank you note. He had given her an early Christmas present.

It was Sunday and she was on call. She thought she would have a few hours respite before the end of the first round of football games, but the first call came in just after 3 p.m. Julie jotted down the address on a blank form, pulled on her coat and a stocking cap and hurried outside after pressing the garage door opener. A light snow was falling and as soon as the cat stuck his nose out the door, he turned and ran back inside before she shut the door.

"I don't blame you, Cat," she muttered as she locked the door, then ran to the garage and got into her car. It would be a good day to snuggle under a blanket on the couch with a mug of hot chocolate and the Sunday edition of *The Denver Post*. Maybe it was time to let someone else take the weekend calls.

The City of Denver was relatively compact, completely surrounded by other cities so it had no room for growth. However, even though it was limited in expansion potential, it was the most populated city in the state of

Colorado and shared a footprint with Denver County. On weekends unless there was a home game for one of the local sports teams, getting almost anywhere in the city didn't take but a few minutes. Julie arrived at a small, well-kept bungalow several blocks from the gold-domed Capitol building and parked. There was only one police cruiser on scene, so because she had arrived so quickly, she assumed this was not a very complicated situation which meant there were no deaths or serious injuries.

She locked her car and tucked the keys into the pocket of her slacks. Sam met her at the door and stepped outside to briefly fill her in.

"It's not a typical domestic," he told her in a low voice. "Just wanted to give you a heads up."

Julie frowned. She still didn't know what to expect.

As he held the door open for her, Sam added, "I'm glad you're here. She scares the shit out of me."

The living room was cluttered, but nothing appeared to be broken or destroyed from a physical fight. A middle-aged man whose slight frame couldn't have been carrying more than 140 pounds sat on one end of the couch, leaning forward with his elbows braced on his knees and his face buried in his hands. On the other end of the couch a woman who outweighed her husband at least double bristled with an angry electricity that filled the air with tension.

As Julie entered the room, the woman jumped to her feet. "Get out of my house! All of you," she demanded.

"Please sit down," Sam told her politely, but firmly.

She continued forward. "*I* didn't call you." She waved toward her husband. "*He* didn't call you. There's no problem here."

"Ma'am, we received a call from your neighbors because they were concerned. We could hear you from the street when we drove up. Now, have a seat so we can get to the bottom of this."

Sam was six feet tall, but the woman towered over him . . . and she wasn't backing down. His hand moved to the can of pepper spray on his utility belt. "Ma'am, sit down." This time, it was clearly a command.

The woman hesitated, standing nose-to-nose with the cop until common sense convinced her that it was in her best interest to return to the couch. Reluctantly, with her eyes shooting poison darts at Sam, she backed up and sat.

"Now, what's going on here?" he asked.

"Nothing!" she shouted. "We were just about to start dinner."

"Mr. Jansen, are you hurt?" Sam asked.

The man slowly lifted his face. His eyes were dull and sad. "I just want some peace and quiet. I worked a twelve-hour shift at the factory. I was hoping to watch the Broncos game, then go to bed . . ."

The woman was back on her feet, this time, facing her husband. "All you do is work and sleep, sleep and work."

"I'm lucky to have a job."

"Don't fuck with me. I know you're sleeping with that slut."

The man shook his head wearily. It was obvious this wasn't the first time he'd had this discussion. "I'm too tired."

"You're having sex with someone. It's certainly not me," Mrs. Jansen accused.

Sam arched an eyebrow that only Julie could see, clearly indicating that he couldn't imagine anyone wanting to have sex with that woman.

"I just want to get some sleep," the man muttered.

The woman lunged toward the man. Sam pushed aside the coffee table and wrapped his arms around her while pulling her back from the man who was cowering in a fetal position on the couch.

"That's it," the cop declared. "You just bought yourself a night in lock up." It was quite a struggle, but he finally got the cuffs on her. "I'm taking her in. Julie, will you be okay here?"

It was understood that the cops would stay if Julie or her staff felt uncomfortable being alone with the victim or if the perpetrator was still at large. Since he had Mrs. Jansen in custody, there was no reason for him to stay unless Julie wanted him to.

"We'll be fine," Julie told him. "I'm going to stick around and talk to Mr. Jansen for a bit."

That was like a shot of adrenalin to the woman who jerked away from Sam and advanced on Julie. "If you screw him, I'll hunt you down and squash you like a roach under my shoe."

Julie didn't doubt the woman's promise. "Mrs. Jansen, I work for the police department, and . . ."

"I don't care if you work for the fucking president of the United States. If you touch my husband, I'll kill you."

Sam grabbed the cuffs and pulled Mrs. Jansen out the front door. Julie and Mr. Jansen could hear her cursing and screaming all the way to the patrol car.

Julie waited until she heard the doors shut and the car start and drive off before turning to Mr. Jansen. "May I sit down?" she asked.

He nodded, and Julie sat on the chair next to the couch.

"My name is Julie, and I'm here to help you."

"I'm Fred," he said, his voice flat and drained of all emotion.

"How long have you two been married?"

After a hesitant start, he eventually poured out a story Julie had heard many times before, but usually told by an abused wife. It was rare to have the husband on the receiving end.

Apparently, Mrs. Jansen had always been overbearing, but it had been focused on their daughter. After their daughter ran off . . . no surprise there . . . two years ago, the woman had turned her aggression on her husband. He, in turn, had started working extra shifts to keep from going home. She had become a frequent shopper on QVC, the evidence of which was crowded on every shelf and flat surface in the room. Every time he mentioned that she should cut back, a fight would follow. And each fight was bigger and worse than the last.

"Does she hit you?" Julie asked gently. It was a question she always asked the women, and although it felt awkward in this situation, she wanted to hear his answer.

His eyes darted around the room as if he was expecting his wife to storm back in. Slowly, he pulled up his t-shirt to reveal a huge purple and black bruise coloring his ribcage.

Julie bit back a gasp. "Fred, when did this happen?"

"Yesterday. I accidentally knocked one of her little dolls off the end table and when I bent over to clean it up, she kicked me."

"Your ribs might be broken. Did you go to a doctor?"

He shook his head. "I don't want to cause trouble for her. She didn't mean to kick me that hard. I shouldn't have been so clumsy."

Julie was exasperated. It was the same excuse she'd heard from countless women. Apparently, abuse had no gender. "I really think you need to have it checked out."

His negative head shake was even more emphatic. "Do you know how it would affect my job if word ever got out? I supervise thirty-two men. They'd never respect me if they knew."

It wasn't really a surprise that he didn't want to be treated. Fewer than one-fourth of all victims ever did. They knew their abuse would have to be reported which would cause on-going repercussions to their home life…and usually more abuse. Since Julie couldn't guarantee that no one would find out if Fred went to the hospital, she couldn't insist. But his injuries needed to be documented. "Is this the only time?"

"Usually, she just screams a lot. Sometimes, she throws things, but I get out of the way if I see it coming."

"Why do you stay?"

He was silent for several minutes, and just when Julie thought he wasn't going to answer, he murmured, "I don't want to be alone."

Julie understood that all too well. People were willing to put up with a lot of misery to keep from being by themselves. Sometimes it was financial. Sometimes it was emotional. Sometimes kids, friends or family were involved. None of those things seem to fit this situation. "Wouldn't it be better to feel safe?"

"It's my home," he stated simply.

"Would she consider couples' therapy?"

"Not a chance."

"I can't give you advice. It's your life and your marriage," Julie told him. "But I think you're in danger. From what I've seen, this isn't a healthy situation. I don't think she'd do it on purpose, but she could kill you."

"She doesn't always hit me," he said, jumping to her defense.

"Verbal abuse can be even more powerful and painful than physical abuse." Julie looked into his eyes, searching for some sign of self-preservation. "Fred, you look exhausted. Your wife can be bailed out tomorrow. That'll give you some time to think about this." She took a card out of her pocket and set it on the table next to him. "Please let me help you. And I mean any time in the future. Just call me, and I'll get you to a safe place."

He nodded, but the slump of his shoulders told her more than words could that he felt defeated and hopeless.

"We need to document this injury. Could I take some photos?" she asked. "I promise I won't do anything with them unless you want me to."

Fred was reluctant, but he lifted his shirt again. Julie snapped a few photos with her cell phone.

"I'll hang onto these just in case," she told him. "You've got a lot going for you. You don't deserve to be treated like this."

A tear slid down his cheek and he brushed it away quickly. "Life doesn't turn out like you expect."

"No, it certainly doesn't." She gave him a warm smile and let herself out the front door.

Monday morning came all too early. Julie was greeted by a chorus of congratulations and pats on the back for her part in the kidnap rescue. Even the chief came up to shake her hand.

"My phone's been ringing off the hook," he told her. "All the TV stations want an interview or a press conference. How's your schedule?"

Julie's heart pounded. The last thing she wanted was to see her face on TV again. "Sir, if it's all the same to you, I want to be left out of it."

"But you're the hero of the moment. It's good publicity."

"I don't think it would be good for my relationship with future victims if they think I'm a publicity hound. I'd rather not be interviewed or have my photo splashed out in the press."

"I see your point," the chief agreed. "I'll do the press conference alone."

"Thank you, sir." She couldn't adequately voice her relief. Before he could change his mind, she scuttled into her office and hid there, plowing through several days of paperwork and putting together the schedule for January. Walt would be back from vacation after Christmas, so she put him on for Sundays because he didn't mind weekends. Sunday nights could be very busy and it was difficult getting to work on Mondays with almost no sleep. Last night had been no exception. She had barely gotten home when the phone rang with another domestic, followed a couple hours later by an apartment fire. She had practically crawled home at three a.m. for a quick shower and a couple hours of sleep.

Maybe it was time she took a break from actually going to calls. After five years, she had to admit she was a little burned out. In her line of work, repeat customers meant failure. Statistics showed that one in four women and one in thirty-three men would be abused or forced to have sex against their will in their lifetime. That guaranteed an abundance of victims which meant that the need for advocates would never go away, even though only about thirty or forty percent of abuses were reported to authorities. Add to that the disturbing fact that most victims were likely to have suffered through seven to ten incidences before they reached a point where they accepted help and tried to change their situation. That is, if they survived. Every day in the

United States three women were killed by their spouse or partner. And for almost all of them, it had not been their first abusive incident.

It was all so overwhelming and hopeless. How long could she go on pounding her head against the wall for these people who usually ended up going back into the arms of their abuser?

Julie leaned back in her chair and stared at the large oil painting of an alpine meadow, lush with wildflowers, alive with a crystal-clear stream curving across it and surrounded by the rugged peaks of the Rocky Mountains. The artist had captured the serenity of the scene, as well as the majesty. Looking at the painting, Julie could almost imagine herself there, sitting on a large boulder by the stream, surrounded by deer and bunnies and other innocent creatures that lived in peace and compatibility. There were no wolves or bears or mountain lions in the meadow. No black eyes, broken bones or deep bruises to a body or a soul. No tears or regrets. Nothing that could hurt anyone or upset the peaceful balance of nature. She felt safe there.

It was probably the only place she felt safe, and sadly, it wasn't real and she couldn't physically hide there.

CHAPTER NINE

Rusty was glad to get back to work. The chief had wanted him to miss a shift to recover, but Rusty had been eager to return. Even though there were no outward scars, it had been an unnerving incident that had shaken Rusty more than he would admit, but after a few days at home and some restless nights punctuated by nightmares, the energy of the firehouse was a comfortable refuge.

The guys didn't cut him any slack, which was oddly comforting. After being fussed over by his parents and the press, it was good to get back to normal. There had been an unusually lingering cold spell. There were still remnants of the last snowfall on the ground, and every other day brought a fresh inch or two. Cold weather brought more than ice on the roads. There was always a rash of fires started by portable heaters and carbon monoxide poisonings from poor ventilation. These cold snaps, frozen pipes and the usual rash of fires fueled by Christmas trees kept the fire trucks on the road almost constantly.

Rusty welcomed the activity. The shift left him exhausted, but invigorated. He took a shower at the firehouse, then stopped for breakfast at Denny's. Working a twenty-four hour shift from 7:30 a.m. to 7:30 a.m. might seem unconventional to most people, but he liked it. Now he had two days off. From the look of the heavy clouds hanging over the mountains, the powder would be fresh and deep, perfect for skiing. He sent texts out to his brothers to see if they were off and wanted to join him.

His eggs and bacon arrived just as answering texts from Sam and Chris came through, both declining his offer. That sucked. He hated skiing alone. Without even asking, he knew his fellow firefighters had families and other responsibilities that would keep them home on their days off. Mentally, he ran through the list of his female acquaintances, but while they were good for a roll in the hay, there wasn't one of them he wanted to spend the whole day with, especially during the car ride there and back.

What about Julie? For some reason, he couldn't quite get her out of his thoughts. At every call last night he had looked for her, but other victim's advocates on her staff had shown up. Maybe she would like to take the day off and go to Breckenridge with him.

He didn't know if she skied. In fact, he knew very little about what she liked or didn't like. What puzzled him was why that mattered. She was pretty in a pure, natural sense, but not beautiful. She was friendly, without being gushy. It wasn't like she was trying to attract his attention or even wanted it. In fact, he felt she was doing everything she could to discourage him.

Rusty didn't get rejected. There was no ego involved; just fact. Maybe that was why Julie lingered in his mind. She was an enigma, an ice cream flavor he hadn't tasted. Just like the dozens of women in his past, once he had licked her, both literally and figuratively, his curiosity would be sated, and he could move on.

He finished his meal, left a generous tip for the waitress who had done everything short of dumping coffee in his lap to get him to notice her. Now that he had a plan of action, he was focused on moving forward.

It was a few blocks to the police station, so he decided to drop in, unannounced and use his charm to convince her to take a day off. Unlike him, she worked at least forty hours a week in the office and an additional ten to fifteen hours on the weekend. She deserved some time away from the stress.

Frankly, Rusty didn't know how she was able to deal with all the drama. He and his fellow firefighters rushed in and tried to save the day by putting out the fire or helping someone who has been hurt. Julie had to come in after the tragedy and try to make things better or help people regroup. She dealt with victims who were at rock bottom. Their homes were gone or their loved ones had died or their own bodies were broken. She gave them clothes, found them someplace to live, helped them with insurance or financial aid, made funeral arrangements or tried to keep them safe from whoever or whatever was hurting them. That had to be even more exhausting than fighting a fire. It certainly would be emotionally draining.

Perhaps that was it. Maybe her job took everything and she had nothing left to give. She definitely needed a getaway day.

In the police station he was greeted by everyone he passed. He knew a lot of cops because of his brothers, but the kidnapping incident last week had made him a sort of civil servant celebrity. Anyone who had almost been killed in the line of duty earned extra respect.

He finally made it to Julie's office. Her door was closed, but that was a minor obstacle. He knocked. When she didn't answer, he opened the door and looked in.

She was alone. At the sound of the door opening, she whirled around in her chair to face him.

"Are you busy?" he asked rhetorically.

"Yeah, swamped," she answered, lifting her hands, then letting them fall back to the arms of the chair. "Are you here for a debriefing?"

"Nah, I did that yesterday . . . between fires."

"I heard you guys were busy."

He shrugged. "People with pets or kids shouldn't have portable heaters. Sixteen apartment units burned because a cat knocked one over."

"People have to stay warm."

She didn't invite him in, but he ignored that, walked to the chair across the desk from her and sat. "You look tired," he told her.

"I *am* tired," she agreed. "I haven't been sleeping well."

"Me either." He flashed her his most charming smile. "But I know what will help us both."

Her eyebrows lifted skeptically.

"Exercise," he continued. "Do you know how to ski?"

"I wouldn't say I'm an expert, but I can get from the top to the bottom without running into a tree. Why?"

He leaned forward enthusiastically. "I'm sure you have some comp time. Let's drive up to Breckenridge."

"Today?" She seemed stunned by the suggestion.

"Why not? There's fresh powder and it's too early in the season for crowds."

"Because I . . ." Her voice trailed off.

"Fresh air . . . nature . . . hot chocolate . . .?" he prompted, trying to tempt her.

"But my staff . . ."

"Can get along without you for a day. You've trained them well." He pointed at the stack of reports on her desk. "Paperwork can wait. You need this change of scenery."

Her gaze lifted to a painting of a peaceful meadow, and he knew he had hit a nerve.

"Come on. You need to recharge your batteries."

She hesitated a moment longer, then, to his surprise, she opened her bottom drawer, took out her purse and stood. "Let's go."

"Really?" He blinked, a little amazed that she had capitulated. It was a small thing, but it felt like a huge victory. He stood and, before she could change her mind, helped her put her coat on and led the way out of her office.

She stopped at her boss's office and the reception desk to make sure everyone knew she would be gone, but not completely out of touch.

"I'm going to run home and get my stuff. I'll pick you up at your place in an hour," Rusty told her. "No chickening out."

She shook her head. "I won't."

He walked her to her car, and once inside, they drove off in different directions.

Julie changed her mind a dozen times on the trip home, and yet she didn't turn back. As she slowed to turn into her driveway, she noticed a car parked across the street from her house. She didn't recognize having seen it before, but then, like most women, cars didn't register on her consciousness. Unless it was a Mustang or a Corvette, it was just a big car or a little car or an SUV. This one was a big car, white and nondescript. As she passed it, she looked in to see if she recognized the driver, but the windows were fogged up. Dismissing it as someone's mid-morning tryst, she averted her eyes, not wanting to see that sort of neighborhood activity. She hit the garage door opener and drove into the garage. The door closed behind her as she unlocked the kitchen door and went inside.

Cat brushed up against her legs and gave her a few croaky meows, obviously disturbed by her messing with his sleep schedule.

"Yeah, I'm not sure what's going on either," she told him as she squatted down and stroked his black-striped gray coat. His purr vibrated against her fingers, an audible appreciation of her hospitality. She had no idea where he had spent the first few years of his life, but he seemed to be quite content to settle here with her.

Julie made sure he had fresh water and some dry kibble before she went to her bedroom to change. It took a couple of minutes to find her ski pants. When she first moved to Denver, she had gone on a few outings with co-workers to the mountains. Julie had grown up in Connecticut with wealthy parents that loved to ski and had spent a few weeks every winter traveling around the country, staying at the finest resorts. Her first time on a Colorado slope had been when she was eight . . . but that was a lifetime ago.

She pulled on a royal blue turtle neck sweater and the tight black ski pants. She didn't own skies or boots, but they would be available for rent on-site. She brought a pullover sweater in case it was really cold and a knit hat with a yarn tassel and put them with her parka and a pair of heavy gloves.

This was so out of character for her. She never did anything impulsive, at least not lately. Rusty had caught her at a particularly vulnerable moment. He had offered a chance to go to the meadow, and she couldn't refuse. She needed to escape if only for a day.

A knock on the back door told her Rusty was there, and she was surprised by the little skip of her heart. She was smiling when she opened the door.

"Ready?" he asked.

She nodded and stepped outside, then locked the door behind her. Cat had resumed his nap on the back of the couch, taking advantage of a sun ray that was warming that spot. He was content to let his person go off and play while he stayed warm and dry.

The car that had been parked in the street was gone. Obviously, just a quickie, she thought, then forgot about it as she and Rusty headed out of the city.

"Aren't you just getting off your shift?" she asked as they headed north on I-25.

He nodded.

"Aren't you tired?"

"I caught a couple hours of sleep between calls last night," he told her. "I try to stay up when I get off so I can keep my sleep schedule regular."

"That's probably smart. Shift work disorder can really mess you up."

"Have you noticed a correlation between shift work and domestic violence?" he asked.

"Actually, I have. Changing your sleep patterns throws off your body clock. It causes insomnia and sleep deprivation. Lack of sleep can make people grumpy and short-tempered which seems to be contagious."

"Then it all escalates and someone gets hurt."

Julie nodded. "It's more that they can't think straight and once they get into an argument, they have more trouble staying calm and finding ways to settle it peacefully. And it doesn't help when their family members expect them to keep up with normal activities which compromises their sleep time."

"I've found that ten to thirty minute naps recharge my batteries and help me get by until I can get a full night's sleep," Rusty commented.

The conversation never lulled during the almost two-hour trip to Breckenridge. Julie had been expecting Rusty to live up to his reputation as a flirt. But he surprised her by keeping up his end of an intelligent dialogue. They talked about everything from their favorite local weathermen, or rather weatherwoman since they agreed that Kathy Sabine was the best, to the last movies they'd seen and even touched on politics. What they didn't talk about was the specifics of their jobs or Rusty's recent brush with death. The topics were heavy, but they kept things light and time passed quickly.

Breckenridge looked like a Christmas card with its thick covering of snow, long icicles hanging from Victorian-looking buildings and flocked trees. Everything was covered in twinkling lights, oversized ornaments and candy canes. The snow had stopped falling and the sky was a vibrant blue against the pure white peaks. Rusty and Julie were anxious to hit the slopes, so they went straight to the resort.

Julie insisted on paying her own way even though Rusty offered. Equipment rental and a day pass for the ski lifts wasn't cheap, but Julie didn't spend a lot of money on entertainment, so she could afford it.

The summit elevation was almost 13,000 feet which was almost two and a half times that of Denver, so even though they were both in good shape, after three runs, they were ready to take a break.

"I'm starving," Julie said as they clumped into the restaurant, their chunky ski boots making their gaits stiff and awkward. She had put on a layer of sunblock, but she could feel her cheeks burning from the wind and the sun. Even though she was winded and her muscles were getting a little sore, she felt good.

They ordered their food, found a table and dug in with the enthusiasm of bears just out of hibernation.

"You're pretty good out there," he commented as he sat back and let the meal he had so quickly devoured settle.

"I skied a lot when I was young, but not so much lately. We had a little ski club going at the station a couple years ago. It kind of fell apart when one of the women got pregnant and one of the men got transferred to a different shift. It's not much fun alone."

"My brothers and I used to go all the time, but we all work different schedules, so it's not easy to arrange it. Holidays are difficult enough to coordinate."

"I don't know how your parents deal with having all of you in such dangerous work."

"My dad was a judge, so he gets it. And Mom tries to be okay with it, but I can tell she worries about us. When my brother got shot earlier this year, none of us told her about it until it was all over." He took a drink of hot chocolate. "Do your parents live around here?"

Julie lifted her cup to her mouth and considered her answer carefully. "My parents are both dead."

Rusty frowned, but before he could offer his condolences, she hurried to add, "It was a long time ago. They were killed by a drunk driver on Christmas Day. I was a junior in college and had decided to spend the holidays with a friend instead of going home." Her gaze lifted to the beauty outside the window, but her eyes didn't see it. Instead, they were glazed with a rush of tears that surprised her. She felt Rusty's hand wrap around hers.

"And you think things would have been different if you'd been there?" he guessed.

"Maybe."

"So you've been trying to make up for it by helping other people get over their losses ever since."

She hadn't really put the two things together before now. Actually, it was events later in her life that had inspired her career, but she couldn't tell him about that. Some secrets were too deep to share.

"It has helped," she agreed.

His smile was gentle and empathetic. Even though his own family was intact, he understood loss. He dealt with it every day, just as she did.

His fingers were warm and distracting. Absently, his thumb was stroking her palm, and he was totally unaware of the disturbing effect it was having on her. Tingles of pleasure streaked up her arm and radiated out from there. It was a feeling she hadn't experienced in a very long time. And one that wasn't entirely welcomed. Abruptly, she pulled her hand away and stood up.

"Let's get in a few more runs," she said.

Rusty was left with no option but to follow. They gathered up their trash and tossed it into the appropriate containers and stomped back outside to where they had left their skis.

It was dark when they drove back into Denver several hours later. They were both physically exhausted and very relaxed. They had picked up dinner from a fried chicken franchise, then headed to her house. With their arms loaded with a bucket of chicken, a bag of sides and Julie's extra clothes, they walked to her back door. She put the key in the lock, but before she could turn it, the slight pressure of her touch pushed the door open.

Julie's eyes widened in alarm. "Someone's been in here."

"Maybe you just forgot to lock it," Rusty suggested.

"No, I'm sure it was locked. A few days ago, I was sure I had left Cat outside, but he was indoors when I got home. So I've been extra careful."

Rusty put his armload of food back in his SUV. "Someone might still be inside. You stay out here, and I'll check it out."

"No, I . . ." She started to protest, but the last thing she wanted was to come face-to-face with an intruder. That was only marginally worse than having Rusty wander around her house and look in all her closets and under her bed. She hoped there wasn't anything horribly embarrassing lying around.

He opened the hatchback of his SUV and took out a small hatchet, then entered her house. She watched as room-by-room, lights went on, marking his progress. Five minutes later he came back out.

"No sign of anyone, and they didn't mess things up. Let's get inside."

He gathered the food and led the way back into her house. Julie followed, looking around nervously as if Rusty might have missed seeing someone hiding behind the door or in the pantry.

"You should check to see if anything is missing," he said.

She nodded, then hesitated. He noticed and smiled.

"I'll go with you," he offered.

Julie was shocked at the rush of relief she felt.

"I don't have anything valuable other than the TV and the microwave, and they're both still here."

"No jewelry or guns?" he asked.

She shook her head. "No, but I'm having second thoughts about not owning a gun."

They retraced his steps through her small bedroom, the spare bedroom and the bathroom. Cat jumped down from his perch on the back of the couch and followed them. Nothing seemed out of place. No drawers were dumped and the closets looked untouched. Feeling relieved, but puzzled, she returned to the kitchen.

He unpacked the food on the kitchen table while she set out plates and flatware.

Julie opened the refrigerator. "I've got some light beer, Diet Coke and a bottle of plum wine. What would you like?"

"I'll take a beer."

She took out a beer for him and a Diet Coke for her and placed them on the table, then sat down. They selected their favorite pieces and dished out coleslaw, mashed potatoes and gravy onto their plates and started eating.

"Any idea why someone would break in and not take anything?" he asked.

"I've been trying to think of something, but I honestly don't have a clue," she answered with a puzzled frown.

He glanced over at the deadbolt lock on the back door. "That's a decent lock, but it's on a wooden door. It would be easy to splinter the frame. But they didn't break in. You don't hide a key outside, do you?"

She blushed. "Yes, under a rock by the gate."

"Bad idea."

"Apparently."

Rusty yawned, which reminded her how long he had gone without sleep.

"You should go home. I'll be fine," Julie told him. There must have been something in her voice that told him she still was on edge because he helped her clean off the table and load the dishwasher.

"Your couch looks pretty comfortable. Why don't I crash there tonight, then tomorrow I can see what I can do to reinforce your doors?" he suggested.

"I couldn't ask you to do that. You're tired. And I'm sure you'd sleep better in a bed."

His blue eyes twinkled. "Are you offering me *your* bed?"

Again her cheeks burned with embarrassment. "Absolutely not. And if that's where your offer was heading, then …"

"Hold on. My offer of sleeping on the couch was honorable." He laughed and gave an unapologetic shrug. "You can't blame me for trying. It's part of the man code."

Julie considered his statement. She was used to living alone and doing everything for herself. It had been a long time since anyone had come to her aid, and she didn't know how to graciously accept it. But the thought of spending the night alone in this house really creeped her out. Someone had been here. Even though there was no obvious sign, she knew it. She felt violated. They had looked in her closets, maybe touched her underwear or her toothbrush. They knew everything about her, and she knew nothing about them.

It bothered her that she didn't know Rusty all that well, but as cocky as he was, she trusted him. She had seen him risk his life to save a parrot. That kind of guy couldn't be all bad. He was big and strong and just being in the same room with him made her feel safe.

As awkward and inconvenient as it was for him, she very much wanted him to stay. But it had to be clear that this wasn't a coy way of agreeing to have sex with him.

"I admit that my nerves are a little on end. I would feel more comfortable with you here," she told him. "But I really mean it about the bed."

He bowed his head in acceptance. "I know you do, and I can be a gentleman. Just don't spread it around. Women will start expecting me to be more sensitive."

She smiled. It was another of his many talents to always be able to make her relax.

He yawned again, and she went to the spare bedroom, that unfortunately had no bed, to get a spare sheet, blanket and pillow. When she walked back into the living room, he handed her the spare key.

"Under the rock, just like you said," he told her.

She dropped it into her pants pocket. "Thanks. I'll think of a better back-up plan. There are clean towels and an extra toothbrush in the bathroom."

"Do you have unexpected guests often?" he asked, one dark eyebrow arched curiously.

"No, you're the first. And don't read too much in me having a spare toothbrush. I got it from my dentist last month when I got my teeth cleaned."

"Likely story," he teased, but she thought he looked relieved.

She made up the couch while he took a shower and made sure all the drapes were closed so the early morning sun wouldn't wake him before he was ready. As she was checking the front door, she looked out the peephole and noticed the white car was back across the street. That was sort of a relief because that meant the neighbor must have traded their old car in. She had only met the young couple a few times at block parties, but it had made her sad to think that one of them was having an affair. Cheating spouses was something with which she had too much experience . . . and zero tolerance.

Rusty came out of the bathroom in a cloud of steam. He was wearing just a short-sleeved white t-shirt, the regular kind you buy in a pack of three, and blue jeans. His dark hair was still wet, and he had combed it back from his face with his fingers, leaving it tousled.

Never had she seen anyone who looked sexier.

She felt her mouth hanging open and quickly turned away to hide her reaction. "This couch isn't too bad. I've fallen asleep on it myself a couple of times. Of course, I'm not as tall as you or as . . ." God, why was she rambling so much? She had almost rattled on about his broad shoulders and his long legs. "Anyway, I turn the heat down at night, so I brought you an extra blanket if you need it."

His full lips stretched into a lazy grin that, no doubt, had set hundreds of feminine hearts pounding just as hers was now. "I'll be fine. I keep my place cool at night, too."

She headed toward her bedroom, then turned back. "I really appreciate this."

He shrugged. "After a twenty-four hour shift and day on the slopes, I could sleep anywhere."

Still she hesitated. "I had a really good time today."

"You sound surprised."

"I was. It was the last thing I expected to be doing."

"You seemed to be in a dark place this morning."

She nodded. "Hazards of the job. You know how that is."

"Yeah, all too well." His expression grew serious. "That's why I act like I do, I guess."

"Yeah, well, you're not as bad as you'd like everyone to believe."

The grin returned. "Actually, I'm very good."

She rolled her eyes. "And that's my cue to say goodnight." This time she made it all the way to her bedroom door before she glanced back at him. "Thanks for asking me to go with you."

"Any time, Julie. Goodnight."

CHAPTER TEN

He was still asleep when she woke up. The blanket had partially fallen off, revealing tanned legs and a broad bare chest. Even relaxed, she could see the definition of well-toned muscles across his shoulders and arms. In sleep, his handsome face looked younger and vulnerable. His dark hair fell across his forehead and the crescent curve of ridiculously thick black lashes fanned his cheeks. Looking down on his magnificent, almost nude body sent a wave of heat curling through her stomach . . . and below. It had been a really long time since she had felt that for anyone. It was not an emotion she had either missed or welcomed.

Julie noticed his blue jeans lying on the floor next to his boots, laid out like he could jump into them at a second's notice, probably a habit of sleeping in the firehouse. His t-shirt, too, had been removed and had been hung neatly over the coffee table. It struck her as ironic since she suspected he was the kind of man who often left women's homes in a hurry.

That brought on a tinge of guilt. She shouldn't be having judgmental thoughts about him when he had sacrificed the comfort of his own bed to calm her nerves last night.

Being careful not to wake him, she went to the kitchen. Her house seemed much less frightening in the light of day, and she felt pretty foolish about allowing him to stay last night. He must think she was a weak, simpering woman . . . an image she had fought long and hard to escape.

There was nothing she could whip up for breakfast. Last Saturday had been her shopping day, but the news people had kept her indoors all day. She tore off a piece of paper out of a tablet and jotted a quick note to Rusty apologizing for having no food and thanking him again for staying. She left him the spare key so he could lock up when he left, poured some kibble into Cat's bowl, filled his water and left.

She cringed as the garage door opened, afraid the sound would wake him up. It took a little maneuvering and two wheels on the grass next to her narrow driveway for her to back out around his SUV, but minutes later, she was heading toward the police station, her attitude vastly improved over yesterday.

Even the paperwork went smoothly. It was amazing how much better she felt after a day off. She still had trouble concentrating, but today it was for a much different reason.

Rusty.

What she had told him was true. No man had been in her house for any reason other than to make a repair or deliver something. In fact, no person other than herself had been there. Her schedule didn't make it easy to develop friendships. She had gone out for a meal or a beer after work with some of the police officers and officer personnel, but always in a group and strictly on a casual basis. As for dating . . . well, that hadn't happened since . . . The years whirled through her mind. Memories she had kept pushed back. Love and pain that had canceled each other out until there was nothing left.

Yesterday she had laughed out loud because she was happy. Last night she had been safe and protected. This morning she had been warmed by the stirrings of desire.

How long had it been since she had felt any of those things? It seemed like forever.

On the second Thursday night of each month, there was a mandatory training class for all of her staff, and she spent the rest of the afternoon finalizing preparation for that. An ER nurse was going to be the guest speaker, and because it was so close to Christmas, Julie had planned a little party with special refreshments and a gift exchange. She had also invited anyone from the department or any of the emergency teams to drop by.

It was almost six o'clock before she left and already dark outside. Her car was parked in the police lot, and she walked out with half a dozen others. Traffic wasn't too bad, so it didn't take long to get home. She was surprised to see lights were on inside her house and Rusty's SUV was still in the driveway. Again, she maneuvered around it to get into the garage and walked into the house, not really knowing what to expect.

She had been a little uncomfortable leaving someone she barely knew in her house this morning. It was more unnerving to have him still there when she returned.

This first thing she noticed was a new back door. Rusty, now fully dressed but still looking incredibly good, was screwing on a new, heavy-duty deadbolt.

"Hey, how did it go today?" he asked, looking up at her with a grin.

"It went fast," she said. "You didn't have to do all this."

"I know, but I like doing stuff like this. My condo is pretty new, so it doesn't need a lot of maintenance." He stood back and admired his handiwork. "What do you think?"

Julie studied the new steel door that had replaced her flimsy wooden one. But even more than that, he had taken out the entire wooden frame and installed a metal one that would resist all but the most professional assaults. The lock had an extra-long latch and a keypad on the outside.

"Now you don't need a key, so you can't lock yourself out."

"Really? That's cool. What's my code?"

"You set it. Right now it's on the default, so if you punch in your four digits twice, it'll change to your numbers." He looked away while she entered her new code.

"Okay," she said. "All done."

"Good. The instruction book and a key to use in case the battery runs down are on the table. I changed out the front door, too. You'll need to set that code. Oh, and you have an alarm system."

"What?" She looked around and noticed a control box mounted on the wall by the back door. "How . . .?"

"I called in a favor, and they were able to make room in their schedule to install it today. There are sensors on every window and both doors. Let me show you how to use it."

She took her checkbook out of her purse. "How much do I owe you?"

Rusty waved it away. "Nothing. I did this for you."

"No, really. I want to pay you. I know that heavy doors like this aren't cheap. Plus, all your time. I'm sure there were a lot of things you'd rather have done on your day off."

He shook his head. "I help out my friends all the time. Consider this a gift."

She scribbled some numbers on a check, tore it out and held it out to him. "It's too much for a gift. I have some extra cash this month. I'll pay you the rest next month, if you don't mind."

He hesitated for a moment, but he must have seen the determination in her eyes, so he reluctantly took the check, folded it and put it in the pocket of his jeans. Then he spent the next fifteen minutes demonstrating the system and calling in to set up her password and testing the alarm. Again, she had to choose four numbers to arm and disarm the system and four more for the front door.

"Wow, I can't believe you did all this in one day," she told him. "I felt bad leaving you here without any breakfast, and then you do all this. Now I feel awful because I don't have anything for dinner either."

He stretched and yawned. "No problem. I'm beat. I'm going to head home, take a hot shower and hit the sack. Your couch wasn't horrible, but it's a little small for me."

A rush of disappointment surprised her. It wasn't until that moment that she realized how glad she had been to see him and think that the evening wouldn't be as long and lonely as all the others.

"I could open a can of chili or something," she offered hopefully.

"Nah, I'll pick up something on the way home." He flashed her that sexy smile that always made her breath catch in her throat. "Now that I know you're safe, I'll get a good night's sleep. I'm on shift at seven-thirty tomorrow morning."

Short of begging, which was definitely not an option, there was no way to keep him there. Julie looked at all the work he had done for her and shook her head. "I don't know how I'm going to be able to thank you for all this. I never thought I needed an alarm, but after yesterday, I'm really glad to have it."

"Helping people is my job," he told her, his eyes twinkling.

"I'm overwhelmed," she admitted, still taking in all the changes.

"You should feel comfortable in your own home," he told her seriously. "And now I'm going to go feel comfortable in mine."

Julie stood awkwardly as he passed her. If he had been a handyman, she would have paid him. If he had been her father, she would have given him a hug. If he had been her boyfriend, she would have thanked him with a kiss. She felt like something more was needed, but nothing seemed appropriate.

Rusty seemed to understand and gave her a grin. "Goodnight, Julie. Sleep well."

She relaxed and returned his smile. "I will, thanks to you." She stood in the doorway and watched as he backed out of her driveway, then she shut and locked her door, immediately feeling safer at the resounding click of the deadbolt. Cat came up to her and twined through her legs.

"Do you want to go out?" she asked.

As if he understood, he walked away from the door and squatted down next to his food bowl and started crunching on his dinner.

"I guess that means you're staying in tonight," Julie said. "I agree. Dinner, first." She punched in the code on the alarm and felt herself relax as the female voice said, *"Armed, Stay, Instant."*

Across the street, the white car idled. A man picked up a cell phone, punched in some numbers and said as soon as the other person answered, "She's home. And she's alone."

Rusty's apartment was dark and cool. He turned the lights on and raised the thermostat by a few degrees. Even though he hadn't awakened until eight this morning, he hadn't felt rested. Of course, he slept briefly in other beds, but not for a whole night. And he never slept on anyone's couch, especially alone.

He took a Styrofoam container filled with a double order of hot wings, opened a beer and flopped down on his favorite recliner. A few clicks of the remote settled on a popular cop show on the TV. As he ate, his attention wandered around the room, touching briefly on the football and bowling trophies and framed photos on the mantle before moving on to a large family photo on an end table his mom had put there when he moved in as a housewarming present. He'd kind of forgotten it was there. Looking at it now made him realize what was missing from Julie's house.

He hadn't nosed around. During the course of his inspection of her house when they'd first arrived yesterday and then while he helped the crew install the alarm system, he had spent some time in each room of her house. Something had struck him as odd, but it wasn't until now that he'd been able to actually put his finger on it.

Julie's house was completely devoid of any personal items. There were no photos, no mementos, no awards or diplomas. Other than a few pairs of pierced earrings in a small tray on her dresser, she had no jewelry. Her closets weren't full to overflowing like all the other women he knew. The clothing appeared to be good quality, but not flashy or too dressy. Stranger still, there had been only six pairs of shoes, two neutral pairs of high heels, two pairs of mid-heel everyday shoes, one pair of tennis shoes and a pair of flip-flops. Even he had more shoes than that.

Bottom line, she had left no personal stamp on the house. Any one or no one could have lived there. It wouldn't take much for her to pack up and move, leaving no sign of herself behind. Or simply disappear and leave it all. Like she had said, there was nothing of any value other than the TV.

It wasn't normal in his experience for a female to live so simply. He didn't know what that meant. Was she starting over from something or someone who had left her with nothing? It was unimaginable for him to think that she didn't spend anything on herself. Was she saving for something special? A trip to Europe? A new car? A wedding? *Her* wedding?

That would explain a lot about her total lack of flirtation. He was used to girls who were all over him, touching him, both innocently and inappropriately, rubbing their bodies against his, flipping their hair and passing him provocative looks. Julie was friendly, but she met his gaze without pretension. He had been a little disappointed that she hadn't thrown her arms around his neck and given him a big kiss as a thank you. He certainly wouldn't have pushed her away.

Of course, he hadn't done it for her gratitude. He was genuinely concerned for her safety. Being alone in that house made her vulnerable to any nut job out there. And there were plenty of those in Denver.

There were many pieces of the Julie puzzle that didn't quite fit. Rusty liked puzzles. But he needed to find out about the wedding thing. The one thing he didn't do was to mark another man's territory. There were plenty of women out there, and he didn't need to trespass.

Why then wasn't he on the phone right now calling Kim or Ava or Lisa? Why was he sitting here, watching reruns and eating hot wings all by himself . . . and wondering what lucky man was in Julie's life?

The only male in Julie's life right now was short and gray with black stripes with fishy breath. He was curled up on the pillow next to her when she woke up the next morning. For several minutes, Julie lingered in the warmth of her bed. She had slept better last night since . . . well, since as long as she could remember. Finally, a look at the clock reminded her that she had a lot to do today to get things together for the meeting tonight.

She grabbed a granola bar for breakfast, fed Cat and punched in the security code to disarm the system. After putting on her coat and gathering her things, she entered the code again to re-arm the system. As Rusty had explained, she had forty-five seconds to exit, so she didn't have to hurry. The door closed solidly behind her, and she put a code into the lock pad and turned the bolt. No one would be walking in and out of that door without making some noise.

Julie backed her car down the driveway and stopped at the end. There was a plastic bag with what looked like a phone book in it. She didn't want to leave it out where the pages would blow litter all over the neighborhood, so she got out to retrieve it.

She noticed the neighbor across the street picking up his newspaper and phone book bag, so she called out, "Need an extra phone book?"

He laughed. "I was about to offer you the same thing. I never use them."

"Me either. This will go straight to the recycle bin. Too bad we can't opt out."

"Yeah, save a tree . . . or a whole forest," he agreed.

"I saw you got a new car," she mentioned.

"Me? No, I'm still driving my old Toyota. And Sue loves her Prius. She drove it to Omaha to visit her mother."

"Oh. She's out of town?"

"Yes, since last Friday. She's supposed to be back on Saturday though."

"That's good. I'm sure you miss her."

He nodded. "The house is quiet without her and the kids."

"I can imagine. Well, I've got to get to work. See you later," Julie said.

"Me too." He headed back toward his house.

Julie was frowning as she got back into her car. If the car wasn't his or his wife's, then who had been parking across the street from her house? Maybe it had something to do with her break in.

A cold chill raced down her spine. For every victim of domestic abuse, there was an aggressor who usually spent at least one night in jail. Another consistency was that the abusers never blamed themselves. They blamed their wife, girlfriend, boyfriend, kids, boss, God . . . and the victim's advocate. Could someone whose partner she had helped be planning a payback? Had they somehow found out where she lived and were watching her, waiting for their chance to ruin her life like she had ruined theirs?

Nervously, Julie looked up and down the narrow street. There was no sign of the white car which might mean they had given up. Surely if they had been hanging out yesterday they would have noticed all the activity as Rusty beefed up her security. Maybe they just wanted to frighten her, to make her aware that they didn't like for her to interfere in their life.

Julie spent most of the morning going through old files of past cases, trying to remember which abusers she had met. On the drive over, she had decided that it was unlikely someone would have held a grudge on her personally if they hadn't actually come face-to-face. They might be angry at the system, but probably didn't blame her.

However, she remembered many angry glares as the men or, in a very few cases, the women were taken away in handcuffs while Julie stayed behind with the victim, often helping them get medical or psychological treatment, hire a handyman to replace locks or broken windows or doors and sometimes even finding the victim a safe place to live that would cut the abuser out of their lives forever.

It was easy to understand the abuser's misplaced assignment of guilt. As they sat in jail or worked through the emotional and financial burden of a trial, their anger and resentment against Julie would grow until she had somehow become the cause of all their troubles. In their twisted minds, she became the villain of their homemade drama. If it wasn't for Julie, their relationship would be happy and normal just like before the incident. Of course, there were also men, like Carlos, who had never been caught.

She tucked the files in her briefcase so she could study them at home after the meeting. Reluctantly, she pushed the white car out of her mind and forced her focus back on finalizing the schedule so she could pass it out tonight and making sure everything was ready. Maybe she was worrying about nothing. After all, it was just a car. It could have belonged to someone visiting one of the other neighbors or, even though it wasn't a cool vehicle, it could be a kid who had borrowed his dad's car for a date.

By the time Julie was heading toward the meeting room at the end of the day, she had almost completely dismissed the threat. After all, it was unlikely any of the abusers had been able to find her address. She had zero presence on any of the internet websites, had no landline phone at her house, a blocked cell phone and her vehicle's license plates had a security shield on them, just like that on all personal cars of most civil servants. Besides, she had a world-class security system now.

Thanks to Rusty.

CHAPTER ELEVEN

Everyone was in good spirits. The lights from the small artificial Christmas tree in the corner of the meeting room twinkled merrily. Julie knew that while her staff was interested in hearing about the speaker's emergency room experiences, they were all ready to party.

They stuck to their usual agenda of going over activity sheets, discussing unusual cases and results, listening to stories of success and failure and passing out the schedules for January. Julie introduced the ER nurse, and she talked about patients she had treated, especially those who had some sort of domestic violence or child abuse history. There was a lively discussion of what the victim's advocates could do to cut down the recidivism rates and a general disappointment that they couldn't do more.

Julie finally called the meeting to an end and started the white elephant gift exchange. As usual, there were very popular items that got passed around until all the gifts had been opened ended with everyone laughing and milling around the food and drink table. Alcohol was prohibited, but that didn't keep everyone from having fun socializing. Of course, there was a lot of shop talk especially when some of the cops they'd worked with dropped by for a cookie and other goodies. Julie mingled, glad to spend some down-time with her staff. The work they did was serious and so often tragedy-centric that it was a pleasure to see them smile and hear their laughter.

After about the dozenth time, she realized she was keeping an unusually close watch on the door. She actually heard his voice in the hallway before he entered the room and she tried to ignore that funny little flutter in the pit of her stomach. She would have dismissed it as a hunger pain if she hadn't been nibbling on the hors d'oeuvres for the last half hour.

Rusty and four other firefighters entered the room. They apparently were on-shift because they were all dressed in their navy blue cargo pants and t-shirts. The refreshment table caught their attention, and they filtered into the crowd, heading for the food.

Except for Rusty. He stood in the doorway, taller than everyone around him, his gaze searching the room. Julie was riveted in place, unable and unwilling to turn away. She hoped he was looking for her, and she was not disappointed. As soon as his eyes met hers, he smiled, that sexy crooked grin that took her breath away. Without further hesitation, he walked straight toward her.

"Nice party," he said as he stopped in front of her.

"I'm glad you made it."

His blue eyes twinkled. "I was hoping the boys and I would be able to slip away for a few minutes . . . to spend some time with your crew."

"I'm sure it means a lot to them that you all are here. It's so much nicer to spend time around a Christmas tree rather than a burning building."

"In so many ways," he agreed. "How's the alarm system working?"

"So far, so good. I slept like a baby last night."

"Are you taking shifts this weekend?"

"Yes, until the end of the year, then I'm just going to be a back-up. I think I need to take a break from the drama."

"Yeah, well that's the line of work we're in, isn't it?"

Julie nodded toward the food table. "You should get something before it's all gone. I highly recommend the spinach artichoke dip." God, what an inane conversation. She wouldn't be surprised if he decided the cupcakes were more interesting. Julie shook her head. And what difference did it make whether or not he stayed with her? She was shocked to realize that it actually did matter. She liked being with him and was truly glad to see him.

"Did you make it?"

She laughed. "Now you're making fun of me. You've seen my kitchen. Does it look like I cook much?"

"The only refrigerator I've seen that has less in it is mine."

"I'm actually going grocery shopping tomorrow after work. As you recall, I was sort of busy last Friday," she said.

"Yeah, me too. I was all tied up," he teased, but the sparkle had left his eyes.

Julie noticed that he seemed a little uncomfortable talking about it. "Have you had a chance to talk to the department psychologist about it?"

"Not yet," he admitted, lowering his voice. "I thought I could work through it, but I'm still having nightmares."

"Any time you want to talk, no matter how late, just call me."

"Actually, it occurred to me today that I don't have your cell phone number. I asked around, but I could get the president of the United States' number easier than I could get yours."

"That's good to hear," she told him. "I had a little panic attack this morning when I thought one of my cases had come back to haunt me. It's good to know that I'm not that easy to find." She took her phone out of her pocket. "While we're at it, what's yours?"

They exchanged numbers, adding them to their Contacts' lists.

"Good, I'll give you a call. How about dinner tomorrow night . . . after your grocery trip?"

"Only if you let it be my treat," she said. "I owe you for all your work the other day."

"If that's the only way I can get you to agree to dinner, then okay. I'll pick you up around seven?"

Julie smiled. She would have expected a little anxiety and not the relief she was feeling. "Sounds good."

They split up and circulated, but until he and his fellow firefighters left a half hour later, every time Julie searched him out with her gaze, she found him looking at her. It didn't escape her notice that all the single women, regardless of their ages, and most of the married ones gravitated to him. He was literally a babe magnet. But she was the only one who had a date with him tomorrow night. She felt like she was back in high school.

The giddiness stayed with her the rest of the evening and the entire next day. It had been years since she'd been on anything even remotely like a date. A voice in the back of her head told her she shouldn't go. There was absolutely no future in any relationship. She held her phone in her hand. It would be so easy to find his name and call him to cancel. Instead, the phone went back into her pocket as she got out of her car in the grocery store's parking lot. She was looking forward to the date. She'd worry about the consequences later.

It had been a several weeks since she had done some serious grocery shopping. Normally, she just ran in and out, grabbing up a couple of things at a time. It wasn't because she didn't have the money; she just didn't have the time. Or rather, she had better things to do with her time because she really hated shopping. But tonight, she pushed her cart up and down every aisle, picking up everything from staples to a dozen fresh croissants from the bakery. Then when she got to the check-out, there were long lines. Apparently, she wasn't the only person stocking up for the weekend.

The entire process had taken much longer than she expected, and she was running a little late. She helped the boy bag her groceries into the canvas sacks she had brought with her, then she quickly pushed her loaded cart across the parking lot to her car. The bags filled her trunk and she even had to put the paper towels and toilet paper in the back seat. It felt good to know that her refrigerator and pantry would be well-stocked at least until Christmas.

Julie opened the driver's door and sat down. It was cold outside, so she hurried to shut the door. After fastening her seatbelt, she started the car and carefully backed out of the space. It was six forty-five. If she hit absolutely no traffic, she could make it home in time. Unfortunately, it seemed like all of Denver was on the road tonight.

She sat at a traffic light only a few blocks from her house, her fingers strumming on the steering wheel as she waited for the light to change. Suddenly, something crawled over her foot. She automatically kicked out and leaned over to see what it was. The light blinked from red to green and the cars around her started to move. Behind her, an impatient driver leaned on his horn, and she jerked upright.

Her instincts were to drive on and check out what it was when she reached her house. But she hadn't gone half a block until she felt it crawling up her leg. She flinched, her foot pressed down on the gas and the car lurched forward. She tried to steer, but was distracted by the icky sensation of something slimy on her leg. It was impossible to tell what it was, but she definitely didn't want it touching her.

Afterward, she couldn't remember what happened. The next thing she knew, she had plowed into a telephone pole and her air bag was slowly deflating.

The air bag plate had hit her in the chest, knocking the air out of her. It took her a couple of minutes to catch her breath and clear her head enough to remember that feeling of something crawling on her. She opened the door and tried to get out, but was held back. It took another few seconds to realize she hadn't unfastened her seat belt. Her fingers fumbled with the latch and finally she was able to crawl out of the car, almost falling over a pile of snow left when the sidewalk had been plowed. She had to cling to the door to pull herself to her feet.

Someone must have called 911 because the sounds of sirens pierced the night, getting closer until she could see red and blue lights chasing each other around the buildings as the emergency vehicles approached from opposite directions and stopped at her accident scene.

An ambulance parked at the curb, the closest to her car and two paramedics jumped out. She recognized the man as Rusty's brother which reminded her that he must be thinking that she had stood him up.

"Hey, take it easy," the paramedic told her.

She glanced at his badge because she didn't remember hearing his name at the kidnapping. "Chris, you're Rusty's brother, aren't you?"

"Yes, but right now, I need you to come with me. Can you walk?"

She nodded. "My head and my chest hurts, but I'm okay." Even though she didn't feel bad, her legs were rubbery, and she allowed Chris and his female partner to walk on each side of her with their arms wrapped around her back as they guided her to the open back door of the ambulance. "I don't need to go to the hospital."

"Maybe . . . maybe not," Chris said. "We need to check you out to see."

"I need you to do me a huge favor," she told him as she sat on the pram inside the ambulance. "Rusty and I had a date tonight, and I need you to call him so he'll know where I'm at."

Chris didn't say anything, but the arch of his eyebrows showed his surprise.

A police officer walked up that Julie recognized.

"Julie, are you okay?" Officer Don Vincent asked with genuine concern. "I don't usually see you on this side of the ambulance."

"Hi Don. I'm fine, or at least I will be once I get something for this headache."

He looked over at her car. She hadn't been going very fast, so the impact had been minimal, but the cheap metal had crumpled in a deep V with the telephone pole buried in the middle.

"Something was crawling up my leg, and I guess I lost control." She massaged her forehead. "I really don't remember much."

"Any alcohol or drugs?" he asked.

"No, I'd just left the grocery store and was headed home."

He walked over to the car and leaned into the open driver's side door and started looking around. Chris checked Julie's vitals and shined a small flashlight in her eyes while his partner did a body check to see if anything was broken.

"Everything looks fine," he told Julie.

His partner whose name tag identified her as Sara agreed. "Nothing's broken, but you have a significant bruise on your chest. Your breathing may feel a little labored, and we need to make sure your lungs don't collect any fluid."

Julie automatically tried to take a deep breath, but it caught midway as pain shot through her. She moaned.

"You're also showing signs of a mild concussion," Chris continued. "I recommend that you spend the night in the hospital for observation."

"No, I'd rather not. I . . . I don't like hospitals," Julie rushed to say.

"You really should consider it," Sara added. "You shouldn't be alone tonight."

"I'll take care of her."

The deep voice everyone on scene recognized came from beside the ambulance, and everyone turned to look at Rusty as he hurried forward.

"She needs to be in a hospital," Chris insisted, giving his brother a meaningful look.

"I don't like hospitals either," Rusty told him. "I'll keep an eye on her. I know a little first aid." The corner of his mouth lifted ironically. They all knew how many hours firefighters had to take each year to keep current on medical emergencies.

Chris threw up his hands, then took off his rubber gloves with a snap and tossed them inside the ambulance. Sara gave Julie a friendly smile, then stepped away. Rusty moved closer and with a finger crooked under her chin, he tilted her head up so he could see her better.

"You've got a couple of impressive black eyes. What happened?"

"As I was pulling out of the parking lot, I felt something on my foot . . . a big spider or a mouse or a snake . . . I don't know, but when it started going up my leg, I must have hit the accelerator or jerked the wheel . . . I don't remember. I guess it knocked me out for a second because I woke up against the pole. My air bag saved me."

Just then Don returned, holding out at arm's length a two-foot long snake with red-yellow-and-black bands around its thin, shiny body. "Look what I found," he said with a mixture of surprise and distaste. He had a tight grip on the reptile just behind its small oval head.

"It *was* a snake!" Julie exclaimed. "Is it poisonous? Aren't coral snakes red, yellow and black?"

"Yes, but this is a milk snake, and they're harmless," Rusty told her. "*Red touch yellow, kill a fellow; red touch black, venom lack.* It's a rhyme my dad taught us so we wouldn't pick one up."

"Harmless if you don't count scaring me to death." Julie shivered, thinking about the creepy creature crawling on her. "How did it get in my car?"

"That's a little weird. They aren't native to Colorado, and they aren't active in the winter," Rusty explained.

"So it's not likely he just crawled up from underneath?" she asked, almost afraid to hear the answer.

"Probably about the same odds as winning the lottery," Don confirmed. "What do you want me to do with this thing?"

"Take him home to your kids," Rusty suggested. "Those things cost about $50 in a pet store."

Don held him out toward Julie and she cringed. "Are you sure you don't want him?" he teased.

"Get him away from me. He's all yours."

Don took out a specimen bag, dropped the snake into it and zipped the top closed. "I'd better get going before he runs out of air."

"Hey, what about the accident?" Julie asked.

"Don't worry about it," Don told her. "Doesn't look like much damage except to your car. Get it towed right away. I'll give you a report for your insurance company, but I won't give you a ticket."

"Thanks," she said, relieved that she wasn't going to get a ticket, but still distracted by how the snake could have gotten into her vehicle. She looked up at Rusty. "I'm sorry about our date."

"I got here as soon as Chris called. Are you sure you don't want to get this checked out at the hospital?"

"No, I'm feeling better already. Do you know someone who can tow my car?"

"Sure. I'll make a call, then I'll take you home." He looked up a name on his Contacts list and hit the call button. "Do you have a body shop you like to use?"

She shook her head. The reliable car had never needed any attention other than an occasional oil change and a new set of tires at the beginning of the winter. "Oh, but I need to get my phone and my purse out of there. And the groceries. The trunk is full."

Rusty nodded and started talking to someone on the other end of the phone line as he walked toward her car. He gave them the location and the information about her car. When he hung up, he reached in and retrieved her purse, her phone and her keys, then popped the trunk open. "He's on his way," Rusty called over his shoulder as he began the process of transferring her grocery bags from her vehicle to his that was parked close by.

An hour later, Julie was settled comfortably on her couch with a soft plush throw tucked around her and a bowl of soup on a tray on her lap. The three Advil she had taken as soon as they arrived weren't doing much to dull the pain that was throbbing in her head. She watched through the open doorway into the kitchen where Rusty was unpacking her groceries and putting things away. He had insisted that she relax on the couch and had provided her with the food.

"How's it going?" she called to him.

"I'm almost through," he answered, pausing to look at her. "You should find everything sooner or later. You had so many empty shelves, I kind of had to guess where things go."

"You don't have to do that," she told him. "As long as the refrigerated stuff gets put away."

"I did that first. Now, eat your soup while I finish."

She obediently took a few spoonsful until it seemed too much of an effort to swallow. There was the sound of the pantry door shutting before Rusty walked into the room, carrying a ham and cheese sandwich.

"I hope you don't mind. I made myself a sandwich. Do you want one?"

"Of course, I don't mind. And no, I don't want one. I'm just sorry that I ruined our evening."

"I still have hope that someday we'll actually eat at a real restaurant." His boyish grin told her he wasn't upset.

He settled on the couch next to her and even shared the other end of her throw. He took control of the remote and flipped through the channels until they settled on a silly Christmas movie that required absolutely no concentration to keep up with the storyline about an elf falling in love with a yard gnome.

"I hate the holidays," Julie muttered.

"Really? I kind of like them," Rusty admitted. "Of course with our weird schedules, we can't always make the whole day, but those of us who can go to my parents' house around noon. There's so many of us that we draw names, even my parents, so everyone gets just one gift, but it's a good one. We take turns playing Santa, without the dressing up part, and hand out the presents. After we open them, we all sit down to dinner. It's always the same, turkey, dressing, gravy, mashed potatoes, green bean casserole, cranberry sauce, hot rolls and pumpkin pie. All homemade, of course." He smiled and licked his lips. "It's my favorite meal."

Julie's smile was wistful. "That sounds nice. Holidays were always like that when my parents were alive, but after . . . well, it's never been the same since. Now it's just another day."

Rusty's vivid blue eyes softened. "Are you going to be alone on Christmas?"

She shrugged. "Yeah, but that's okay. It's usually a busy day for victim's advocates. A lot of people behave badly on holidays. After all the hype, it's a big disappointment, you know. It can never meet our expectations after we're grown up."

"You just haven't spent them with the right person."

CHAPTER TWELVE

Rusty shifted, trying to relieve the crick in his neck. It took him a minute to get his bearings. For some reason he was sitting up and someone was sleeping in his arms. The morning sun was just starting to peek through the cracks where the drapes didn't quite overlap. Slowly, all the events of last night came back to him . . . Julie's accident, the snake, her concussion.

He sat up straighter. He was supposed to have been watching her and keeping her awake. And here they were, asleep on the couch. He looked down at Julie, slumped over with her head resting on his chest. Her hair smelled like flowers and vanilla and was soft against his chin. At work she always wore it pulled back into a ponytail or clipped up in a bun. He'd seen it down only twice, the first night he had dropped by and surprised her and last night when her head had been hurting, and she had taken the rubber band out and combed her fingers through the silky strands, releasing it to fall long and loose around her shoulders.

It had surprised him how sexy she was, even with two black eyes. He had thought she was sort of pretty before, but now that he had gotten to know her, he realized she was beautiful, in a totally natural way. Her skin was flawless and her body was slender but had the right amount of curves. He was very aware of her firm, full breasts that were pressed against him right now. One of her hands was lying on the couch, but the other was draped over his lap, her fingers dangerously close to the morning bulge in his jeans. The thought of her actually touching him, stroking him made his erection grow even more.

She wore very little makeup, but she didn't really need any. There was nothing artificial about her. Except for the brown contact lens, which he still didn't understand. The natural color of her eyes was a soft, cornflower blue that made her look younger and more vulnerable. If anything, she was a little too thin which made her eyes look almost too large and her cheekbones more prominent than they would if she took the time to eat properly. She was so busy taking care of other people that she didn't take very good care of herself.

And for some reason, she did everything she could to make herself look plain and unattractive. It was like she didn't want anyone to notice her; sort of like she wanted to blend in with the wallpaper. Maybe that was why people trusted her and let her inside their private lives so easily. She came across as honest, compassionate and non-threatening.

Rusty looked down at her and lightly brushed her hair off her face. His feelings toward her confused him. Of course, he could be counted on to help out a buddy who needed an extra hand to repair their roof or install a fence. The girls he knew were attracted to his muscles or his sexual prowess or even how he looked in a uniform. He wasn't known as being emotionally available.

Why then was he spending all his spare time with a woman who was even less emotionally available than he was?

He could tell she liked him and appreciated his help, even that she enjoyed being with him and was glad to see him. What she hadn't done was flirt with him or send him any of those feminine messages that told him they wanted him to make a move. She didn't caress his cheek or squeeze his arm or lick her lips, making sure he was watching. She either had no interest in him other than as a friend . . . or she had absolutely no game.

And why did it make a difference to him? Hell, if he knew. It just did. Around Julie Lawrence, Rusty had absolutely no game either.

Gently, he shook her shoulder.

"Julie, wake up."

She moved slowly, going through the same disorientation that he had. It was clear when she realized she was lying on him because she immediately jerked upright and put a little distance between them. But the abrupt movement caused her to gasp in pain.

"I was supposed to keep you awake," he admitted sheepishly. "I should probably be fired."

"Don't be silly. I'm fine. I didn't need a babysitter." She pressed her fingers against her throbbing temples. "But I could use some Advil."

He went to the kitchen and shook out three Advil pills and filled a glass with water from the sink. As he approached, she looked up at him and held out her hand.

"You must think I'm the most pathetic person on earth," she moaned as she popped the pills in her mouth, took a drink and swallowed. "All you do is take care of me."

"It seems that way, but I have to say that you have some original problems. Are you up for breakfast?"

"Actually, I'm starving." She started to push to her feet, but paused halfway, struggling to let a wave of dizziness pass.

"I can handle it," he offered. "You stay here."

"No, I'll be fine . . . just give me a minute." She closed her eyes and clung to the edge of the coffee table for support.

Rusty knew she wouldn't give up, so he decided to help her out a little. Careful not to move too quickly, he swept her into his arms and carried her to the kitchen where he sat her gently on one of the chairs. "Now you can supervise me while I cook. I know where everything is since I put it away last night. Of course, after I'm gone, you won't be able to find anything."

"I always loved hunting for Easter eggs when I was a kid. I guess the adult version is hunting for corn and beans."

Rusty took the eggs, butter and bacon out of the refrigerator. "I'm better at grilling, but I make great scrambled eggs." He cracked several eggs into a bowl, then searched the drawers for a whisk. Finding none, he beat them with a fork while waiting for the bacon to fry.

A half hour later, they had cleaned their plates and Rusty reached for the last piece of toast. "Want this?" he asked.

"No, I'm stuffed." Her eyebrows arched with surprise. "For a single guy, you're a pretty good cook."

"My mom insisted all of us boys know how to cook basic things and how to sew on buttons. She wanted us to be able to take care of ourselves should we not find a woman crazy enough to marry us."

"That seems unlikely. You're all pretty good catches," she teased. "I saw your photo in this year's Firefighters' calendar. Hot stuff."

He could feel himself blush. He knew he was considered attractive, but posing for the calendar had been the most embarrassing moment of his life. Since its release in August, he couldn't count the number of calendars that had been thrust in front of him for his autograph. All the other guys and one girl had been similarly undressed and in comparatively beefcake poses, but that didn't make it any easier to look at his own half-naked body, oiled and glistening as he stood, holding an axe next to a burning building while water showered down over him. As a joke Sam had entered him in the competition, and Rusty had gone through with it because the sales from the calendar benefited the Children's Hospital Burn Center.

"Yeah, that was the one and only time I'll ever do anything like that," he groaned.

"It's a worthy cause, and I have to admit, I have one hanging in my bathroom."

"I saw it when I was checking out your house the other night. I was hoping you wouldn't realize it was me."

"Are you kidding? I can't wait for July so I can check out your abs while I'm brushing my teeth every day."

Of course she was teasing, but for a moment, he felt an unexpected pang of disappointment that she hadn't really meant it. What would it take for her to actually look at him like all the other women did? Then again, he didn't want her to be like all the others. She was different . . . and special.

"So, I guess I'd better call in and get someone to cover for me tonight." Julie shook her head. "I've never missed so much work."

"You've never had someone put a snake in your car," he commented.

Julie's eyes widened. "You don't think he just crawled inside for warmth?"

Rusty shook his head. "No, he wasn't out there just wandering around. He was probably a pet, but even if he had escaped his cage, he would have been hibernating somewhere, not out crawling in the snow. Cold-blooded creatures can't survive these temperatures."

"Then where . . .?"

"They're not poisonous. They sell them in lots of pet stores. It looks like someone wanted to frighten you." He studied her for a moment. "Any idea who might want you to back off?"

Julie looked up at him. Her eyes were cautious, but worried. "I think it might have something to do with one of my victims. Maybe someone wants to pay me back for taking away his or her partner. They need to blame anyone but themselves for their lives being disrupted by jail or divorce or separation, and they might see me as the person in the middle." She frowned. "I think someone in a white car has been watching my house, probably the guy that broke in."

"That might explain why he didn't take anything. Any idea who?"

"I brought the files home, and I was going to check them out this weekend." She frowned. "I left them in the car."

"I'll stop by the body shop where they towed your car and pick them up for you."

"Oh no, I can get them . . ."

"Are you going to walk there? You don't even know the address."

Her shoulders slumped. "I can't keep depending on you to do everything for me. I'm sure your girlfriends are wondering where you've been."

"For the record, no girlfriends, no missing person reports, and I don't mind helping you out. You're just used to being the person who helps other people. You have no idea how to accept help."

She opened her mouth to continue her protest, but then leaned back in her chair and smiled.

Rusty was dazzled. Most of their time together had been so serious, even to the point of being life and death. Especially since they found the door open, Julie had been worried and distracted, and he had rarely seen her smile. But now, even with her long dark hair tousled and the purple bruises under her eyes, she looked relaxed and happy. Not for the first time, his body reacted in a totally masculine way. She hadn't noticed his earlier erection, but she couldn't help but notice the telltale bulge pushing against the fly of his jeans right now. He quickly turned away, too confused by his own thoughts to deal with the obvious issue that he was very attracted to this woman.

No one was more surprised than he was. She didn't flash her cleavage, wear a ton of makeup, spend hours on her hair or show off her legs. And yet, here he was, spending almost every waking hour with her . . . and enjoying it.

Last night as he tried to keep her awake, they had talked for hours about their favorite movies, their ideal vacations and their childhoods. Having grown up as an only child, she had been very interested in his family, especially the interaction between his brothers. Of course, their jobs had come into the conversation, and it had been really nice to be able to discuss the dark side along with the more mundane. It was a subject Rusty never discussed with anyone else except, occasionally, his brothers. Some things were too raw and painful, but Julie understood. She saw the bad, ugly sides of life every day and could relate to his experiences. It was such a release to be able to talk about it openly.

Rusty busied himself with the dishes, thankful that his back was turned so Julie wouldn't notice his physical attraction to her. He didn't notice that she had stood and joined him at the sink until he reached for the sponge and his arm brushed across her breasts. He froze, his startled eyes looking down into hers.

"You're supposed to be taking it easy," he managed to say.

"I'm feeling much better. You cooked, so I should clean up."

Her long hair felt like silk against his bare arm. She was standing way too close for his libido to ignore. He wanted to grab her, pull her against him and to taste her full, pink lips. He wanted to see if the curves of her body matched his imagination and how his name would sound when she called it out as she climaxed.

Suddenly, he knew he had to get out of here before he made the biggest mistake of his life by doing something really stupid . . . like making a move that would both shock and insult her. She had given him no sign that she wanted him . . . and he knew how to read the signs. He had seen them often enough from other women who couldn't keep their hands off his belt buckle.

Rusty grabbed a dish towel and wiped his hands. What he really needed tonight was to get laid. And clearly, it wasn't going to be by Julie.

"I just remembered that I have a date tonight. I'd better get going so I won't be late."

Julie glanced at the digital clock on the microwave. "It's only ten a.m. How much preparation does it take?"

"You think looking this hot is easy?" He tried to joke as he held the dish towel in front of him so she wouldn't notice his erection. "Are you sure you're going to be okay?"

"I'll be fine." She touched his arm, completely unaware of the electricity that streaked from her fingertips through his body. "The snake could have been one of those freak coincidences, couldn't it?"

He could tell that she needed his assurance, so he told her what she wanted to hear. "Sure, it could have been an escaped pet." He didn't add that cops and firefighters didn't believe in coincidences, but he left her with the hope that it had been an accident.

Her sigh of relief was audible. "Thank you for staying with me last night. I really enjoyed it. You're a good friend."

Rusty pulled away, anxious to break the connection before his self-control shattered. He tossed the towel on the counter as he hurried to the door. "I'll pick up your files and drop them off tomorrow."

"Aren't you working tomorrow?"

"No, it's my Kelly Day," Rusty told her, referring to the extra day all firefighters got every seventh shift. "Gotta run." He didn't look back but hurried out the back door.

He didn't actually have a date, but a call to Heather remedied that. He hadn't planned on ever asking her out again after her boring behavior at the barbecue. Of course, she had to go through the whole pouting inquisition about why hadn't he called her and who had he been with? He avoided her questions by distracting her with dining options and promises for dessert at his place. They both knew that that dessert would be calorie and clothing free.

As promised, he dropped by the body shop and picked up the files from Julie's wrecked car. Fortunately, the damage wasn't fatal, and his friend promised it would be ready for her by Wednesday. Next, he stopped at the liquor store and stocked up for tonight. Heather liked expensive chardonnay, and he picked up a case of Corona Light beer for himself. Another stop at the grocery store for cheese and crackers and something for breakfast. Not that Heather would be staying for breakfast. He never let a woman stay all night. Nor did he spend the night at her place. It sent the wrong message, and one of the things he was most careful about was not to make any promises, either spoken or implied, that he wasn't going to keep.

The afternoon stretched long and lonely, even as he switched back and forth between the two football games that were on television. Neither were teams he particularly cared about, and he often caught his thoughts drifting back to Julie. Finally, he gave up and went to the gym in his complex and worked out for two hours. That was something else he'd been neglecting, and he felt much better afterward.

A long shower and it was time to dress for his date.

As usual, Heather wasn't ready when he got there. She met him at the front door with a towel wrapped around her.

"Come on in." She shut the door behind him. "There's some wine in the fridge. Help yourself." She stopped and looked over her shoulder provocatively. With a flick of her fingers, the towel fell to the floor, revealing a naked, perfect body.

Rusty had seen it before, and he knew how it felt to fill his hands with her full, rounded ass. Odd that he wasn't tempted to take her up on her blatant offer.

"We have a reservation at seven-thirty," he told her. "We can't be late or they'll give our table away."

"We can call out and have something delivered." Her eyelids lowered as she added, "Later."

Rusty dragged his fingers through his hair. He was horny. It had been a couple weeks since he'd had sex, before the whole kidnap thing. And he knew Heather was up for anything he wanted. Why wasn't he following her into her bedroom? Why was his dick lying motionless in his boxer-briefs?

"Nah, let's get dinner first. Do you have any beer?"

Two beers later, Heather returned to the living room. The wait had been totally worth it because she looked terrific with her shapely curves packed into a red bandage dress and her dark hair pinned up in a fashionably messy bun.

"You look great," he told her and rested his hand on her back as they exited her apartment.

"You look pretty hot, yourself," she told him as she leaned against him. She was almost a foot shorter and her compact body fit well against his as she wrapped her arms around his neck and pulled his head down for a hungry kiss. "Hmmm, I've been waiting for that all evening," she purred.

Nothing. The same kiss that would have revved his engines only weeks before now had absolutely no effect on him. God, what had happened to him? He leaned down and kissed her again, more deeply and aggressively than before, searching for that familiar reaction.

"Whoa," Heather gasped for breath as the kiss ended. "Are you sure you don't want to miss dinner and go back to my apartment?"

Unfortunately, no. But he wasn't giving up yet. "We'd better go. We've got plenty of time for dessert."

He opened the door and helped her climb inside his SUV. It was pretty high off the ground, and it was a big step for her short legs, hampered even further by her tight dress. She giggled as he lifted her up until she reached the seat.

"When are you going to get a sports car like everyone else? The new Camaros are nice."

"I like my Explorer. It gets me everywhere I need to go, no matter what kind of weather Denver throws at me." He walked around and got into the driver's side.

"So how many people did you save this week?" she asked as she placed her hand on his thigh.

"None. Everyone got out all by themselves," he answered, a little bored by her usual questions.

"I have your calendar hanging next to my bed. I can't wait until July."

Funny. That was almost exactly what Julie had said, but somehow it had meant more coming from her. They pulled up in front of the restaurant and the valet opened

Heather's door and helped her down while Rusty stepped out and walked around the back.

It was one of his favorite restaurants. He often took dates here because the chef had a great selection of lighter meals and salads. But he always ordered one of their steaks, medium and smothered in sautéed mushrooms. He sat across from Heather and tried to listen as she rattled on about the shoe sale at Macy's and her bad experience getting a pedicure. She paused slightly when their dinner salads arrived, then picked right back up after their entrees were served. Rusty nodded and focused on his food, trying not to be too obvious about his complete lack of interest in the conversation. Although having sex with Heather was a sure thing, avoiding a lengthy apology session about not paying attention was high on his agenda.

He wondered what Julie was having for dinner. At least she had plenty of groceries so she wouldn't starve since she didn't have a car. It occurred to him that he hadn't told her that her car would be ready on Wednesday. He glanced at his phone and saw it was almost eight-thirty. He really should let her know so she wouldn't worry.

"Excuse me a minute," he told Heather as he pushed his chair back. "I'll be right back."

"Uh . . . sure," Heather said, pausing in mid-sentence about who one of the Kardashians was sleeping with. As far as Rusty was concerned, it was one of the mysteries of the universe why anyone cared about any of the Kardashians.

Rusty picked up his cell phone and headed toward the restrooms. He stopped in the small open area between the men's and the women's bathrooms and dialed Julie's number. It rang once, twice, three times before she answered just before it went to voice mail.

"Hello."

He felt his body relax at the sound of her voice. It was soft and husky, like she had been asleep. "Hi, it's me."

"Rusty? I thought you had a date tonight."

"I do. I mean, I'm on it now, but I just wanted to tell you that I dropped by the body shop and picked up your files."

"Thanks, but you didn't have to call for that."

Now he felt like a fool. What the hell was he doing, calling her in the middle of his date? Why was he jeopardizing an evening that was guaranteed to end in a blow job? "I just wanted to tell you about your car while I was thinking about it."

"Is it totaled?" she asked reluctantly.

"No, it's not too bad. It'll be ready on . . ."

All of a sudden her home alarm shrieked, the sound coming through so loudly that Rusty had to pull the phone away from his ear.

"Julie," he yelled. "Are you there? Can you hear me?"

There was a clatter as her phone hit the floor and slid across the hard wood.

Then she screamed.

CHAPTER THIRTEEN

Rusty's heart was pumping as he charged out of the restaurant. As he ran, he managed to dial *911* and report the alarm, even though he knew the monitoring company would also call. It might shorten the response time by a couple of minutes which could be the difference between life and death.

Oh God, if anything happened to Julie . . . he didn't even want to consider that possibility. As he burst outside he saw his Explorer parked in a lot across the street, so he grabbed his keys off the valet board, and without waiting for their assistance, he ran across the street, jumped into his vehicle and left the lot with a squeal of tires and smoking rubber.

He cursed every red light as he raced through the icy streets, sliding around corners and passing anyone driving slower . . . which was everyone he encountered. He turned onto Julie's street and saw he had beaten the cops to the scene. As he slid to a stop in front of her house, his headlights momentarily caught a big man as he ran out the front door and sprinted down the street. Rusty jumped out and gave chase, his slick-soled dress shoes sliding on the ice. Adding a new curse that he wasn't wearing his water-proof boots with their heavy rubber soles, he followed the man's trail across the front lawns and driveways of Julie's neighbors. The man slipped between two houses and vaulted over a decorative iron fence. Rusty was several yards back and gaining ground. He reached the fence, but as he started to vault over it, his foot hit a patch of ice and he went down hard. Luckily, he had avoided the iron rails, but he had to hang onto them to help him stand up.

"Fuck!" he growled as he scrambled over the fence. By the time he got to the backyard, the man was gone. He continued down to the corner where all four streets were visible, but there was no sign of anyone out on such a cold night. The man could have gone in any direction. "Fuck, fuck, fuck!"

He turned and ran back to Julie's house, arriving just as two patrol cars slid to a stop. Out of breath and not pausing to explain, he ran in the open front door, followed closely by the cops.

"Julie!" he called, running from room to room. The alarm's shrill siren was deafening as he checked in every closet and under the bed. She wasn't there.

Rusty didn't know whether to be relieved or worried. The man he had seen leaving hadn't had her with him. But that didn't mean someone else hadn't already taken her away somewhere.

"No sign of the resident or the perp," one of the cops said.

"No shit," Rusty muttered as he slumped down on one of the dining chairs. He wanted to go outside and search for clues, but he knew the cops wouldn't appreciate his interference in their investigation. With his elbows on the table, he rested his head in his hands as his mind raced with all the possibilities. He felt dangerously close to tears of frustration and . . . what else? It felt like there was a rock in the pit of his stomach. Where was she? Was she okay? Was she still alive? Had she been kidnapped?

"Rusty."

The voice was so close to his ear that he jumped. He whirled around to see Julie standing behind him punching in the code to stop the ear-splitting siren. Suddenly, there was silence which, after the high decibel sound, was almost painful.

He stood so abruptly that the chair skidded and fell backward. He grabbed her by the shoulders and realized by her wince that his grip was too tight, so he softened his hold but didn't release her. "Julie, are you okay? Did he hurt you?"

Her voice was a little breathless and shaky, but she answered, "I'm fine. As soon as I heard the glass break in the kitchen and the alarm go off, I ran out the front door."

"I heard you scream."

"I tripped over the coffee table and dropped my phone. I don't remember, but I must have screamed. I just knew I had to get out of here before whoever it was made it inside."

"It was a man, about five foot ten, heavy-set. I saw him as I arrived. I tried to catch him, but these damn shoes are worthless on the ice. Any idea who it could have been?"

She shrugged. "Any one of a dozen guys I've dealt with. Of course, I usually meet just the victims. I don't see the men unless I'm called into court to testify."

"I think that's the files we'll start with."

The two cops came back inside the house. One of them approached Julie.

"I assume you're the resident," he said. "I need you to tell me everything you saw or heard. Could we sit here at the table?"

She nodded, then repeated the whole story while the cop took notes on his pocket-sized spiral notepad. The other cop walked in.

"I just got another call. I'm heading out," he told them, then left.

Rusty paced restlessly during the interview. He could tell by the cop's attitude that he was dismissing this as a standard breaking and entering, not as a threat on Julie's life. He would file a report, then move on to the half dozen other calls he would respond to tonight.

But Rusty suspected that this was anything but a typical B&E. He knew it was useless to express that to the cop. They were busy and overworked, and in this instance, there were no bodies and no blood. Time to move on to something more critical.

Several minutes later, the cop was gone and Rusty was nailing a piece of wood over the broken window. Luckily, Julie had some leftover scraps from her home remodeling in the garage, and one of them fit well enough to provide minimal protection until she could get the glass replaced tomorrow. She followed him closely, using the excuse that she had to show him where everything was, but he suspected it was because she didn't want to be inside the house alone.

When the window was as secure as possible, they went back inside. Cat, who had been hiding somewhere in Julie's bedroom, dared come out and join them. Julie bent over, scooped him up in her arms and hugged him close to her. She buried her face in his soft fur. Cat put up with it for a couple of minutes, but then he squirmed out of her grasp, stalked over to his food dish, hunched down and started crunching his kibbles.

Rusty saw that Julie's head was still bent with her face buried in her hands. It didn't take a genius to see that she was crying. His heart twisted in his chest, and he stepped closer and pulled her into his arms. She didn't resist and actually leaned against him. The shock was wearing off, and she was trembling so much he had to hold on tight to keep her from collapsing to the floor.

Gently, he bent and swept her into his arms and carried her to the living room where he sat on the couch and cradled her on his lap. She sobbed quietly against his chest, the only outward signs was the shaking of her shoulders and the growing dampness of his shirt.

He didn't say anything because he sensed she didn't need encouraging words so much as she needed the comfort of knowing he was there and he would take care of her. This whole on-going assault on her security was unnerving because it was so far out of her control. She rarely needed other people, and even more rarely accepted their help. It was significant that she was accepting his.

He stroked her back and rested his cheek against the top of her head. Slowly, his intention to comfort her began to be replaced by an awareness of the very feminine body in his arms. Her fragrance was intoxicating and his fingertips burned through the thin layers of her gown and robe. She was clearly not wearing a bra and the soft mounds of her breasts pressed against his chest.

Rusty shifted as the blood rushed to his groin in a totally masculine response to the woman on his lap. He hoped she was too distracted to notice. She had made it clear that she valued his friendship and didn't want a more intimate relationship. But right now, being intimate with her was all he could think about.

He became aware that she had gotten very still. There was no evidence that she was still crying or even trembling. His hand stilled on her back and he held his breath. She had felt his arousal and was upset.

As much as he didn't want her to be angry, he didn't want her out of his arms. He was struck by how much he cared about this woman. She was like a female version of himself, ready to run into a disaster to help people but not ready to let someone get inside her own defenses. Neither of them let anyone get too close . . . until now. Rusty tightened his grip on her. He wanted her even closer.

Her head moved and he felt her looking up at him. Reluctantly, afraid that he would see condemnation in her eyes, he leaned back and looked down at her.

Instead of anger, he saw confusion. Instead of rejection, he saw desire. Still he hesitated, not wanting to be too presumptuous or misinterpreting the signals because of his own feelings.

Julie studied him for a moment longer, then, to his surprise, she lifted her hand to his cheek and stretched up until her lips touched his.

A jolt of electricity shot through him. As much as he wanted to show restraint, the softness of her mouth ignited a desire whose intensity shocked even him. He lowered his head to deepen the kiss. She shifted in his arms until she was at a more comfortable angle to return his embrace.

Encouraged, Rusty's lips moved over hers. When the tip of her tongue slipped into his open mouth, he gasped. The taste of her pushed him over the edge. Slowly, he eased her back on the couch and stretched out on top of her, supporting his weight so he didn't crush her.

Her kisses were as hungry and eager as his own. Her fingers threaded through his hair, holding him close . . . as if he was likely to move away. He couldn't remember ever being so turned on. But he had to hold back so he didn't frighten her away.

It quickly became clear that she wasn't going to stop him. When she moved her hand to his waist and slid under his shirt, his breath sucked in with a whoosh. Her fingers slid over his skin, and his penis instantly responded, swelling even larger.

"Make love to me," she whispered.

But he was afraid she was offering herself as a way of showing her gratitude. The last thing he wanted was a thank-you fuck. He wouldn't have hesitated had she been anyone else. But with Julie, he wanted it to be more than just a quickie.

"I know you're thinking this is because of everything that has happened," she told him with her usual intuitiveness. "This has nothing to do with that. Right now, it's just about you and me."

"Oh God, Julie, you're making me crazy."

"Then do something about it."

Still Rusty paused as he tried to convince himself that she wouldn't regret this in the morning. He didn't know where this relationship was going, but he didn't want her to be sorry for anything that happened.

Julie's hand slid lower until it skipped over his belt buckle and spread over the hardness beneath his zipper. She stroked him, then closed her hand to grip him through the cotton. He almost came in his pants.

Rusty rolled off of her and in one smooth movement, scooped her up into his arms and carried her to her bedroom. Instead of laying her down, he set her on her feet, giving her one last chance to call it off. As she stood in front of him, her gaze was open and steady. Her hands moved to the belt that held her robe closed. Rusty watched, mesmerized as her fingers loosened the knot. With a shrug, the silky fabric fell off her shoulders and slithered to the floor. Now only a thin layer of almost sheer cloth hid her body from his view, and he grew more anxious by the second that it be gone.

His hands moved up to cup her breasts and as his thumbs brushed her nipples, they thrust against the gown, begging to be freed. He couldn't resist leaning over and taking one in his mouth, letting his tongue roll around the hardened bud, moistening the material until it clung to her. Julie moaned and reached for his belt buckle, fumbling with the leather in her eagerness.

Heat curled in his stomach, pulsing and growing more excited by the moment. He helped her by unbuttoning his shirt and tossing it aside. She had succeeded in releasing his buckle and her fingers slid his zipper down then moved back up to the waistband of his slacks.

It was the final signal he needed. He kicked off his shoes, striped off his socks, pushed his slacks and briefs down in one hasty thrust and stepped out of them. Then his fingers moved to the thin straps of her gown. It took only the slightest nudge to ease them off her shoulders and the gown fell to the floor with a whisper.

The sight of her fully naked body drove him past the point of no return. His breath exhaled in a low groan as he pulled her into his arms and gently guided her backwards to the bed. He felt like a teenager . . . overheated and ready to explode. At this point, he hoped he could hold on long enough to satisfy her.

She pushed aside the bedspread and scooted to the middle of the bed. Rusty couldn't stand even the brief separation and quickly stretched out on the cool sheets next to her, anxious to feel the warmth and smoothness of her naked body against his.

They hadn't paused long enough to turn the lights out in the living room, so the bedroom was not totally dark. He wanted to look at her . . . to taste her . . . to touch her from the top of her head to the tips of her toes. He levered over her, his large, muscular body dwarfing hers, but belying the tenderness of his touch as his lips brushed over her eyelids, moved to her mouth for a deep, hungry kiss, then trailed down her neck and over her breasts until they closed around one of her pert nipples.

Julie gasped and arched her body as he nipped and suckled one nipple, then the other. Her moaning and writhing sabotaged his intentions to take it slowly. He felt her fingernails digging into his back, urging him on.

"Oh, Julie, I want you . . . now," he breathed, his words hot against the tender skin of her breasts.

"Take me," she answered, equally anxious.

A flash of sanity sobered him. "I don't have any condoms with me. Do you?"

"Are you kidding?" she scoffed, then smiled. "But I can't get pregnant, so we don't need one." She pulled him up until their lips met in a kiss so heated they almost melted together.

He moved between her legs and lowered himself until his penis pressed against her. She was moist and swollen, ready for him to enter her. He forced himself to go slowly, but the sensation of her warmth closing around him, pulling him deeper was almost more than any man could bear. With a groan, he pushed all the way in, burying himself in her sweetness, then pulled back before plunging in again. Julie wrapped her legs around him, clinging to him as they joined in the rhythm of love.

Rusty had long ago lost count of his lovers. It wasn't that he was promiscuous, but at the ripe old age of thirty, he'd had dozens of girlfriends and even a few one-night stands. But with Julie, it was like the first time.

He had to struggle to hold back, waiting for her. Her hips lifted off the sheets as she welcomed him deeper and deeper until, with a cry, her fingers dug into his ass and he felt the ripples of her orgasm stroke his penis until he buried himself in her one more time and poured out his passion in a heated rush.

For a few seconds, time stood still as the pleasure was so intense he couldn't register a single thought. All he wanted was to hang on to the feeling for as long as possible.

Gradually, he drifted back to reality and realized he was lying halfway on top of her. He eased off, but didn't pull away. His eyes, still glazed with desire looked at her and saw that she was lying very still, with her eyes closed.

"Julie . . . are you okay?" he asked gently, desperately afraid that she was flushed with regrets.

Her long, dark eyelashes swept open and her big blue eyes gazed up at him. A slow, sexy smile turned up the corners of her mouth. "I passed okay about a half an hour ago. Now, I'm feeling terrific."

He relaxed, lying on his side with his arm crooked and his head propped up on his hand. "That was . . .," he struggled for an adequate word and settled for, "amazing."

"I know now why you have so many groupies. Firefighters *do* do it better."

"Hey," he pretended to be upset. "Don't lump me in with all those other jokers. I'm in a class by myself."

She chuckled. "I would argue with you on principal, but I've just been thoroughly ravaged. I can't bring myself to criticize you."

"Hmmm, glad to hear it." His hand had been resting on her hip, but he began idly stroking her belly, then moved up to cup her breast. The light in her eyes immediately changed from teasing to sensual. Her nipples reacted, swelling from his touch, tempting him to take them in his mouth, one-at-a-time, back-and-forth until her head lolled back and her eyelids drifted closed.

His mouth covered hers, the tip of his tongue dipping inside and mating with hers. His penis leaped back to life and once again he moved over her. This time their love making was slow, as they took their time exploring each other's body with their hands and their mouths. And although they stretched it out, their shared climax was every bit as explosive as the first.

Rusty rolled over. Now was when he usually got out of bed, dressed and went home. Instead, he pulled Julie into his arms and rested his head on the pillow of her silky hair. She cuddled against him with her cheek nestled on his chest. His eyes closed, and as he drifted off to sleep, he realized he was smiling.

CHAPTER FOURTEEN

What had she done? Was her first thought when she woke up. *So that's what great sex is!* Was her second thought. Julie felt she should be regretting what happened, but all she could think of was how Rusty's hands had set her body on fire . . . a fire that only he could put out.

She hadn't moved since she had fallen into a completely relaxed and totally satiated sleep, cuddled against his chest. It was still dark outside, but she couldn't see the clock, so she had no idea what time it was. And she was not inclined to move for fear it would break the intimacy between them. She could tell by the slow, steady beat of his heart that he was still asleep, and she took advantage of the quiet time to savor the moment.

One of her hands was pinned beneath her, but the other was flung over his waist. She couldn't actually see his body, but the image branded in her brain would stay with her forever. The photo on the Firefighters' Calendar didn't do him justice. Broad, muscular shoulders, a well-defined chest, trim waist and abs that Hercules would envy proved he took good care of himself. Other, more sexy memories of how magnificent his manhood had been, large and proud . . . and justifiably so.

Granted, Julie hadn't seen that many men naked, so she didn't have a lot of data to go on. But surely his maleness was uncommonly impressive.

Julie felt her cheeks flush hotly at the thoughts about how he had felt buried deep inside her and how he had grown in her hand as she stroked him. It had been almost six years since she had even kissed a man, so the things they had done to each other had been unexpected and breathlessly exciting. She was actually shocked at her uninhibited responses to his kisses. That was completely out of character for her. She had been avoiding a relationship and saying *no* to everything, even the most innocent coffee dates for so long, that she thought she had forgotten how to say *yes*.

But as Rusty cradled her in his arms last night on the couch, she had become aware of exactly how glad she was that he was in her life, however temporary.

Julie had no misconceptions about how long this relationship would last. Rusty was not a forever kind of guy. He hadn't offered her any hint of more. She would never have guessed she would settle for less, but with this guy, she was willing to take whatever he wanted to give her, for as long as he chose. As long as her heart didn't get involved, what was the harm in living in the moment? God only knew how long she had not been living at all.

Perhaps they would have just that one night. It was entirely possible that when he woke up, he would drive away and their paths would cross only when they were on the job.

Julie sighed. That would be disappointing, and she would definitely miss having him around. In a very short period of time, she had grown accustomed to seeing him and sitting around talking and laughing almost every day. Other than their lifestyles, they had a lot in common, and she had immediately felt comfortable around him. She would be sad to think she might be a one-night stand . . . but, oh, what a night to remember.

She felt a change in his breathing and the rhythm of his heart sped up. She didn't move, savoring a few more seconds of lying in his arms, inhaling the musky scent of his body and feeling safe and protected in his arms. No one had ever held her like this, and that was almost as good as the sex. Almost.

He buried his face in her hair. Her legs were pressed against his and as his passion grew, she could feel his manhood harden. Her desire to touch him overcame her intention to remain still, and she moved her hand down to his erection. As her fingers tightened around him, he instantly doubled in size.

Neither of them spoke as they adjusted until their mouths found each other's. One kiss turned into another as they quickly rekindled the passion they had felt before. His hands were large and his palms rough as they caressed her hyper-sensitive skin. The heat coiled in her groin, and she ripened eagerly. Her nipples rubbed against his chest as he moved over her. His fingers slid down until they dipped inside her, taunting her already swollen femininity until she writhed and moaned beneath him.

Rusty accepted her invitation and replaced his hand with his penis, sliding in easily. Her warmth and wetness welcomed him, and he drove deeper. They moved together, taking their time and enjoying the way their bodies fit together. He came first, then finished her pleasure with his mouth suckling her nipple and his fingers inside her, tweaking and teasing until she arched against his hand and screamed out loud. Lights flashed and the air pounded in her ears as she launched into the clouds and slowly drifted back down to earth.

Her eyes fluttered open and she saw that he was staring down at her, that sexy crooked grin lifting one corner of his mouth.

"Good morning, Julie." His voice was husky. "Sleep well?"

"Best night ever," she answered, not making any effort at coyness. They were both consenting adults, and she figured the time to play games was past. "I'm glad you stayed."

His eyes narrowed slightly. "Because you needed a bodyguard?"

She sensed that her answer was much more important than it seemed. She leaned over and gave him a long, deep kiss. "No, because you're an amazing lover," she answered with a smile.

His expression relaxed and his eyes grew solemn. "I want you to know that I didn't plan this."

"Neither did I," she agreed.

"No regrets?"

"Only that sooner or later we're going to have to get out of this bed."

Satisfied with her answer, he rested his head on her pillow so that their noses were only inches away from each other. "But not for a while."

They dozed, still wrapped in each other's arms. When they awoke, the weak winter sun was creeping through the cracks in the draperies. They made love again before they got up and shared a shower that would have included a stand-up quickie if the shower wasn't ridiculously small. Julie put on a pair of stretch pants and a loose sweater. Rusty's wandering hands quickly discovered that she wasn't wearing a bra, and that concession seemed to delight him.

He had been wearing slacks and a dress shirt and jacket last night for his date, but he pulled on just the slacks. Julie was temporarily distracted by the sight of his tanned bare torso, and when he caught her staring at him, she blushed.

"Uh . . . I'll make breakfast. How do you like your eggs?" she asked, struggling to drag her attention away.

"Surprise me." He flashed his grin. "Actually, you already have. Let me help."

Her house that had always seemed roomy was dwarfed not only by the size of his body but the power of his personality. As they worked together in her kitchen, they were constantly brushing up against each other, either accidentally or on purpose. Julie was reminded of a pair of kissing cats her mother had had. Whenever they were within inches of each other, the magnets in their lips pulled them together. She smiled at the thought. Yes, there was definitely something magnetic about Rusty's lips. She couldn't resist them, nor could she stay away.

They finally got breakfast on the table and gobbled it down as if they were starving. Cat was equally glad they had finally gotten up because he had fresh kibble in his bowl. Rusty had retrieved her newspaper from the driveway, and they sat on the couch, each leaning on one end, their legs stretched out in the middle with hers on top as they had another cup of coffee and shared the paper.

It was a cozy scene as if they did this every Sunday morning. Julie couldn't help but sneak an occasional glance over the section she was reading. This man fit into her life very well. She hoped he wasn't too anxious to move on.

"Do you mind if I turn on the TV? There's an early game on today."

She shook her head. "Go ahead. I like football."

"God, you're too good to be true," he teased as he picked up the remote, flicked on the TV and found the channel broadcasting the game. His phone that had been sitting on the end table buzzed and vibrated, and he picked it up and checked the message.

"Uh oh," he said.

She was trying not to be nosy, but he must have noticed her curiosity because he held his phone out for her to see.

Asshole! U owe me $200 for the meal and taxi ride home. Call me.

"Your date?

He nodded. "When I heard your alarm, I just ran out of the restaurant. I forgot all about her."

"Sounds like she's ready to negotiate." Julie kept her tone casual. The last thing she wanted to do was to sound like a jealous shrew and scare him away, even though her heart ached at the thought he might leave her and go straight to the other woman.

Rusty shrugged. "I'll mail her a check. I feel bad about deserting her, but I had to get here."

Julie felt some of the tension melt away. That didn't sound like the woman was someone he really cared about.

He folded the section of paper he had just finished and tossed it on the pile on the floor. "Did you ever find your phone?"

"No, I was sitting here when you called, but I don't remember where I was when I dropped it."

Rusty called her number and they listened, but there was no ring.

"The battery could have run down," she suggested.

They got up and started looking around the room for the phone. They crawled around on their knees and looked under furniture and pulled all the cushions off the couch and the chairs. They even searched in the kitchen and the bedroom, but her phone was nowhere to be found.

"Do you think the man took it?" she asked, bewildered and horrified at what he might do with it.

"It looks like that's a possibility. Just to be safe, let's run to the mall and get you a new number. I'm not comfortable with someone having that kind of access to you. Did you have anything important saved on it, like your alarm code?"

She shook her head. "No, just some music. I can download it again."

"Well, let's go now so we can shut your old number down. When we get back, I want us to look over your case files to see if we can figure out who this guy is."

Julie's emotions were mixed as she finished getting dressed. On one hand, the thought of some strange man having all her personal contacts and her own phone number was terrifying, but on the other hand Rusty had said "*when we get back*" which meant he wasn't just going to hit and run. But there was also the option that he felt compelled to help her with this problem, and once it was solved, he would be free to move on.

Shaking off that depressing thought, Julie returned to the living room where Rusty had put on his shirt, although he had left the tails out and the top two buttons undone.

"I want to stop by my condo on the way so I can change clothes," he said. "Ready?"

It was a beautiful, sunny day and Cat was eager to go out and do whatever it was that he did when wandering the neighborhood. Even though he was a stray that stayed, Julie had taken him to a vet and gotten all his shots up-to-date so she wouldn't worry about him picking up some sort of cat disease during his Romeo roaming.

Julie set the alarm and locked the door. Rusty measured the window and told her they would stop at The Home Depot on the way back to see if they could find a replacement.

"You're a man of many talents," she told him.

He waggled his eyebrows suggestively. "And you've only seen a few of them."

"I don't know if I could survive anymore." She fanned her face with her hand as if the very thought overwhelmed her.

"I promise you'll like them."

"I'm sure I will." She laughed and climbed into the passenger seat of his SUV. He closed her door, then got in and turned on the engine. They fastened their seatbelts out of habit. They had both seen too many bodies thrown out of cars in their line of work.

His condo was in a new area of mixed-use homes. There were blocks of condos mixed with small and large single-family homes built around a small town square and several small parks and green spaces. The whole area used to be Stapleton Airport, but had been transformed into a well-planned community when Denver International Airport opened in 1995. That was many years before Julie moved to the area, so she didn't really know what it had looked like before. But it was very nice now.

Julie had been in the area before on calls, but they were usually in the middle of the night, and she'd been more concerned about getting to the correct address than sightseeing. It was sad proof that domestic violence stretched through all socio-economic levels of the population. These families, so happy and successful-looking on the outside were dealing with many of the same problems as the families who lived in the poorest sections of Denver. It was a pleasure not to be here for an unhappy reason.

Rusty parked on the street and ran around to open Julie's door for her. He led the way to the front door of a contemporary metal and glass industrial designed building. They rode the elevator up to the third floor which opened to an airy hallway made brighter by a row of skylights. There were only four condos on each floor, each nestled in a corner to take advantage of the views. He unlocked the door on the southwest corner and held it open for her to enter first.

"It's not big, but I like the open floor plan. Plus I can see the mountains from my deck and the bedroom. Come on, I'll give you a tour."

She followed him through a large room that was a kitchen on the left with granite counters and a large eat-at bar that overlooked a dining area and the living area beyond. The ceilings were tall and open as if the apartment was carved out of an old loft instead of being designed for new construction. The living room was furnished with a brown leather couch and two matching over-sized recliners, all of which faced the biggest television she'd ever seen.

"It must have been quite a change to watch football on my little 25" Magnavox," she commented.

He shrugged and his mouth twitched into a grin. "The scenery was better at your place."

She blushed, and she welcomed the blast of cold air as she opened the patio door and walked outside on the deck that stretched almost the entire length of the apartment and overlooked a beautifully landscaped courtyard that had a large pool with a rock waterfall that was also a fountain, several barbecue pits and volleyball poles sitting empty and waiting for spring. In the distance, the snow-covered Rocky Mountains cut jagged holes in the crystal blue sky. "That's hard to believe," she challenged as he joined her at the wrought iron railing. "This view is pretty awesome."

"There's a gym and a game room in that building on the end. And we're only a couple blocks from stores and restaurants in the town center and a really nice park where they have concerts and show movies on an inflatable screen in the summer."

"Sounds nice."

"It is. I grew up in Parker, about twenty-five miles from here. My brothers and I had horses and played paintball, mostly running wild." He laughed at the memories. "I never thought I'd like living in the city, but this place is okay. I've gotten used to the convenience."

"You don't live all that far from me. I can almost see my neighborhood from here."

"It's probably less than a mile as the crow flies, but sticking to the speed limits makes it take longer than it should."

They went back inside and Rusty locked the door behind them. He led the way down another hall and opened a door to a small bedroom at the end that he was using as an office. There was a hall bathroom, then they returned to the beginning of the hall and he walked into a large master bedroom with a full bath, complete with a huge shower, a jetted garden tub and a walk-in closet that was way too big for his few clothes.

Rusty ran his hand over his day-old stubble. "Make yourself at home. It won't take me but a few minutes to get changed . . . unless you want to stick around and help me." Both of their gazes gravitated to the king-sized bed.

"As tempting as that is," she said, sincerely regretful, "we'd never make it to the mall today."

He nodded in acceptance. "Okay, then wait out there so I'm not distracted. I'm used to dressing quickly."

Julie decided she'd better get out of the room quickly or she'd change her mind. There was nothing she wanted more than to spend the day in bed with Rusty, but they needed to have time to catch their breath. Even though they weren't establishing a long-term relationship, it wasn't healthy to have only one shared activity. Besides, she was anxious to get her old phone disconnected before her psycho-stalker did something crazy with it.

She returned to the living area and was drawn to the corner fireplace. The front was a slab of white granite with a rectangular hole cut out for the firebox. Inside was a layer of cobalt blue glass. She flipped the switch next to it and flames leaped up, flickering and reflecting off the glass. It was a beautiful play of colors and textures that she could have stared at for hours. It was easy to picture herself curled up on the couch on a cold evening with a bowl of popcorn on her lap and Rusty's arm around her shoulders, holding her close.

With a flick of the switch the flames disappeared, breaking the spell. There was no mantel to mar the beautiful silver and grey-veined granite face, so she moved to stand in front of the bookshelf on the other side of the television screen. Dozens of books, mostly history and science-fiction/fantasy filled the lower shelves, but the upper shelves were crowded with trophies and sports memorabilia among framed photos of his family and friends. She studied each one and recognized his brothers and a few of the other firefighters who were casually dressed for a softball league, bowling team or a game of golf. There were a few women in the photos, but they were part of the group rather than featured.

For some reason, Julie was relieved. There were no 8 x 10 glossies of supermodels or cheerleaders standing next to Rusty with smug, possessive smiles. She glanced around. The whole condo reflected his personality, big, warm and unpretentious. The kitchen cabinets were black with countertops that matched the fireplace. Just to keep things from being too designer chic, there was a black velvet Elvis painting in the dining area and a leg lamp reproduction like the one Ralphie's dad won in her favorite holiday movie "*A*

Christmas Story" on one end table. Stainless appliances looked mostly unused. Glass panels in the cabinet doors revealed red dishes and glasses that brought a pop of color to the kitchen. Darker cranberry-colored draperies were hung over the windows and patio door. Overall, it was a very masculine condo with no evidence of a woman's touch.

"You're admiring my decorating skills, aren't you?"

She turned around and saw him standing in the doorway. His blue eyes twinkled and that sexy grin lifted one corner of his mouth. He was dressed in a navy blue sweater and jeans, and his face was clean-shaven. He looked so handsome Julie felt her heart do that crazy little flip-flop she was becoming used to when he was around.

"It's a beautiful place. And I love your fireplace," she told him as she tried to distract her wayward thoughts.

"It was an upgrade," he admitted. "I see enough wood burning every day. I wanted to have something more interesting."

Julie smiled and nodded. "You've got a lot of trophies."

"They go all the way back to my t-ball league. As soon as I bought this place, my mom boxed them all up and brought them over. She said she had run out of room. We Wilsons are a pretty competitive bunch. She tried to be supportive and put all of our trophies out on the mantel, but I think she was relieved to have her mantel cleared. Now it's full of frou-frou stuff like candles and flowers."

"With three boys, she didn't get much of a chance to have frou-frou around," Julie commented.

"You're right. The day after I moved out, she painted my room yellow. It was great motivation for me to never be tempted to move back."

"You clearly prefer red."

"Yeah, it's my favorite color. I was sort of disappointed that Denver's trucks aren't red. It's every little boy's dream to drive a big red fire truck."

"So, you've wanted to be a firefighter forever?"

He nodded. "As far back as I can remember," he confirmed. "Fires always fascinated me. When I was a kid, I would set them, watch how they burned, then put them out."

"I'll bet your parents loved that," she said with a chuckle.

He grimaced. "I almost started a brush fire once when it was a really dry summer, but it actually taught us a lesson about keeping a clear space around our house for protection. You can't believe how fast even short grass fires can spread."

Julie laughed. "I almost feel sorry for your mom, putting up with three active boys."

"We probably caused her a few sleepless nights," he admitted. "But I think our careers bother her even more. Not that she would say anything, because she wants us to make our own choices."

Julie lifted her hand to his smooth cheek. "Your mom did a great job. All of you boys turned out to be fine men." Impulsively, she stretched up on her tiptoes and kissed him. His arms wrapped around her, pulling her tight against him as he returned her kiss with equal passion.

Reluctantly, she took a step backward. "We need to go."

His hands dropped back to his sides, but the heat in his eyes told her he would much rather stay.

CHAPTER FIFTEEN

The mall was super-crowded with everyone shopping the last-minute sales for Christmas gifts. It took Rusty several circles of the parking lot to find a space. As they walked along, not in a particular hurry to get to the phone kiosk, he caught her hand and entwined his fingers with hers. It was a ridiculously simple gesture that made Julie, for the first time in a long time, feel really special. Christmas music filled the air, along with the fresh smell of pine that came from the large trees that were elaborately decorated and placed throughout the mall.

Christmas had once been Julie's favorite time of the year, but it was a holiday for kids. For the last five years, she hadn't been able to bring herself to celebrate. With no family, she didn't have any presents to buy except a few for her co-workers and staff, and she did that early to avoid the rush. So, as they strolled along, looking at the elaborate window displays, she realized she had missed all the color and sparkle. And the sentiment.

As they faced one of the big display windows, she saw their reflection in the glass. She and Rusty stood, side-by-side, her hand still snugly inside his much larger one. He was so tall and gorgeous that it took her breath away. The blue of the sweater brought out the intense color of his eyes and the delicious fragrance of his aftershave was driving her wild. How wonderful it would be to actually be a part of a happy couple, especially this time of year.

"Hey, Rusty . . . Julie," a masculine voice called and they turned around.

Sam, Rusty's younger brother and his fiancée Kate approached, their arms loaded with bags. Their gazes immediately took in Rusty's hand gripping Julie's possessively. Sam didn't even pretend not to notice. Instead, he gave them a "gotcha" smile. "So, what's new?" he asked.

"Oh, you mean my sweater?" Rusty bantered back. "Yeah, it is. Do you like it?"

"Looks good on you," Sam answered. "I think you made a good choice, much better than some of the other sweaters you've worn."

Rusty squeezed her hand. "This one is a good fit." He nodded toward their purchases. "Looks like you two have been busy. What did you get Mom?"

Sam rolled his eyes. "She's the only one left. I just can't find anything."

"She saves those Snow Village house thingies," Rusty suggested.

"She's got dozens of them. I have no idea which ones she needs."

"How about a Painted Pony statue? I noticed she has started collecting them."

Sam smiled and nodded. "Great idea."

"We just passed a store that sells them," Julie spoke up.

"So what did you get her?" Sam asked. "No, wait, don't tell me . . . another gift certificate to Red Lobster?"

"No, I got her that last year," Rusty scoffed. "This year, it's for Carrabba's."

"That's such a cop out."

"No, it's not. It's a thoughtful, useful gift. She likes to eat. And I usually tag along when she uses it, so I get a good meal and some quality time with her. What's wrong with that?"

"It's just lazy. You don't have to think about it or fight these crowds."

Rusty grinned. "Yeah, pretty smart, huh?" He turned to Julie. "You've met Kate, haven't you?"

"Yes." Julie smiled at Kate. "It's getting close to the Music Hall's last performance, isn't it?"

"Yes, I'm really sad about it," Kate told her. "I've had a blast working there. In the last six months, we've put on four different plays, plus the children's shows on Saturday. I'm really going to miss the cast. They're such nice people."

"Do you have something else lined up?" Julie asked.

"Not yet, but I just auditioned for a local production that will be at one of the smaller theaters in the Denver Center for the Performing Arts," Kate answered.

"Isn't that where . . . ?" Julie hesitated.

"Yes, I was almost killed there, but I can't let that ruin it for me. The guy's dead, so it's over. I try not to think about it." Kate shivered, still affected by the memory. "But the whole incident was how Sam and I got together and fell in love, so the good outweighs the bad, don't you think?"

Julie nodded. "Absolutely. You can be a victim or you can be victorious. It's good you've chosen to move on."

"Chris told us about your car accident," Sam said to Julie. "A snake? That's pretty weird, isn't it?"

"It really creeped me out," Julie admitted. "I'm just glad I didn't hurt anyone."

"If that had happened to me, I probably would have climbed out the window," Kate said with a grimace. "I hate snakes."

"Me, too," Julie agreed. "I couldn't get out of that car fast enough."

"Don's son gave it a good home," Sam said, then turned to Rusty, "So, bro, are you coming on Christmas Day?"

"I get off at 7:30 that morning. Depending on how busy we are the night before, I might go straight to Mom and Dad's or I might catch a few hours' sleep."

"We'll open presents around noon and eat at two," Sam told him. "Don't oversleep."

"And be late for turkey and dressing and pumpkin pie? No way."

Sam and Kate looked over at Julie. They obviously wanted to ask if she was going to be there, but they didn't dare.

The silence stretched awkwardly. Julie certainly didn't want to think she expected an invitation when one wasn't forthcoming, so she hurried to say, "Well, I have to work all day Christmas. I usually take the whole 24-hour shift so my staff can spend the time with their families."

"That's really nice," Kate said. "I'm sure they appreciate that."

"They're all volunteers, so it's the right thing to do," Julie told her.

Sam gave Kate a little shoulder bump. "We'd better get going. "I've got to go to work tonight."

"Let's go get one of those horses for your mom," Kate reminded him.

"See you two later," Rusty said.

Sam gave them both a smile and a nod and Kate gave Julie a conspiratorial wink.

Rusty and Julie watched them walk away for a moment, then turned back to each other. "They're so cute together," Julie commented, surprised by the wistfulness in her voice. Hoping Rusty didn't notice, she quickly added, "Let's go find that phone store."

Monday morning Julie arrived at the office in a much better frame of mind. She felt relaxed and invigorated, even though she had to explain to everyone why she had the remnants of two black eyes. The color had faded to a sort of sick-looking green which she hoped would disappear completely by the end of the week.

Once in her office, she flipped through the incident reports and the pile of missed call slips and sorted them by importance, then set about catching up. Weekends usually generated as much activity as all five other days. But on top of her pile was an urgent message from one of her staff.

Brenda was one of the volunteers that had been with her the longest. Very reliable and generous with her time and her compassion, she very rarely called off a shift. Julie dialed Brenda's number.

"Hello." The voice on the other end of the line was distracted and upset.

"Brenda, this is Julie. What's wrong?"

The sound of muffled sobs filtered through the phone. *"It's my mom. She was just diagnosed with breast cancer, and I've got to go back to Kansas City and take care of her."* Brenda sniffled and tried to get her emotions under control. *"I hate to leave you short, especially on the holidays . . ."*

"Don't worry about us," Julie interrupted. "You need to be with your mother. I'm so sorry to hear about her diagnosis. They've got some amazing treatments now, but it's going to be a rough road for her. I'm sure she'll feel so much better with you there."

"She's always been so healthy. This was such a shock."

"It's good that she's strong. You can help her fight this. I think attitude has a lot to do with recovery."

Brenda sniffled again. *"I think you're right. I've got to make sure she's getting the right treatment and staying positive."*

"What about your children?"

"They're out of school, so they're going with me at least until after New Year's Day. After that, my husband can take care of them. He'll just have to come home a little earlier than usual."

"Let me know if I can help in any way," Julie offered sincerely. "Tell Richard to call me if he needs a backup."

"I will. Thanks, Julie. I just hate to leave with such short notice."

"I've been taking some time off, so I can take your shift."

"I don't know when I'll be back."

"There will always be a spot for you on our team," Julie promised. "Just focus on your family for now and let me know when you're ready to come back."

"Thank you. You know how much I love the work."

They wished each other a Merry Christmas, said their goodbyes and Julie hung up. She opened the schedule file on her computer screen and studied it. This was the worst time of year to ask for the other volunteers to take an extra shift. As Brenda had implied, the holidays brought out the dark sides to many relationships. Disappointments blew out of proportion and arguments ensued, followed all too often by physical fights or mental abuse. And of course, there was an increase in fires and robberies and personal assaults, all of which provided her with more victims who needed help.

Julie would have to reshuffle the schedule for January, but she would take all of Brenda's shifts for the rest of December. Cat wouldn't mind if she was gone an extra night each week and Julie didn't have any other family who would care. Of course, there was Rusty.

That brought a soft smile to her lips. The weekend had been wonderful. Julie couldn't remember a time where she felt happier or more relaxed. And then there was the sex. Just the thought of him lying next to her or walking with a complete lack of modesty, naked from the bathroom caused that now-familiar stir of desire to ignite in the pit of her stomach. He had a perfect body, and she had unabashedly stared at it.

And he had spent plenty of time staring at hers, although her body wasn't anywhere close to being perfect. But he had made her feel beautiful. It wasn't just the words, but the way his eyes glowed with appreciation and how his hands caressed her with such tenderness that she felt treasured and very, very special.

How long would it last? Probably until another girl caught his eye. While that thought should have revolted her, it had been so long since she had felt so happy and satisfied, she pushed the thought aside. She knew he would eventually break her heart. Hopefully not today . . . or tomorrow . . . or next week.

The follow-up calls and official reports took the rest of her day. It was after six when she finally left her office and headed down to the parking lot. The rental car was much smaller than her Sportage and didn't have four-wheel drive. However, the roads were in pretty good condition and the traffic kept her speed slow, so it didn't take too long to get home. Her house was dark, and she tried to swallow back the fear that someone might be in there, waiting for her.

Rusty had replaced her window yesterday, and she hadn't received a text alert from the alarm company, so she had no reason to believe the man, whoever he was, had come back.

It made her angry, furious even that this stranger had taken away her serenity and made her be afraid in her own home. It was her safe haven, and now it had been violated. The only time she wouldn't be listening for every little sound and jumping at shadows was when Rusty was there.

Julie pulled into the garage and quickly moved from the car to the house, turning off the alarm and locking the back door, then hitting the garage door button. Cat came strolling out of the living room, and that was all the reassurance she needed that no one else was there. Otherwise, he would have been hiding in one of his secret places.

"Hey there, boy. Are you hungry? You ate all your kibble today." She rattled on as if he understood while he twined around her ankles. "I think we both deserve a treat tonight," she told him as she took a can of cat food out of the cabinet and pulled back the tab. Cat reacted immediately, starting up a cross between a loud meow and an impatient howl. Wet food was such an unusual extravagance that he completely lost his cool and started begging shamelessly.

She dumped the food onto a saucer and set it next to his water dish, then added a scoop of dry kibble to the empty bowl. Now it was time to put together her own meal.

The knock on her door startled her so much that she dropped the can of tomato sauce she'd been holding.

"Julie, it's me," Rusty's voice filtered through the door, and she hurried to open it, not trying to hide her relief and pleasure that he was here.

"I was just about to make spaghetti," she told him. "Are you staying for dinner."

His azure eyes twinkled. "I was hoping you'd ask." He held up a bottle of wine and a box. "I stopped by Pino's on the way here."

"You're going to make me fat, then dump me for a super model," she teased.

"I can think of a couple ways to burn off the calories. And they're completely healthy."

"Oh. Are they really?"

"You're looking pretty good, and I can't remember when I felt better."

She smiled. "Maybe Kim Kardashian and Pam Anderson should repackage their sex tapes as exercise DVDs."

"They've got nothing on you." He set the wine and the dessert box on the table, then pulled her into his arms. "I've been wanting this all day. Girl, I don't know what you've done to me, but you're all I can think about.

Julie melted against him, loving the way their bodies fit together and the way his lips were both soft and firm at the same time. It took all their self-control and growling stomachs to make them finally pull away.

"I can boil the water," he offered after he stepped away.

She was glad to see that he was having as much trouble controlling his breathing as she was. "I make great spaghetti sauce. It's my one culinary talent, but I'll admit that I take a shortcut with the meatballs. I buy them by the bag from Costco, and they're as good as homemade." Julie took the bag out of the freezer and poured about a dozen into a bowl, then put them in the microwave to defrost.

They worked together in comfortable harmony, laughing and talking about their day. The conversation rarely lulled, and when it did, it wasn't awkward.
He opened the wine and they sipped while they cooked, then finished the bottle off with the meal. After they cleaned the kitchen, they watched television for a little while, but almost all the shows were repeats and much less interesting than the promise of what could happen in the bedroom.

They cuddled on the couch with her sitting on his lap. His hands had slipped under her sweater and with a talent whose source she didn't want to question, he removed her bra and released her breasts to his caresses. It didn't take much of that kind of playing for her to feel the moistness wet her panties. He nibbled her neck and her earlobe, then whispered, "Can I stay?"

She cupped his ruggedly beautiful face in her hands. "You don't ever need to ask."

"Yes, I do. I don't want you to think I'm taking you for granted."

"Shhh," she breathed against his lips. "I know where you can take me . . . to bed."

He didn't need a second invitation, but swept her into his arms and carried her to her bedroom where he set her on her feet. Impatiently, they shed their own clothes until they were standing in front of each other, totally naked.

"My God, you have the body of a super hero," she told him, constantly amazed by the rippling muscles, toned abs and impressive erection that was now standing at full alert. "They should make an action figure of you."

"Anatomically correct?"

"No, I don't particularly want to share that with the world," she admitted.

He grinned, and his blue eyes smoldered. "Good. Because I don't want to be shared."

"Show me what you *do* want," her voice was husky and she felt her knees grow weak as she read the desire in his eyes.

"I want you."

He pulled her into his arms and they collapsed on the bed.

CHAPTER SIXTEEN

Smoke curled around the man's face before it found its way out through the crack in the window. Calls crackled back and forth through the portable police scanner he had plugged into the lighter. Listening to the pulse of the city was more interesting than any radio station, and it was live twenty-four hours a day.

He took a final drag on his cigarette, flicked it out the partial opening, then hit the button to roll the window up. It was cold, too damn cold to be sitting in a car on a sleepy street in the middle of the night.

He should have been tired, but anger was a powerful motivator. It had kept him awake for the last week, staring at a small red brick bungalow. He thought it was an ugly house, old and square with a low gabled roof. There was a single car garage in the back with a narrow driveway leading to it. Wooden pillars formed the corners of a raised, almost square concrete porch. The multi-paned windows should have allowed him easy access to the interior of the house, but he hadn't considered that she would install an alarm system. He knew, for certain, that it hadn't been there a week and a half ago.

That had been an almost fatal miscalculation. He knew how long it took the Denver PD to respond to a home alarm, so he'd known he had plenty of time. But he hadn't counted on that firefighter to storm up like a bat out of hell. Another miscalculation. It had to be his last. He was too close to the end to screw up again.

Headlights flashed in his rearview mirror as a car turned onto the quiet street. The man ducked down and the car didn't slow down as it passed him. He peeked up over the dashboard in time to see the car turn into the drive, hesitate for a moment while the garage door rolled up, then continued inside. Only seconds later, a woman walked briskly out of the garage, unlocked the back door and hurried into the house. Lights flashed on in the kitchen, then in the living room. Draperies covered the windows, but he could see her silhouette as she moved through the house.

Only minutes later, another set of headlights turned onto the street, and the guy dropped down again. He knew without looking that it was a red SUV and that it turned into the driveway and parked in front of the garage.

The man sat up. Yes, he had been right. He watched as the firefighter got out of the SUV. The back door opened, allowing a wave of light to splash out. The woman stood in the doorway. The firefighter took her in his arms and gave her a long, deep kiss, then they walked inside and shut the door behind them, blocking the rest of their passionate reunion from the man in the car's view.

The man pounded the steering wheel. Fuck. The firefighter was there again. Ever since the man had staked out the house, the woman had not spent the night alone.

Slut.

Whore.

Bitch.

He knew the woman's name was Julie Lawrence. It hadn't been easy finding that out. It had been even more difficult to discover where she lived. She was well-protected in her police department cocoon. For the last week he had been following her, watching her, planning how and when to make a move on her.

The firefighter complicated things. He was big and strong, obviously in great physical condition. It would be a challenge to beat him in a fair fight. The man's thick lips curled into a smile. Then he would just have to make sure to have an advantage should the two of them ever actually meet.

In a perfect world, the man preferred getting Julie alone. There were things that needed to be discussed. He wanted to make sure she knew just how much she had ruined his life . . . and just how much he hated her for it. He wanted to make her suffer as much as he had. She thought she was so high and mighty, rushing to the aid of every whiny woman or cowardly child, especially considering she couldn't even take care of herself.

He had thought the snake was a good touch. It had been easy enough to pop the lock on her car door while she was in the grocery store and let the little guy loose on her floorboard. Too bad she hadn't been going fifty-five when she found him. A crash at that speed would have done some major damage, maybe even killed her.

That thought made him frown. He didn't really want her dead. That would be too easy. After all the anguish she had caused, she needed to live with the knowledge that she didn't know jack shit about how to make a man happy . . . or how to make a marriage work. A woman had to know who the boss was in any relationship. Sometimes, it was a lesson not quickly learned.

If ever a woman deserved to be punished . . . it was Julie.

And it had to be soon. He was fucking tired of sitting out in the cold while she was inside a warm house with a goddamn firefighter, fucking his brains out. The man knew her routine. Now he needed a plan . . . and a place where the firefucker was unlikely to be.

An idea sparked in his brain. He could wait a few more days. This time there would be no miscalculations. This time she would get the lesson of her life . . . maybe her last. It would be risky, but once she understood how much damage she had caused, he really didn't care what happened to him. He had nothing left to lose.

Inside the house, Julie collapsed on one of the dining chairs. "That was a tough one. A man decided he needed to discipline his step-son . . . with his fists. Apparently, the boy had admitted he was gay, and the man thought he could beat it out of him."

"That's grim," Rusty agreed. "How old was the boy?"

"Sixteen. The mother sided with the step-dad, so now the boy is with Child Welfare. I doubt the foster system will be any more understanding or kind." She leaned forward and rested her head on her arms on the table.

"Want a glass of wine?" Rusty asked.

"No, it's too late." She lifted her head enough to glance at the kitchen clock and noted it was two-thirty in the morning. "Actually, it's too early. I hope that's the last call tonight."

He moved behind her and massaged her shoulders. "I wasn't sure if I'd hear from you tonight."

"Are you kidding?" Her head lolled forward as she felt the tension ease out of her. "And miss this?"

He leaned down and nibbled on the tender flesh of her exposed neck. His fingers threaded into her ponytail and he pulled off the elastic band, releasing her long dark hair to spill over her shoulders. "How about this? Did you miss this, too?"

"Hmmm," she murmured, loving the feel of his hands on her skin.

His hands slid down her arms and entwined with her fingers. Gently, he pulled her to her feet. "Let's go to bed. You've been working too hard."

As much as she wanted to stay there and let him caress her, she had to admit that she was dead on her feet. These last few days had been the best and the worst of her life. She and Rusty had spent almost every non-working moment together which had been wonderful. They had even run into each other on several calls when they had both been on-shift.

But as with all holidays, victim's advocate calls were double what they were on a normal night. The closer it got to Christmas, the more the number and the intensity increased. She had taken Brenda's shifts as well as her own, so she had had to work three of the last six nights.

She let him lead her to the bedroom. With a yawn, she went into the bathroom, took out the brown contact lens and left them soaking in their container. Another yawn as she squeezed toothpaste on the brush. It was almost more of an effort to move her hand up and down than it was worth. She spit and rinsed, then quickly stripped out of her clothes, pulled on a short, soft cotton nightgown and returned to the bedroom.

Rusty was already in bed, naked of course because he didn't even own a pair of pajamas. He pulled the covers back, revealing the most desirable place on earth . . . a spot next to him. She switched off the lamp and crawled in, immediately scooting over until her back was spooned against his chest. He covered her with the comforter, then wrapped his arms around her.

"Goodnight, angel," he whispered, his breath warm against her ear.

"Night, Rusty," she said, barely able to get the words out before her eyes closed. As much as she loved the sex, she treasured the time when they just cuddled or, like now, slept in each other's arms.

Thankfully, her phone didn't ring again and they were able to sleep through until the alarm went off at seven a.m. They hadn't moved much during the night and woke up still lying closely. Julie rolled over and buried her face in the curve of his neck. He leaned back and kissed her closed eyelids.

"Can't you call in sick today? You didn't get enough sleep." He brushed the silky mass of hair back from her face.

"I've got a couple interviews for new volunteers this morning," she told him without enthusiasm. "Besides, it's the last day before Christmas Eve, so I really have to go in. What are you going to do today?"

"Nothing special." He stretched. "I need to take my Explorer into the shop to get the oil changed and it needs a bath. With all the slush on the roads, you can barely tell it's red."

Reluctantly she threw back the covers and sat up. A glance back at his sleepy eyes and the sexy grin proved irresistible and she leaned over and gave him a lazy good-morning kiss.

He groaned. "Are you sure you can't be late?"

"I'm sure, but I'm not on call tonight, so I'll be home early."

"Promises, promises," he grumbled, but he knew she was as devoted to her career as he was.

She shuffled into the bathroom where she started her preparations for the day. When she was putting in the contact lens, he walked in behind her. She looked up and saw he was studying her in the mirror.

"I still don't understand why you wear brown contacts. You don't need the vision correction, your blue eyes are way more beautiful, and you're not a vain person, so I'm not buying the looks excuse."

It was a conversation she had been dreading. Since she didn't know how long the relationship was going to last, she hadn't really volunteered any more personal information than he had asked for. As she thought about how to answer, she brushed her hair, twisted it and clipped it on top of her head.

"And this?" he asked, perversely taking out the clip and letting her hair fall free. "Why don't you let your hair hang down like this." He ran his fingers through the silky strands and let them fall back in place. "You're an attractive woman. Why do you go to such lengths to make yourself appear ordinary?"

Julie sighed and dropped her head. "I'm not sure now is the right time for this discussion."

He gripped her shoulders and turned her around until she faced him. "Actually, I think now is the perfect time. You and I have spent a lot of intimate moments together these last two weeks. We've shared everything. I've told you about my family, my friends and even my ex-girlfriends. You've never told me anything about yourself. Other than a vague reference to Connecticut, I don't know where you grew up, where you went to college or why you've been living like a nun." He cupped his hand under her chin and lifted her face so she was forced to look into his eyes. "Julie, what are you running away from?"

She shook her head. "I don't want to talk about it. It's . . . it's just too painful."

And you don't trust me enough . . .?"

"No, it's not that at all," she hurried to assure him. "I really do have to get to the office. We'll talk about it tonight."

"Promise?"

She nodded. "Promise." Anxious to push the disapproval from his eyes, she stretched up and kissed him. "I've got to run. Please set the alarm when you leave."

Rusty watched as she rushed from the room, practically threw on some clothes and hurried out of the house. She was clearly keeping something from him. As he showered, all the possibilities ran through his mind. But none seemed logical or plausible. He thought he had gotten to know her relatively well. They talked for hours about everything imaginable.

Apparently, not everything.

He dressed, turned on the alarm and locked the door as he left. She had given him the code several days ago so he could let himself in when she was out on a call. She trusted him with her home, her safety and her body. She just hadn't trusted him with her secrets.

It was two days before Christmas, and he knew all his friends would be busy. Most of them had kids, and that meant there was always last minute shopping, gift wrapping and whatever else parents did to keep the myth of Santa Claus alive. His brothers were both sleeping today because they worked nights. That left only his mom. She would probably be busy baking pies and cookies. Even though her sons were all grown up and she didn't have any grandkids yet, she still went all out with the decorating and the goodies. Maybe it was a perfect day to visit his mom after all.

He dropped by his condo for a change of clothes. As much as he was enjoying his nights with Julie, not ever sleeping at his own place was getting old. He felt silly carrying his personal items in a little travel bag. It gave him a little insight into how women must feel after spending the night with a lover. It was awkward, kind of the masculine version of the walk of shame.

His mother, Pat, tried to get everyone together for family dinners at least once a month. It was difficult with the three boys working shifts and often called in for overtime. She didn't let that discourage her, and most of the boys were able to make the dinners. However, the rules were more strict for holidays, especially Christmas, Thanksgiving, Easter and Mother's Day. It wasn't so important to his dad who preferred to spend Father's Day golfing or at a baseball game, but no one dared make excuses to Mom.

It took him about forty minutes to drive to Parker. There was snow in the forecast and everyone was hoping for a white Christmas, but so far the only signs were some thick clouds building over the mountains. Denver seldom had snow on Christmas Day, so it was more likely that the storm would wear itself out before reaching them. The sun was shining brightly as he turned into the familiar driveway that led to his parents' home.

His parents had bought five acres and had the house built in the early Eighties, and all three boys had grown up there. A few years ago, after Rusty and Sam had moved out and Chris was in the military, his parents had completely remodeled the interior, so it looked like a new house. Even with new appliances and flooring, the place still looked the same at Christmas. Every year just after Thanksgiving, Mom carried dozens of boxes up from the basement and hung garland on the stairs, stockings on the fireplace and a big wreath on the front door. She always insisted on having a real tree that almost touched the fourteen-foot peak of the vaulted ceiling in the family room and decorated it with ornaments that ranged from delicate blown glass to handmade items from the boys' childhood.

Rusty knocked on the front door, then walked in without waiting for a response. The fragrance of freshly baked pies pulled him to the kitchen as if he was being led by a leash.

His mom was rolling out red-colored dough on the granite countertop. "Hey, kiddo. You're just in time to help me make cookies."

He plucked off a chunk of dough and put it into his mouth. "Hmmm . . . how did you know I was coming?"

"Mom's have a sixth sense about these things."

"Your sugar cookies are the best."

"Don't tell anyone, but I use powdered sugar instead of granulated. It makes them lighter and more crispy."

He pinched off another piece and she swatted his hand away.

When she had the dough at the correct thickness, he picked up a cookie cutter shaped like a tree and started stamping out shapes. His mom reached out and grabbed it away from him.

"Wait until I bring out the green dough for the trees and the wreaths. You know better than that."

Rusty smiled and picked up a star. "I like red trees."

"You've always been a rebel," she accused, but her expression was indulgent. "So, what's going on in your life?"

"Nothing." He stamped out a row of stars, then switched to a stocking.

"That's not what I heard."

He looked up at her curiously. "Oh?"

"Sam and Kate invited Dad and me over for dinner yesterday. They said you've been dating a new woman and it looked pretty serious."

He hesitated. He honestly didn't know how to respond. Was it serious? Had his relationship with Julie moved out of the friend zone and into . . . What? What was the next phase? He'd never been there before, so he didn't recognize it or know how to proceed. He sighed. Even if his feelings were changing, he didn't think Julie's were.

There was no doubt that they were compatible sexually. All he had to do was think about the way she looked, all soft and glowing, after they made love or the way she touched him, so tentative, yet so eager or how her hair smelled or . . . God, he realized he was getting hard and he shook his head to clear his thoughts. Yes, she turned him on. Lots of women had. It was just that Julie was so much more.

She challenged him intellectually so that their conversations were never reduced to inane discussions about shoes or Heidi Klum's latest boyfriend. He didn't have to explain how it felt to recover a body from a fire or the huge sense of accomplishment when you carried out a live one that you knew would survive. She fit in his life like no one else ever had. He was relaxed and comfortable around her.

All of which terrified him to his core.

Besides, she had showed him no signs that she was interested in anything beyond what they had. Unlike other women, she never dropped hints about getting married. She hadn't even hesitated at the mall when they passed a jewelry store window that was filled with sparkling engagement rings. There wasn't a single issue of *Bride* magazine in her house and she never dropped hints such as what sort of flowers she wanted at her wedding or where she'd like to go on a honeymoon. She didn't mention wanting children or that her clock was ticking, whatever the hell that meant.

And there was that whole thing about her contact lens and severe hair-dos that made no sense to him. To add to the mystery, she wasn't very forthcoming about it either. For a woman who encouraged people to talk about their troubled past, innermost fears and worst problems, she was surprisingly silent about hers.

"I've been dating someone, but I don't know how serious it is," Rusty finally answered his mom with total honesty.

"Why don't you invite her to join us for Christmas . . . unless she has her own family?"

"No, she wouldn't come. Actually, she's working that day. She's the head of the Victim's Advocate Dept."

"Is she the one I met that awful day you were kidnapped? The one who saved your life?"

"Yes, that was her."

Pat nodded her approval. "She seemed very nice . . . and genuinely concerned about you."

They transferred the cookies to a cookie sheet. Rusty picked up a container of colored sprinkles and shook a generous amount on each cookie. His mom put the pans in the oven and set the timer.

"Do you want a glass of milk while we wait?"

"Sure," he answered, having a flashback to when he was twenty years younger and sitting in this same kitchen, drinking a glass of milk with his mom while they waited for the cookies to bake. Instead of making him feel comforted, he was a little shaken by the thought at how time was passing him by.

He was thirty years old, loved his job and his condo, but was that all there was to life?

The irony was not lost on him that for a man who had never spent a whole night with a woman or woke up in someone else's bed, he was now practically living in the home of a woman who was basically using him for sex and safety. It was more than ironic; it was humiliating. He felt a hint of shame at how he had treated women in the past with the same cavalier attitude.

"So, what's the problem?" his mom asked after setting a full glass of milk in front of him.

"No problem."

She pinned him with one of her don't-bullshit-your-mother looks, although she would never actually have phrased it like that. "You don't just drop by unless something's bothering you."

The corner of his mouth lifted in a grin. "Ah, come on. Can't a son come see his mother just for fun?"

"No," she answered bluntly.

Rusty grew serious. Her ears had heard all of his childhood complaints about friends, teachers, grades, college and girls. Her advice had always been good, even if he had sometimes chosen not to take it . . . often regretting that decision later. Maybe she could give him some kind of insight into the female mind.

"Pull up a stool. This is going to take a while," he told her.

CHAPTER SEVENTEEN

Julie had been distracted all day. Several times she realized she was staring at the painting of the meadow on the wall while her mind wandered over her conversation with Rusty.

It wasn't unreasonable that he should want to know why she was doing what she was doing. She could see how it could be viewed as peculiar behavior. But her reasons were good. Would he understand or would he judge her?

They had spent so much time together and shared everything in the last few days. Actually, to be fair, he had shared; she had listened. Was it her turn?

She had been tempted, many times as they relaxed on the couch, talking about his family or laying in the dark when their inhibitions were gone and their personal walls down. It would have been easier to tell him when the lights were off, and she couldn't see the disappointment and shock in his eyes.

Now he was insisting they have the conversation tonight, probably sitting across the dining table from each other with the lights in the small chandelier blazing. She wasn't sure she could go through with it.

If her relationship with Rusty was for the long haul, she could see opening up to him. However, since she knew it was just a matter of time before his eyes wandered and he lived up to his reputation of loving 'em and leaving 'em, she would risk chasing him away even sooner. It was one of the reasons she hadn't wanted everyone to know they were dating . . . if that was what you could call it. If that had gotten out, she would have been the brunt of office chatter. Working in the police station where the majority of employees were male, she had quickly discovered that men gossiped as much as women, although they would never admit it. When Rusty did move on, she didn't want everyone to be either pitying her or thinking she was a slut.

Her reputation was important, not just personally but professionally. Once Rusty was out of her life, that's all she would have left.

Julie leaned back in her chair. She would never have believed that she would risk so much to be with a man . . . especially with no promises or chance of a future. For five, actually, almost six years, she had gotten along quite well without any type of relationships, either male or female. The trauma she had gone through that had triggered her move to Denver had left her without the slightest desire for sex or even dating. She not only hadn't missed it, but she hadn't even given it much thought.

Until Rusty appeared on the scene.

Other than the delightful fact that he made her bones melt with his passionate lovemaking, he made her laugh. It had been a very long time since Julie had been happy. She couldn't even remember the last time she had smiled so much or felt so relaxed.

Even with the threat of her crazy stalker in the background, she wasn't afraid when Rusty was around. He was big and strong and used to running into burning buildings to save puppies. How could she not fall in love with such a man?

Fall in love? Oh God, no! she groaned. That would be the worst possible scenario. Not only would her reputation be ruined, but her heart would be broken. As much as she had tried to protect herself, she had slipped up.

So, tonight he wanted to hear the whole truth. That would probably be the impetus for his departure. He wouldn't want her after he knew. It would be his excuse to walk away. Not that he needed an excuse, but this would just speed up the process. By now he was probably already getting a little bored and antsy. She had no false hopes that she was fascinating or sexy enough to keep his interest for very long.

Julie had ignored the alarm bells clanging in her brain. She had pushed aside her morals and brushed off the potential for the personal pain of a broken heart for the temporary love of a man. Not just any man . . . her lover was a hero. But even heroes can hurt people.

She forced herself to focus on the two interviews she had scheduled. One was an adrenalin junkie who had probably applied in the hopes she would get to hang out with cops and firefighters. The other was also a woman, but she was happily married with spare time she wanted to use to help other people which made her an ideal candidate. There were a dozen more interviews set up for after Christmas, and hopefully, Julie would be able to bring at least three more people on staff. Number two went in the "to-be-considered" pile while number one went in the "not-even-if-there's-no-one-else" pile, a.k.a. the shredder.

After a few follow-up calls to some of the victims from recent events, she confirmed that her staff would be working their scheduled shifts. When her desk top was clean, she gave up trying to put off the inevitable and headed home.

She hadn't heard from Rusty all day, but that wasn't unusual. He knew she was planning on being home early, so he would probably get in touch with her or drop by early in the evening. It would have to be an early night because he was on shift at 7:30 on Christmas Eve morning and wouldn't be off until 7:30 Christmas Day.

She dropped by their favorite Chinese restaurant for take-out. Maybe a dose of MSG would make her confession go down more smoothly. It was already dark when she pulled into her driveway and watched the garage door open. She gathered up the bag of take-out, her briefcase and purse and hurried to the house.

The door was unlocked and swung open at her touch.

A cold chill ran through her. Someone had been here.

But then she dismissed that possibility. The alarm hadn't gone off. More than likely Rusty had hurried out and forgotten to set it and lock the door. That seemed highly unlikely, considering how aware he was of the situation. Possibly he had set it, but then came back and just popped out for a minute.

Her chuckle was shaky. Hopefully, he hadn't gone out to pick up dinner, too. Of course, if he had, that would leave her with a lot of leftovers for Christmas, which would be good since so few restaurants were open that day. It was clear he wasn't going to invite her to have dinner with his family. Not that she expected that or even wanted it.

Who was she trying to fool? She wanted it very much. But theirs wasn't that type of relationship.

She hesitated a moment longer, considering and dismissing the option of calling the police before she went in. When they walked through her house and found nothing wrong, she would feel silly. Her thoughts kept going back to the fact that the alarm hadn't gone off, so it had to be safe.

Julie flipped on the light switch, pushed the door the rest of the way open and stepped inside. Her gaze immediately focused on the small body tied to her antique chandelier. The bags dropped from her arms and she screamed.

Cat, with a rope tied around his neck, hung limply from the light fixture over the table, clearly dead. She rushed forward, her first instinct to cut him down, but she knew that she shouldn't. There could be all sorts of evidence she would contaminate. But oh, God, she wanted to save him. Her head dropped and she noticed that the person, whoever they were, had left her a message. Carved deeply in crude jagged letters on the wooden surface was the word *WHORE*.

Rusty heard Julie's address broadcast over the scanner in his Explorer. His hands gripped tighter on the steering wheel. He was still about ten minutes away and traffic was heavy. His mother had talked him into staying for dinner, so he'd gotten away from his parents' house later than planned. Using all the skills he had learned in one of his firefighter academy classes, he made the ten minutes in seven, squealing to a stop behind a patrol car parked on the street in front of her neighbor's house. Another patrol car was parked across the street and an unmarked car was directly in front of her house.

It took him only seconds to jump out and jog to the front door that stood open, even though the temperature was near freezing. Julie was perched stiffly on the edge of the couch as if she was poised to leap to her feet and run away. A cop was sitting next to her, jotting notes onto his pad. Her back was to him, so she wasn't yet aware he had arrived. It gave him a moment to assess the situation.

Through the doorway to the kitchen, Rusty could see the shocking and gruesome site of the gray-and-black-striped cat still hanging from the chandelier while the other cop and the detective took photos and dusted for fingerprints.

What kind of monster had done this? Over the last few days Rusty and Julie had combed her files and compiled a list of possible suspects. Sam had run them through the National Instant Criminal Background Check, also known as NICS and other systems which had helped them to eliminate almost half of the suspects who were in prison or dead. A little amateur detective work had discovered that fifteen or twenty percent of those left seemed to have gotten their acts together and had, at least outwardly, straightened out their lives. The rest were still in the area, had moved out of state or simply disappeared which kept them all as possible suspects.

That left a list that was still long and anything but definitive. Julie had made a second list that was little more than gut instinct about which of the aggressors would have the motive and ability to track her down.

Whether or not a person actually meant to harm her or simply frighten her and make her life miserable hadn't been clear until now. The fact that he had murdered her pet changed everything. He was sending her a message. She was next.

When the cop stood and went to join the others in the kitchen, Rusty stepped forward and joined Julie on the couch. She was surprisingly dry-eyed, but obviously in shock.

"I wanted to cut him down," she told him. "But I knew the cops needed to process it first."

"I'll take care of him for you," Rusty offered.

"He was just an innocent cat. He never did anything wrong."

"Of course he didn't."

A lone teardrop rolled down her cheek. "He always hid when strangers were in the house."

"Then how . . .?" Rusty jumped to the conclusion that maybe it was someone Julie knew, but she offered an alternative.

"They had a can of cat food. Cat never could resist the sound of that lid popping open." A tear trickled down her other cheek. "Silly Cat. It was his special treat. I couldn't afford it very often." That memory opened the flood gates, and she buried her face in her hands and sobbed.

Nothing made Rusty feel more helpless than tears. A child crying over his lost dog, an old man grieving for his deceased wife or a woman sobbing over the grizzly death of a beloved pet, all touched him to the core. He put his arms around Julie and pulled her against his chest.

The police officers walked through the living room, and Rusty nodded as they left. They didn't have any answers and had collected all the data possible. The holidays would delay the processing of any evidence . . . *if* they had found any. Rusty suspected they hadn't. Dinner tables were always covered in fingerprints, so even if the man hadn't worn gloves, it was unlikely the cops had been able to pull any clear prints off. The rope would be even more difficult, but Rusty could see that they had taken it with them. Poor Cat lay on a newspaper on top of the table. Apparently, they hadn't believed they could gather any evidence off of his body.

Several moments later, Julie's tears were spent and she pulled away. "I'll take you up on your offer. There's a place under that old cottonwood in the backyard. He loved climbing that tree and trying to catch the squirrels." She sniffled. "He never caught one, but he never gave up."

Rusty knew it would be hard on her, but she was a trouper. She wrapped his limp body in a soft wool shawl and cradled him in her arms while Rusty struggled to dig a hole in the frozen ground. She gently laid Cat in the fresh hole, then said a silent prayer before she tossed one of his favorite catnip mice in the hole and watched as Rusty carefully refilled the hole. The wind had picked up, lowering the temperature to close to zero. Julie pulled her coat tighter and stared down at the small mound of dirt for several minutes, silently grieving for the sad little stray who had welcomed the warmth of her house and the generosity of her heart for the last few years of his life.

"He didn't even have a real name," she mourned.

"Of course he did. He answered to Cat, so he knew that was his name."

"I should have been more original. I should have done a better job."

"Come on. It's freezing out here." Rusty knew he couldn't talk her out of her misery, so he put his arm around her shoulders and guided her back inside the house. He noticed the raw scratches on the table top, but neither of them mentioned it as they passed through the kitchen. "Go pack your things. You're going to spend the night at my place," he told her, leaving her no chance to argue.

While she was in her bathroom, gathering the personal items she would need, he went through the house and collected all of Cat's toys and dishes and packed them in a box so it wouldn't be such a harsh reminder of his absence when she returned. He cleaned up the spilled Chinese food and tossed the open can of cat food in the garbage. It was full. The psycho that had killed Cat hadn't even let him eat any first.

Julie walked back into the room. "I'll follow you over there in my car. We both have to work tomorrow."

Rusty started to protest but accepted that what she said was true. "Stay here. I'll lock up and we'll walk out together." He locked the front door, turned off all the lights except for one lamp in the living room, then went back to the kitchen. She set the alarm and they left, locking the back door behind them. He escorted her to her car inside the garage, not letting her out of his sight as she backed out. The garage door closed, and she waited until he got into his SUV, then followed him to his condo.

She was unusually quiet as they sat on the couch, warmed by the fireplace and shared a bottle of wine. He knew he had to get up early the next day for his shift, so she actually did most of the drinking.

As Rusty leaned against the corner of the couch with Julie nestled against him, their legs covered by a Denver Broncos blanket, he thought about his earlier conversation with his mother. After he had told her all about Julie, leaving out the juicy parts, of course, his mother had looked him straight in the eyes and gave him the benefit of her years of dealing with her husband and sons.

"I've never seen that look in your eyes when you've talked about a woman. Maybe she's the one. Or maybe not. You won't know unless you give it a chance. You need to tell her how you feel."

"But I don't know how I feel," he had protested.

"Yes, you do. And it scares you to death. This one is special. Don't screw it up."

Rusty looked down at Julie who was staring with misty eyes at the flames dancing among the glass pieces. His mother was absolutely right. He knew how he felt . . . and he *was* scared to death.

But tonight was not the night to talk about her past or their future. He would be at the fire house until 7:30 Christmas morning, then he had to go to his parents' and she had to work. There would be plenty of time Christmas night. Maybe they could put all this behind them and decide how to move forward.

For the first time ever, Rusty welcomed a woman into his bed with no expectation of sex. All he wanted to do was hold her and make her pain go away. As she moaned in her sleep and he felt fresh tears drip onto his arm, his confidence wavered. What if he couldn't?

CHAPTER EIGHTEEN

Rusty had already left for work when she woke up. It felt odd to be in a strange bed. She lay there, for a moment, and took in her surroundings. The room was totally masculine, with heavy oak furniture and framed photographs of Colorado scenery. There was an expensive Nikon DSLR camera and a powerful telescopic lens next to a case of accessories on the dresser. Was Rusty the photographer?

She climbed out of the sprawling king-sized bed and walked closer to one of the photos. It was a photo of Echo Lake on a calm, clear day. The line of evergreens and aspens that came down to the water's edge and the snow-capped peaks behind were mirror-imaged onto the surface of the lake with such perfection that the photo would have looked almost exactly the same if flipped upside down. She moved to the next, a scene of two giant bull elks, their heads lowered, frosted breath billowing from their flared nostrils as they measured each other's worthiness for battle. An interested herd of females watched from a distance.

Julie continued around the room, admiring the beauty and balance of each photo until she reached the last, and her breath caught in her throat. It was her meadow. Well, not *her* meadow, but the one in the painting in her office. She hadn't been sure it actually existed, but here it was, in vibrant color, splashed with wildflowers. The stream running through it was so vivid that she could almost hear it bubbling over the rocks. Rusty had been there . . . in her meadow.

Somehow, she was not surprised. It wasn't the first time they had shared something so obscure. It was as if they had been walking down parallel paths all their lives until, they finally, accidentally crossed . . . and merged. Julie's heart ached. There were so many reasons why those paths could not stay joined. His was inclined to wander endlessly and hers wasn't wide enough for anyone else.

Julie thought about the scene back at her house and shivered. She loved that little house, even though the counters were old and chipped and the windows were only single-paned and completely inefficient. But she didn't know how she would ever feel comfortable there again. Maybe it was time for her path to take her out of Denver. She could move to Salt Lake City or Reno or wherever, and start over. She would escape from her stalker and run away before Rusty had a chance to move on to someone new.

However, it was Christmas Eve, and she had to get to work. It would take a couple weeks to find a replacement and to get her house on the market. She needed to make some calls and check with the Chief of Police who might know of another department in a different state who needed a Victim's Advocate manager or maybe even start a new department. It would be tricky, but her excellent history with the DPD should help. Or she would take a completely different path and go into teaching and take some art classes. She had loved oil painting in college, but had never touched another paintbrush after she had graduated except to change the color of the walls. She had waitressed before, and she could certainly do it again if necessary. There were many options and she was young enough to make a change . . . even if she wasn't particularly enthusiastic about it.

After a quick shower, she dressed for the office and made the bed. In the kitchen there was a note next to a plate of cookies, which when she opened it, a key fell out and clattered to the table.

You were sleeping so deeply I didn't want to wake you. Here's a key for the front door. I'll be back tomorrow morning around eight. Help yourself to these cookies. Keep in mind that I made them myself with my own two hands. ☺ Make yourself at home. R

Smiling, she picked up a red Christmas tree and took a bite. Did he really have to sign it "R"? Who else would be leaving her a note in this condo? It was sweet of him to leave her a key . . . and he was sharing his cookies. She finished the tree and took a green reindeer with her as she left the condo and pocketed the key.

Obviously, the Police Dept. didn't close for holidays, but most of the office staff either took a day of vacation or left at noon. Julie had planned to leave at noon, but she wasn't anxious to go back to the empty condo and even less enthusiastic about going to her own house, so she stayed until after six. She stopped and picked up a Subway flatbread sandwich and took it back to the condo where she ate it in front of the fireplace while watching the news.

Even though Rusty wasn't there, his personality filled the rooms. It wasn't just the photos of his family and friends or the artistic shots he had taken with his camera, or even the mementoes from his sports and firefighter career. It was his leather jacket draped over the back of a chair and his Nikes by the front door and the scent of his after shave that hung in the air in his bathroom. There was an indentation in the seat of his favorite recliner and a set of hand weights in the corner.

When she went to bed after a long soak in the jetted tub, she snuggled against his pillow. She was almost asleep when her phone beeped, indicating that she'd just gotten a text.

"Real busy 2 nite. Just wanted u to know that I'm thinking of u & wish I was there beside u."

She typed a response. *"Missing you, too. Nice bed. Love the tub and the fireplace.*

Keep the bed warm. I'll be beside u before u wake up."

"Promises, promises. BTW, the cookies were great. I left some for Santa," she answered.

"Good. Wouldn't want him to pass by without stopping. He's got a present for u."

"Oh no! He better not."

"Santa does his own thing. Another alarm. Gotta go. Night, darling."

"Be safe."

"Always."

She held her phone against her chest as if she could feel his heartbeat through it. With his pillow under her cheek, she drifted off to sleep.

Julie felt the covers lift and the mattress move as a weight lowered onto it. The pillow was replaced by warm skin. A bristle-rough cheek rubbed against hers and soft, gentle lips pressed against her forehead, her closed eyelids and finally captured her mouth. She stirred and reached out for him, responding automatically to his familiar touch, his scent, his taste.

He lifted her short nightgown and slid his hand down her belly and below, dipping his fingers inside her, encouraged by her wetness. She lifted her hips, pressing against his hand until he moved over her and replaced his fingers with his rigid flesh.

They made love with a passionate urgency that had more to do with their night apart. It was pulsing with the fragility of their future and heightened by the danger they constantly faced. They were both adrenalin junkies, each in their own way. He handled his obsession by running into burning buildings; she by facing her worst fears and trying to help victims take control of their lives.

She lost all coherent thought as she reached a bone-melting climax, crying out his name before floating off into oblivion. Vaguely she was aware of him plunging deeply inside her and filling her with his heated liquid before he collapsed on her.

Slowly she drifted back to reality.

"Merry Christmas baby," Rusty whispered in her ear.

"Thank you, Santa. That was the best gift ever."

He chuckled. She could feel the vibrations move through her chest.

The ringing of her phone shattered the moment.

"Hello," she spoke into the mouthpiece. "Yes, just a minute." She picked up a pen and a clipboard that she had left next to the bed. "Go ahead." She jotted notes as the dispatcher gave her the information. After hanging up, she turned to Rusty and sighed. "It's already started. Someone is having a bad Christmas morning."

He pulled her back down into his arms for a last lingering kiss. "Last night was crazy, too. We weren't in the station for more than five minutes before we'd get another call." He yawned and stretched. "I'm going to grab a nap, then go over to my parents. Call me if things calm down."

"I will," she promised and reluctantly left his bed. A few minutes later she was in her car and heading for her first call.

As she had predicted, people did ugly things to each other on holidays. The economy was bad. People were unemployed or underemployed. A father who couldn't provide that special gift his child had been wanting or hadn't received a Christmas bonus that would help pay off some overdue bills would sometimes act out his frustration. It might start as an argument or an accusation to deflect the blame. But it always ended in tears and pain . . . and in the case of the first call, a trip to the hospital.

There was barely enough time to grab a sausage biscuit from 7-11 before the dispatcher called with another incident. Julie arrived just after the fire department and watched, helplessly as a family's house burned, started by a dry Christmas tree and taking with it all hope for a happy holiday. It would be months before their lives returned to normal. As the dad, mom and their four kids watched everything they owned being ruined by the flames, smoke and water, Julie took some blankets out of her trunk and handed them out. She made some calls and arranged for a free Christmas dinner at a local restaurant, one of the few that were open today, and talked the manager of the local Salvation Army into opening up so the family could get some clothes and a few toys for the kids. Finally, she found them a room at a nearby motel so they could clean up and have a place to stay until their insurance company stepped in. The family was understandably in shock, but at least she had helped them stay warm and dry and to have a good holiday meal.

After calling in her notification that she was finished, Julie was trying to find a fast food restaurant that was open so she could eat lunch when the dispatcher called with an address that was all too familiar. As she wrote 238 W. Maple

Ave. on her incident sheet, her heart sank. It was Gloria's address.

Of course, there was a chance that there were new residents in the house and that Gloria had kept her son, Danny and the new baby safe at her relative's. As much as she wished she was wrong, as Julie parked in front of the house, behind a cop car, she had a bad feeling that this was the same family she had visited three times before.

This was one of those frustrating cases because no matter how much he hurt her or how terrified she had been, the wife continued to take the husband back. He had probably cried and begged and said he would never do it again. They always promised. They rarely kept those promises. But the women were hopeful . . . or gullible . . . and they believed what they wanted to believe. Everyone wanted that fairy tale ending. In the fairy tales, the prince used his sword to slay dragons, not his fists to punish the princess. Julie never had met any princes on her calls.

In her mind, the men who came the closest to being heroes were the ones who came to help. The cops, the firefighters, the paramedics who arrived in the middle of the turmoil and tried to fix things. They, too, had their dark sides. Some of them took their jobs home. Some of them hit their wives or abused their children. Some of them were alcoholics and drug addicts. They just knew how to hide it better. And they had the brotherhood to protect them.

Julie looked at the small stucco house with its freshly painted shutters and strings of colorful lights hung around the porch and she thought how happy it looked. The wreath hid the anger and hurt that was behind the front door. The Christmas tree visible through the large front window masked the fragile family inside.

She noticed Danny was sitting on the top step, his thin body hunched over with his chin on his knees and his arms wrapped around his legs. Julie took a minute to sit next to him before going in.

"How have you been?" she asked him.

He shrugged.

"Are you doing well in school?"

Again he shrugged.

"Did Santa bring you something good?"

His lower lip quivered. "Dad told me Santa wasn't real. Then he smashed all the presents."

Julie swallowed back her disgust. What kind of dickhead would ruin Christmas? She decided it would be safer to change the subject. "Are you going to play Little League next year?"

"Probably not."

"That would be too bad. Your mom told me you're an excellent first baseman."

"Yeah, I'm pretty good," he agreed, lifting his head. "I've done some pitching, too."

"The Rockies always need good pitching. Maybe someday you'll play for them."

His expression brightened. "That would be epic. I saw a game last summer with my scout troop. We got to walk on the field."

"Wow, that's pretty cool."

"Yeah, maybe I'll get to play."

"I'll see if there's anything I can do to help," Julie promised. "I've got to go inside to talk with your mom. Could you stay out here a little longer?" She wanted to be able to speak freely with Gloria, and she had no idea how bad things were inside, so she was glad Danny was wearing his coat and the day was not too cold. Julie didn't want him to overhear something he shouldn't . . . not that his young ears hadn't already heard too much.

"I'm okay," he said, looking anything but.

Julie stood and walked inside. Gloria was curled into a corner of the couch. Her lip was split and her face was bruised and swollen. Blood was dried in streaks from the cuts on her arms that had probably been made by the shattered lamp on the floor. She was still wearing a long flannel nightgown, showing that the fight had probably been going on since early that morning. The cop stood across the room, taking photos of a pile of destroyed presents and the baseball bat that had probably been used in a fit of rage. Julie suspected there were some bruises on Gloria's body that matched the size and shape of the bat.

As soon as Gloria saw her, a mixture of relief and embarrassment crossed her face. "Julie, I'm so sorry . . ."

Julie sat on the couch next to the shaking woman. "I've told you before that you have nothing to be sorry about. Where's Carlos?"

She shook her head. "I don't know. He ran out the back door when he heard the cops arrive."

"Is your baby okay?"

Her expression softened. "She's in the bedroom. She slept through the whole thing."

"You need to go to the hospital and be checked out," Julie said to Gloria, then turned to the cop. "Have you called for an ambulance?"

"They've already come and gone," he replied. "She refused treatment."

"Why?" Julie looked back at Gloria. "You might have broken ribs."

Gloria shook her head adamantly. "I can't. Carlos told me . . ." She didn't finish the sentence, but Julie could guess that he had threatened the children. That was a classic way abusive spouses controlled their victims.

"What happened?" she asked Gloria.

"I got up early and made pancakes, but Carlos said we had to open the presents before we ate breakfast." She hesitated.

"And . . .?"

"I told him the pancakes would get cold," she continued in a small voice. "I shouldn't have said that. He was right."

"You didn't do anything wrong."

"Yes, I did. I should have waited. Carlos threw the pancakes against the wall, then took a bat to the presents. "He said I shouldn't talk back and that he was the one who paid for everything." She buried her face in her hands.

Julie rested a comforting hand on the woman's shoulders. "Gloria, none of this was your fault. Making pancakes was very thoughtful. Carlos has anger issues and needs to learn how to control his temper."

"He's been much better since . . ." She hesitated, not wanting to admit that she had let him come back even though it was obvious that she had.

"I thought you were going to move out of state."

"I tried, but Carlos found me and talked me into coming back with him. He can be really charming when he wants to."

Yeah, when he's not pummeling you within an inch of your life, Julie thought ruefully. Where had she heard that before?

"And look how nice our landlord fixed the house up." Gloria waved her hand to indicate the new paint and carpet. "You can't even tell there was a fire."

"What are you going to . . . ?" Julie started to ask but was interrupted by the dispatcher's voice over the cop's radio.

"Shots fired. Shooter unknown. 288 W. Maple Ave."

The cop looked at Julie. "That's only a few houses down the street." He paced restlessly, then leaned down so only she could hear, "I know this is still a hot scene, but the perp here is probably long gone. I'm going to run down there and see what's going on."

Julie wasn't really concerned. In the past Carlos had always disappeared for several days after an incident. However, after all of her and Rusty's cross-checking her files, Carlos was at the top of her list. If a man would threaten to hurt or kill his own children, he wouldn't hesitate to harm the woman he viewed as having ruined into his life. "I don't know if that's a good idea," she told him.

The cop went to the door and glanced down the street. He was clearly anxious to trade this quiet scene for one that promised to be more active. Cops and firefighters shared many interests, one of which was that they didn't like to be on the sidelines. They weren't born to be spectators. "I won't be far away. I'll come back as soon as backup arrives."

"This is Renfro and I'm less than a block away. I'll check it out, but I need backup," he spoke into the radio as he ran out the front door.

Julie looked at Gloria and tried not to act worried. "Have you called your mother?"

Gloria avoided eye contact. "No. She hasn't spoken to me since I moved back in with Carlos."

"Maybe she doesn't want to see you dead. You know that's how this could end, don't you?"

"Oh, he wouldn't do that."

"Really? Would you have believed he would beat the crap out of you like he has . . . over and over? Would you have believed he would try to kill your baby or threaten your son? Don't you know that the longer you stay with him, the higher the odds are that you won't make it out alive?"

"Maybe he's just trying to keep his family together," a strange, masculine voice commented. Both women jerked around to look at the man. Neither had heard him enter through the back door, and now he stood in the living room doorway, a large, imposing figure.

Gloria's expression showed her confusion.

Julie's face had gone pale.

"Who are you?" Gloria demanded.

The man stepped forward until he was directly in front of the couch. His eyes never left Julie's. He nodded toward her. "Ask her. She knows me."

Gloria looked back at Julie. "Do you know this man?"

Julie had been struck dumb. All the saliva had disappeared from her mouth, and she couldn't have spoken if her life depended on it. She was terribly afraid that it did.

The man reached down, grabbed Julie's ponytail and yanked her to her feet. "Tell her, *Julie*."

Old habits die hard and Julie felt that same old fear that had paralyzed her in the past sweep over her. Cold sweat bathed her body and her knees went weak.

The man looked directly at Gloria for the first time. "I don't know who the fuck you are, but this bitch . . .," he shook Julie like a rag doll, "is my wife."

CHAPTER NINETEEN

"Dinner's ready," Pat called as she found a spot on the crowded table for a gravy boat. Sara filled the water glasses while Kate got the bread out of the oven. In the family room, the men were still focused on a football game on TV, but the delicious smells of roasted turkey, marshmallow-topped yams and fresh bread got their attention, and they all joined the women in the dining room.

Jack and Pat took their places at the head and foot of the long table while the younger family members jostled for their favorite chair. When everyone was finally seated, they all bowed their heads and said grace. It was the last quiet moment for the next thirty minutes.

Bowls and plates filled with food passed from one to the other until the plates were filled and they all settled into the act of devouring the meal.

"Where's Julie today?" Chris asked. "The way you two have been all over each other, I would have thought she'd be here."

Rusty looked at his brothers. This was the first Christmas Sam had known Kate, so she was new at the table. Sara had come with Chris, but theirs was a platonic relationship. She had grown up with all the boys, even though she was several years younger than Rusty and Sam, they were accustomed to having her around as if she was a member of the family. For the first time, Rusty felt like the odd man out. And yet he had never been tempted to invite any of his girlfriends . . . before now. He realized the day was kind of flat without Julie here with him.

"She had to work today," Rusty explained, keeping it simple.

"You can take her a plate," Pat offered.

"I'm sure she'd enjoy that."

"So, are you two getting serious?" Sara asked, apparently not realizing what a sensitive subject she had breached.

All eyes turned on Rusty as they waited.

He wished he could answer definitively, but he didn't know.

"Oh my God! He's been bitten!" Sam exclaimed. "Romeo has been taken off the market."

"I never thought I'd see the day," Sara chimed in. "You always claimed you'd be a bachelor for life."

"Hey, I didn't say a word," Rusty said defensively. "What made you think that?"

"It's that look in your eyes when you talk about her," Pat added her opinion.

"You act differently around her," Sam pointed out. "I've seen you around a lot of women, and you never held their hands or kept them close like you thought someone was going to steal them."

Rusty opened his mouth to protest, but snapped it shut. He couldn't deny any of it. The truth was that, as much as he loved his family and all the excitement of Christmas with them, he would rather be with Julie. He felt bad that she was out working, dealing with drama and tragedy without even a special dinner or a present to open.

The doorbell rang. "Now who could that be?" Jack asked. He went to the front door and came back a few minutes later holding a small cardboard box. "Does this belong to anyone?"

Almost everyone stared blankly, but when a tiny, but demanding meow came from the box, Rusty jumped up.

"That's mine." He took the box from his dad and opened it. From within he took out a ball of black-and-white fur with two crystal blue eyes.

"A kitten! It's so cute," Kate gushed, unable to resist petting it.

"I assume that's not for you," Sam guessed.

"You assume correctly," Rusty confirmed. "And right now I've got to take it to its new owner."

"But we haven't had pie," his mother protested.

"Could I take mine to go? I hate to eat and run, but there's someplace I need to be."

Pat smiled with motherly understanding. "I'll wrap up some leftovers." She stood and went to the kitchen.

As usual because even as grown-ups the boys couldn't wait, they had opened their presents before the meal. The rest of the day would be spent playing board or card games and watching football. Rusty wasn't even tempted. He was determined to find Julie, wherever she was and share as much of the day as possible with her.

He said his goodbyes and wished everyone a Merry Christmas. Pat walked him to his car, carrying a larger cardboard box that had two plates heaped with food and protected by foil and half of a pumpkin pie. She placed it in the backseat while Rusty settled the kitten box in the front passenger seat. He turned and gave her a big hug.

"Go to your girl," she encouraged.

Rusty's grin was broad and excited. "I am, Mom. Thanks."

As he drove away, he called Julie, but her phone went to voicemail. He figured she was on-scene, so he called the dispatcher office and asked the woman who answered if she would see if Julie was on a job.

"She arrived at a DV about an hour ago. We haven't heard from her since," the dispatcher told him.

"Could you give me the address? I want to swing by and check on her."

"It's 238 W. Maple Ave.," the dispatcher told him without hesitation. *"Oh, wait, there's been a second call from the same street. A shooting in progress. We've got two patrol cars on their way. Renfro, the cop on-scene at the first call is checking it out."*

For some reason a chill ran down his back. Something didn't feel right. "Thanks." He tossed his phone on the seat and pressed down on the accelerator. He recognized the address. It was the place that had burned the first night he and Julie had talked. It was also where that wife-beater Carlos lived. Every time Rusty and Julie had refined their suspect lists, Carlos had always been on it. The thought of him touching Julie ignited a fire in Rusty, and he drove as fast as safety allowed.

Julie's worst nightmare had come true. "How did you find me?" she asked as she grasped her ponytail at the scalp to keep Ray from jerking her hair out. He didn't relax his grip as he held her in front of him.

"It wasn't easy. I'll give you that. When I went to the hospital to pick you up so we could go to the funeral and you were gone, I went crazy. It's taken me five years, but, by God, I found you."

"How . . .?"

"I hired a private detective. Your trail was completely cold until a cop buddy thought he saw you on a call. My PI staked out your house, but we weren't sure it was you 'cause he couldn't find any photos or anything that tied you to who you really are. And you don't look liked you used to. Then I saw you on the news, saving that firefighter." Ray's smile was more of a smirk. "It was easy after that."

White hot anger flashed through her. So that was who had broken into her house the first time. "Did he kill my cat?"

Ray snorted. "I did. You know how much I fuckin' hate cats."

From deep within her an anger that had been created during their marriage and nurtured through the years welled up. With all the strength she could muster, she balled up her fist and hit him square in his evil face. "That's for Cat!" Blood spurted out of his nose and he roared in pain and anger.

"You crazy cunt!" he bellowed as his hands closed around her neck. "I should have killed you years ago . . . before I lost my job and used all my fuckin' savings to track you down."

He was strong and easily overpowered her . . . like so many times before. Back then, she hadn't fought back, afraid of his anger and retribution. Now, he still terrified her, but she was determined to fight to the end. She clawed at his face, feeling globs of flesh coming off under her nails. She kicked and struggled, trying to land a knee or a foot in his groin. But as his hands tightened and the pressure of his thumb against her windpipe shut off her air, it became more of a challenge just to breathe. Darkness circled her line of vision, slowly closing in as she came closer to blacking out.

"Let her go!" Gloria shouted. Neither had noticed when she got up off the couch and picked up the baseball bat. She swung the aluminum bat and caught him firmly across his back.

Ray staggered and temporarily released his hold on Julie who fell limply to the floor.

"You'll get your turn," Ray yelled, whirling around and jerking the bat out of Gloria's hands. He stood over Julie, his legs straddling her body and hoisted the bat overhead. "I loved you. I never meant to hurt you. You know that. You just made me so angry."

She saw the insanity in his eyes. As if in slow motion, the bat began its arc downward. The image of Rusty's sweet crooked grin and laughing blue eyes filled her senses. She had come so close to true happiness. A smile touched her lips and her eyes closed. She wanted her last memory to be of Rusty's face and not Ray's. Still gasping for breath, she tried to prepare for the last crushing blow that would take her life. Her only hope was that it would be quick.

There was a crash and she felt Ray's body fall heavily next to her. Julie squinted through half-closed lids, wondering what new torture he had in store for her. But the sight of Ray lying flat on his back while Rusty battered him made her eyes fly open. She struggled to scoot away and Gloria ran over and cradled Julie in her arms. Their roles were reversed as the victim helped the comforter.

Ray recovered from the shock and started fighting back. The two men rolled and tumbled, locked in the most serious combat of their lives. Ray struggled to reach his boot. Julie knew that he had always kept a back-up weapon tucked in there for situations like this. Rusty was bigger and stronger, but Ray was fueled by his fury and insanity. They exchanged blow after blow, as all the while Ray continued trying to reach his boot.

Julie's lungs still burned, but she got to her knees. The baseball bat had fallen off to the side, and she scrambled to it just as Ray pulled a switchblade knife from his boot and snapped it open. She recognized the narrow, razor-sharp blade as his back-up weapon of choice. It was fast and deadly.

Rusty saw the blade and grabbed Ray's wrist. But Ray had the leverage advantage. With the pointed blade dangerously close to Rusty's chest, Julie struggled to her feet and lifted the bat over her head. It was tricky trying to wait for a clear shot as the men tumbled across the floor, but finally Ray rolled on top.

"This is for Emma!" Julie cried as she swung the bat down and connected with the back of Ray's head.

He crumpled to the floor and Rusty pushed him away, then got to his knees. He rested there for a moment, breathing deeply. He wiped off a trickle of blood oozing from a cut over his left eye with the back of his hand. Julie dropped the bat and rushed over to him, kneeling beside him and putting her hands on his shoulders.

"Are you okay?" she asked.

"I'm fine," he managed to say between ragged breaths. He looked up at her and saw the bruises around her neck. His eyes narrowed. "He did that to you?"

She nodded.

"Is that Carlos?" Rusty asked.

Julie shook her head. "No, it's Ray Drake."

Rusty frowned. "Who the hell is Ray Drake? He wasn't on any of the lists."

"Ray was . . . *is* my husband." Julie's voice was so soft Rusty had to strain to hear her.

He leaned back on his heels, his expression totally blank. "Well, that's certainly not the answer I was expecting."

"Let me explain . . ."

But she was interrupted when Renfro and another cop came bursting through the front door, their guns drawn.

They quickly assessed the scene and Renfro's face showed his embarrassment.

"There was no one down the street. Someone reported shots fired, but we didn't find any evidence of that," he admitted.

"Probably not, genius," Rusty said as he stood and brushed himself off. "The guy on the floor likely called in a decoy to pull you off."

"Shit!" Renfro muttered. He looked from Julie to Gloria. "I'm really sorry. I thought . . ."

"You're lucky he didn't kill both of them." Rusty was in no mood to be generous. "What's the world coming to when a firefighter has to do your job for you?"

Renfro knew it wasn't an argument he could win. He holstered his gun and cuffed Ray who still hadn't moved but was breathing and called in a request for an ambulance.

Gloria who had been watching the fight with wide eyes walked up to Renfro and tugged his sleeve. "Carlos is hiding in the utility closet in the basement," she told him.

"What?" Renfro had clearly forgotten the original call.

"My husband is downstairs. I want to turn him in," Gloria lifted her chin and met Renfro's gaze.

Renfro and the other cop glanced at the closed door, pulled their guns out and ran down the basement stairs.

Julie recognized the significance of Gloria's action. The two women exchanged knowing looks.

"I saw my future in you," Gloria admitted, "and I can't accept that. This time I'll follow through. I can raise Danny and Isabelle on my own. They deserve a better life than this."

The women hugged, bonded by their pasts. "If there's anything I can do, let me know," Julie offered. "I can get you a new identity and relocate you where your family will be safe. With Carlos' history, he should be in jail for quite a while."

"Thank you. You've always been there for me," Gloria told her.

"I know what you've been going through," Julie admitted. "I didn't have anyone to turn to, so I ran away." She shrugged. "As you can see, that didn't turn out all that well."

Gloria turned to Rusty. "And thank you, too. You risked your life for us."

"Yeah, well, that's what I do," he said modestly.

"You're a hero."

"Not so much. I was lucky to be in the right place at the right time."

Julie knew it was more than luck. Rusty *was* a hero . . . and in spite of his reputation, a gentleman. He hadn't spoken to her since she had admitted that she was married to Ray. His expression masked whatever emotions he was feeling. Or maybe he wasn't feeling anything at all. Her heart plummeted to her toes at the possibility that he had just been doing his job and not risking his lift to protect her.

Then why had he showed up here, at this moment?

Danny came running in from outside and wrapped his arms around Gloria's waist. She hugged him close, keeping his head turned as Renfro escorted a hand-cuffed Carlos up the stairs, across the living room and out the front door. For a man who was such a bully, Carlos was surprisingly meek. Apparently, he felt powerful only when he was beating on women and children. He looked up only once to spear Gloria with a furious glare. To her credit, she lifted her chin and stared right back at him.

Ray was stirring as the ambulance arrived, and by the time they had him loaded, he was awake, but groggy.

Renfro took everyone's statements, and after receiving their promises to stop by downtown later in the week, he left. The ambulance and the other cop had already gone, so almost as suddenly as it had all began, it was over.

As if on cue, the baby started crying and Gloria and Danny left the room to take care of her.

Julie and Rusty, all alone, finally faced each other.

"Rusty, I wanted to tell you . . . and I was going to . . ."

"After all we've been through, you didn't trust me enough to share this?" Instead of sounding angry, his voice was wounded.

"I'd kept the secret for so long . . . and my life depended on it."

"We spent hours going through your files, and you didn't think it was important enough to mention to me that you had a husband who was hunting for you?"

"I honestly thought that he would have given up. Who does that?"

"A man who loves you . . . or hates you very much."

"It was never love. It was always about control."

"So why not go to the police and file charges against him?"

"He *was* a cop."

Rusty looked unconvinced. "That shouldn't matter."

"Are you kidding? You know how cops take care of other cops. It's the same with firefighters." Her legs were still shaking, and she wanted, more than anything, for him to take her into his arms and tell her he understood. "I threatened to go to his captain, but that didn't accomplish anything except get me a beating that broke four ribs. No one believed me because he denied everything, and he was an officer of the law."

Rusty looked around the room, taking in the broken furniture, destroyed gifts and shattered lamp.

"Give me a chance to explain," she begged. "After that, I'll go. But it's important that you know everything."

The muscles in his square jaws flexed. "Follow me."

CHAPTER TWENTY

Julie said her goodbyes to Gloria and Danny and ohhed and ahhed over Isabelle before leaving. Rusty was sitting in his SUV, waiting patiently. Julie unlocked her Kia and climbed in. All the way to Rusty's condo, she ran dialogue through her mind. There was no question that she was going to tell him the truth, but did he really want to hear it all?

The horror that had been her marriage, the terror, the pain, the shame, the guilt . . . would he be able to understand? She had gone into her relationship with Ray with an open heart. Her parents had just died in the middle of her junior year of college, and she used part of her inheritance to finish getting her degree in Communications. Ray had been a handsome young cop who had pulled her over for speeding. He had given her a warning . . . which in retrospect, she should have taken as an omen.

He was charming and persistent and soon they were dating. Ray had been her first and only lover until she met Rusty. They had gotten married the week after her graduation and within a month after that the abuse started. As with most domestic violence, the first time could have been dismissed as being accidental. He apologized, brought her flowers and candy and promised to be more careful, using the excuse that he was in a rough profession and sometimes it carried over.

Each time was progressively worse and the apologies more profuse. At some point she found out he was cheating on her, accepting the favors of the groupies that cops . . . and firefighters . . . attract. She had no confidants. He had isolated her from her college friends and didn't allow her to work, so she couldn't make new friends. Her world grew smaller and smaller until there was only Ray and Julie in it.

She had even gone to the captain once. Ray had been furious and had slammed a door on her fingers, breaking three of them. He'd been immediately contrite and rushed her to the emergency room. As always, she'd lied and told them it was an accident. Ray had treated her really well for several months after that . . . until something else spun him up and the abuse continued. Another report to the captain might have ruined Ray's career, so she kept quiet. Plus, she had heard many stories about how the cops covered up for each other, no matter what the crime. She suspected there were other wives in similar circumstances, but there was never an opportunity to discuss it . . . that is, if she could find a wife who would. And always, in the back of her mind, she'd known Ray would kill her if she talked about it. That's why she hadn't left him until she was sure there would be no trail.

They arrived at Rusty's condo with her not any closer to a decision on how much to share with him. How did she know he wasn't just like Ray, wonderful now, but a devil after sundown. Once he knew, would that be the end of any hope for a relationship? She remembered her plans to move out of state. Now that her stalking issue was over, that was no longer necessary. Except for Rusty.

With a sadness so profound she could hardly breathe, Julie accepted the fact that she had foolishly fallen in love with him. That left her with no options. She couldn't stay. The only thing worse than never seeing him again would be to see him with another woman and knowing that he was holding her and kissing her and making her feel as special as he had with Julie.

She inhaled deeply, trying to steady the sudden rush of nerves that caused her hands to shake as she parked behind him. Always the gentleman, he came back to open her door and walked next to her to the elevator. In his arms he carried two cardboard boxes.

After putting the boxes on the table, he poured her a glass of wine, without asking, selected a beer for himself and they settled on opposite ends of the couch in front of the fireplace that he had switched on.

"So tell me what happened." He took a drink and waited.

When it came right down to it, she told him everything. He may not be interested, but once the words started spilling out of her mouth, she couldn't stop them. Sometimes, biting back tears and other times, ducking her head with shame, she detailed the beatings, the stranglings, the cuts and bruises that were always positioned so they wouldn't be seen. She even tried to explain how it felt to be abused and caught in the endless cycle of violence, guilt and forgiveness, all brought on by an increasing feeling of inadequacy.

"I was actually pretty outgoing and self-confident before our marriage," she said. "I don't know how it happened, but he wore me down until I felt worthless and incapable of surviving on my own."

"What caused you to finally make the decision to leave?"

It was the question that was the most difficult to answer. "I found out I was pregnant." Her eyes filled with tears that slowly slid down her cheeks. "I thought it would be a new beginning, something that would bind us together and make the marriage work. Ray wasn't as excited as I was, but he was okay with it." She looked up at the ceiling and exhaled, struggling to keep her composure. "Then one night when I was about six months along, he came home drunk. They'd suspended him at work for inappropriate behavior with a young woman at a traffic stop. He was upset and bruising for a fight. I was the only person in the room, so he took it out on me.

"I had survived worse, so I just tried my usual escape tactic and went limp. He started kicking me . . . hard. I tried to get away and almost made it, but one last kick and I tumbled down a flight of stairs."

Rusty's hands tightened into fists in his lap, but he didn't speak.

"I lost the baby," she was barely able to whisper. "It was a beautiful little girl. I named her Emma Rose. Ray never even visited me in the hospital. I made all the arrangements for the funeral while I was at the hospital. But as the actual day came closer when I would be released so I could go to it, I knew I could never go back to Ray. And I also knew that he would never let me go."

"That explains the Emma comment when you made that home-run swing," Rusty interrupted.

"I held back a little," she admitted. "I didn't want to kill him. "

"Probably gave him a serious concussion. He'll have a hell of a headache."

Julie shrugged. "Good."

"How did you get away from him?"

"A kind victim's advocate came to visit me in the hospital. I don't know why, but I felt like I could trust her and I told her everything. She was able to do what I thought was a miracle by getting me a new identity, a new look, some clothes and a bus ticket.

"The night before the funeral, I slipped out of the hospital and hitchhiked out of town because I was too afraid Ray would be able to trace the bus ticket even with the disguise. Besides, I didn't really know where to go. All I knew was that I wanted to get as far away as possible and that would buy me almost twenty-four hours because no one would expect me not showing up for Emma." She shook her head with regret. "I hated not being there, but it was my only chance. I had very little money, no credit cards and no extra clothes, just the hygiene items they'd given me at the hospital. I left everything behind, all my photos, things from my parents, my personal papers. I figured if I didn't have anything to tie me to that life, then that woman would be dead."

She looked past him to the impressive view of the mountains. "I fell in love with Denver. It was so different than Connecticut, and I knew that Ray thought anything west of the Mississippi River was wild frontier. I figured he'd try to find me, but I never thought he'd go this far or persist this long. Luckily, I got a job at Tom's Diner where I met Natalie Turner."

"The cop?"

"Yes, she worked for DPD back then. She got a great job with the FBI and moved to DC shortly after that. But when I met her she was going through an ugly divorce. We became friends, and she encouraged me to be a Victim's Advocate volunteer. I worked my way up from there."

"That explains the brown contact lens," Rusty mused. "That's probably not your real hair color either, is it?"

She lifted a shiny black strand and looked at it as if seeing it for the first time. "No, it's naturally a sort of medium brown. I thought Ray would assume I'd go blond, so I went dark."

"And your name isn't really Julie?" he asked.

She shook her head. "It *was* Karen Drake. However, I'm not that girl anymore. She didn't make it. But Julie Lawrence is a survivor."

He leaned back, resting his head on the top of the overstuffed couch as he tried to process the flood of information. It was so much more complicated than he would have imagined. He shut his eyes and rubbed his hand over his forehead. "I guess I'm having trouble getting past the trust issue. I can understand why you didn't make it public, but I don't understand why you didn't tell me. There were so many opportunities."

She wanted to reach out and touch him, to thaw the cold, hard set of his jaw. He was right, of course. There had been times when she had been tempted to tell him everything, but then she would remember the fragility of their relationship. She had no idea how he would have reacted. Even now, after nearly being killed by the man who had haunted her all these years, Rusty wasn't accepting her explanation.

He was an amazing man, but he was still a man. Her experience with the male sex, both personal and through her professional encounters hadn't been all that positive. Trust was a two-way street, and he was upset that she hadn't trusted him. On the other hand, he prided himself on his playboy lifestyle which didn't exactly inspire trust. The fact that he didn't understand that told her he was looking for an excuse to push her away.

It was over. Whatever they had had together had ended. She was no better or worse off than any of his past lovers. Fun and games, then hit the road. Her chest felt like an elephant was sitting on it, and she struggled not to cry. Silly girl. She had thought she was special. In his way, Rusty had hurt her worse than Ray ever had. He had broken her heart.

Julie stood. She glanced back over her shoulder and saw that he hadn't moved. *Please, please don't shut me out. Don't make me leave. Take me in your arms and tell me it all doesn't matter.*

But he didn't move, remaining with his head back and his face buried in his hands as she walked to the bathroom. Julie had brought only a few personal items and some clothes, so it wouldn't take her long to gather them and put them in her tote bag. Even though she felt safe to return to her house for now, she knew it would be just long enough for her to enact Plan B. She no longer had to run from her past. But she couldn't face her future here.

Her fingers fumbled with her toothbrush and she dropped it into the sink. Working blindly now because her eyes were filled with tears, she felt for it, but when she couldn't find it, she leaned over the sink and struggled to get it together. The last thing she wanted was for him to remember her as a weak, crying woman.

He had seen her in that role so often in their relationship. But that wasn't who she was. She had lost a child. She had escaped from an evil creature. She had started a new life with nothing but the clothes on her back. She had helped hundreds of victims survive horrible events. She was strong and brave, and she was not a victim.

She felt his hands on her shoulders and she jumped. She hadn't heard him walk up behind her.

"Julie, you don't have to run anymore," his voice was gentle.

With her head held high, she turned and faced him. "I can't stay."

"Because you can't let yourself fall in love?"

"No." She sighed. "I can't stay because I already have."

To her surprise, his beautiful lips lifted in a grin. "Then you can't leave."

"Why not?"

"Because I'm asking you to stay. I *need* you to stay." His fingers tightened on her shoulders. He shook his head, his expression incredulous. "I've done something totally crazy and out of character . . . I've fallen in love."

Julie blinked, too surprised to respond. Her heart that had been so heavy did a little flip-flop in her chest.

"As I see it, there's just one problem," he continued. "I know I have a bad reputation, but I have one hard-and-fast rule. I don't fool around with married women."

A wave of relief swept over her. "Good, because Julie Lawrence isn't married."

She wrapped her arms around his neck as he pulled her closer. He leaned down and pressed his lips against hers, gently at first, but quickly becoming more insistent.

In the other room one of the cardboard boxes moved, then tumbled off the table and onto the floor.

Rusty looked around, then grabbed Julie's hand and pulled her along behind him. "I almost forgot. Here's your Christmas present."

"Oh no, you didn't. I . . .," she protested.

"Shhh. Just open your gift." He picked the small box up and handed it to her. She hadn't noticed before that it had dozens of holes poked all over it. Carefully, she set it down on the table and unfolded the flaps.

The first thing she saw was a pair of bright blue eyes shining from inside. She reached in and pulled out the puff of fur.

"She's the cutest thing I've ever seen," she declared with excitement as she picked up the kitten and cuddled her against her chest.

"I wish I could say I rescued her out of a tree, but I got her from one of my parents' neighbors who had a litter to give away."

"She's adorable, and she's going to have a proper name." The kitten's tiny body vibrated with the intensity of her purr. "How about Holly?"

"Sounds like a good name," Rusty agreed. "I found out about her when I was at Mom's on Monday, so I had time to pick up a litter box and some Kitten Chow. It's in the utility room"

"She's probably ready to try it out."

Moments later after she had things set up for the kitten and had left her with a small bowl of mushy chow, Julie returned to the kitchen to find the dining table set, complete with candles.

"I assume you didn't have time to eat Christmas dinner," Rusty said.

"I haven't had Christmas dinner in more than five years," she admitted.

Rusty's eyes softened as he held out his hand. "Julie Lawrence, let me show you how happy life can be."

EPILOGUE

Red and yellow tulips filled the flower bed around the big cottonwood tree in the backyard. Julie sat on a free-standing wrought-iron swing and tried to read the book in her hands. One foot was tucked underneath her and the other touched the ground periodically to keep the swing moving while being distracted by the half-grown kitten who was trying to stalk and attack the fat robins that were hopping around the yard. Just as she pounced, the bell around Holly's neck would jingle, warning the bird so it could escape unharmed. But there were plenty of robins and Holly kept trying.

The gate leading into the backyard squeaked, and Julie looked around as Rusty strode through it. His hair was still wet from the shower he had taken at the station before he left.

"Are you just getting home?" he asked as he leaned over the back of the swing and gave her a kiss.

"About an hour ago. But I wanted to wait up for you." She had gotten only one call last night, but unfortunately, it had been just before dawn. "A guy got shot in the ass when he was leaving a bar at closing time."

"We had a three-alarm fire in an historic hotel downtown that they were remodeling. Some homeless guy thought it was a good idea to start a fire in the middle of the dining room."

Julie smiled. As usual, he beat her in their game of one-upmanship. With jobs as stressful as theirs, dark humor helped keep things bearable.

He took her hand and pulled her to her feet. "Eventually, you're going to have to find someone to take your shift. You're going to have to take care of yourself . . . and him . . . or her." His hand slid down to her stomach. It was still flat, but they both knew that deep inside her, a tiny heartbeat fluttered. She wouldn't be showing for at least another month, but Rusty was already treating her like she was made out of porcelain . . . which was ironic considering the abuse she had survived.

The doctor had been wrong. No one had been more surprised than Julie when she started suffering from morning sickness and missed periods. She had been told she would never be able to have children, but this child had defied science and had somehow made it to the fourth month. Her new doctor was hopeful and said it looked like the baby would go full term.

Julie had been a little hesitant to tell Rusty, but she dared not hold back. They had worked through their trust issues, and it would be a betrayal not to share the news, especially as important as this. To her relief, he had been delighted.

She looked into his eyes, searching and finding the warm glow of love. He hadn't, even for a moment, made her doubt it. After a lengthy discussion, they had sold his condo and moved into her house. She hadn't been sure they would be comfortable here, but with his help, the remodeling had continued until the place looked new. They had even been able to add a fireplace. Plus, the house had the added space and a large backyard that would come in handy when the baby arrived.

He yawned and pulled her into his arms. "I'm exhausted. Are you going to tuck me in?"

"How exhausted?" she teased.

"Never *that* exhausted," he assured her with a flirtatious wink. He bent and swept her into his arms.

Julie cupped her hand against his handsome face. She would never tire of looking at this man, and best of all, she would never fear him. The sunlight sparkled off the big diamond in her engagement ring. They planned to be married in May after her divorce was final and her name would officially be changed to Julie Lawrence Wilson. She was looking forward to this new stage in her life . . . as Rusty's wife.

She had always known he was a hero. Now he was her's.

ABOUT THE AUTHOR

Kathy Clark's 23 women's fiction (romance) novels have sold over 3 million copies in more than 10 languages and have been on the *New York Times'* bestsellers' list and won her numerous awards.

In September 2012 she broke away from the romance genre and launched a new suspense series, *Denver After Dark* that is centered on three brothers, one a cop, one a firefighter and one a paramedic. The first book, **After Midnight** has been named as the Best Indie Suspense of 2013 and won third place in the prestigious Readers' Favorite Suspense Awards 2013. **Cries in the Night** is Book #2 in the Series and **Graveyard Shift**, Book #3 will be released in summer, 2014.

Also in 2012 Kathy teamed up with her husband Bob Wernly to write a Young Adult Time Travel Mystery/Romance series called CUL8R (See You Later) under the pen name of Bob Kat. Book #1 **OMG (Oh My God)**, when they go back to 1966 to save a girl's life, was released in October, 2012 and was named as the Best Indie Young Adult Suspense of 2013 and was a Beverly Hills Book Awards finalist. Book #2 **BRB (Be Right Back)**, when they travel back to 1980, recently won First Place in the Readers' Favorite Young Adult Awards 2013. Book #3 **BION (Believe It Or Not)**, when they go back to 1927 and join a circus to save a boy, was just released in July, 2013. All three books in this series have received rave reviews and 4 and 5 star ratings. Book #4 **RIP (Rest in Peace)**, a ghost story set at the famous Stanley Hotel will be released in January, 2014. Also, under the Bob Kat pen name, Kathy and Bob wrote a fictionalized version of his fraternity days at Kent State University in 1970 that mixes the drama of senior year with the first military draft lottery, the Vietnam war and the Kent State shootings. This novel was named as a finalist in the Best Indie Mainstream Book of 2013 Awards.

Kathy and Bob are also working on a New Adult series called Scandals with the first book **Baby Daddy** scheduled for release in November, 2013.

Kathy is currently a member of Mystery Writers of America, Sisters in Crime, Austin Romance Writers of America and Rocky Mountain Fiction Writers, and was on the board of directors of national RWA and Colorado Romance Writers for several years. Her books and screenplays have won numerous awards, including top honors from Romantic Times, Colorado Romance Writer of the Year, two RITAs and several film festival screenwriting competitions. When not writing, she and Bob love to travel, hang out on beaches, spend time with their five sons and two grandsons, go to movies or just play with their dogs.

http://www.NightWriter93.com
http://www.CUL8Rseries.com

COMING SOON FROM KATHY CLARK

SCANDALS: BABY DADDY Book #1 scheduled November, 2013
GRAVEYARD SHIFT Book #3 scheduled Fall, 2014

Direct Link to Purchase all of Kathy Clark's and Bob Kat's books:

http://astore.amazon.com/nightwriter93-20

If you enjoyed **_Cries In The Night_**, don't miss Kathy Clark's (also writing as Bob Kat) latest novels. Please enjoy the following excerpts.

AFTER MIDNIGHT

CHAPTER 1

PLAYBOY Magazine once called Colfax "*the longest, wickedest street in America*". But to anyone who knew it, that's what made it interesting.

Colfax had originally been the main road through Denver and stretched from the eastern plains to the Rocky Mountain foothills. In the shadow of the spectacular state capitol's golden dome, businesses thrived, some legitimate, but most not. Populated by prostitutes, dealers, artists and certifiable crazies, several blocks were part of District 6, fondly known as District Shit because of its concentration of degenerates and crime.

For the last five years Sam Morgan had called that section of Colfax Home. Not as a resident but as a police officer on the night shift. The clock started at 11 p.m., but the fun didn't begin until after midnight. After the Phantom had left the Opera. After the Black Crowes had flown the Fillmore. And after someone had the last laugh at Comedy Works. As the entertainment venues emptied, the streets and the bars filled, mixing yuppies, coeds and players. LoDo, the rejuvenated Lower Downtown area with its cozy sports bars and upscale clubs attracted the cream. Colfax welcomed the rest without bias or prejudice. You didn't have to have a job or money or nice clothes or even shoes to fit in. Especially on a warm summer night like tonight.

Sam made his usual loops through the area, passing through neighborhoods of stately mansions that struggled to retain their dignity just blocks from low income housing and run-down apartment buildings. With the windows down on the patrol car, Sam could stop and chat with the local kids or call out to a dealer he'd busted a half dozen times in the past. He knew them and they knew him. It was an oddly effective way to be visible without being aggressive.

Music, laughter and streams of conversation flowed into the car as he drove along, competing with the constant chatter on the police band radio. It was starting out like a typical Saturday night, with one exception.

Sam slid a sideways glance at the man sitting in the passenger's seat. Ridealongs could be a blessing or a curse. Most cops dreaded having strangers tag along. Other than the challenge of dealing with an unknown personality…dull, dumb, chatty or flirtatious that bordered on stalking…there was the possibility of added danger, both to the ridealong and the cop. In a crisis, the last thing a cop wanted was to have another civilian in the mix.

But Sam didn't mind. With only one officer per patrol car, having someone to talk to on quiet nights made the time pass more quickly. Usually.

Oh, the guy had asked all the normal questions. "How long have you been a cop?" "Is this what you always wanted to be?" "What kind of gun do you carry?" "Have you ever shot anyone?" Then the conversation ended. Sam had tried to make small talk, but after the first hour, he gave up and, at times, almost forgot he had a passenger. Truth was…his passenger was completely forgettable.

Average height, average weight, short reddish-blond hair, the man was so unremarkable that Sam, even with his keen observational skills, would have had trouble picking the man out of a crowd of two. Sam slid a sideways glance at the man and mentally noted…gray Broncos hoodie, jeans that were faded by age, not fashion and a green camouflage t-shirt. Blue eyes, short, chewed nails, holes in his earlobes indicating he had, at some point, worn ear metal. Completely nondescript, almost like he was trying to be invisible.

He sat stiffly in his seat, his attention focused outside the car except when he looked at his watch for at least the tenth time in the last hour.

"Hey, we can swing by the station," Sam offered. "I can drop you off if you need to…go somewhere or do something else." The guy was starting to be annoying.

"Oh no, I'm fine. Just wondered what time it is."

"How about a break?"

"Sure. Sounds good," the ridealong answered with the first burst of enthusiasm he had shown all night.

Maybe he just was tired of riding around in a car for so long or maybe he had to hit the john and was embarrassed to ask. Cops were used to spending a lot of time in their rolling offices, but now, in the lull between midnight and the 2:00 a.m. witching hour when the bars closed and the drunks staggered out to the streets to find other entertainment, it was a good time to grab a sandwich. Sam picked up the microphone, switched from the main to the car-to-car frequency and pressed the button. "Hey, Larry. Ready for coffee?

"I thought you'd never ask," a raspy voice responded over the radio.

"We're heading to Tom's."

"Be there in ten."

Sam replaced the microphone on its hook, and turned west onto Colfax. Not coincidentally, they were only a few blocks from Tom's 24 Hour Diner. Strong coffee and homemade pie had made it a favorite cop hangout for years, and he and his old partner, Larry, usually timed their patrols to be in the area at about the same time every night.

They rolled along, passing buildings decorated with splashes of graffiti and protected by wrought iron bars on the windows and doors. Most parts of the city were already asleep, but Colfax stayed up late. People of all ages, genders (not limited to just male or female) and eras, from old hippies with scraggly beards and tie-dyed shirts to young goths with pitch black hair and more eyeliner than Lady GaGa drifted in and out of the tattoo parlors, quaint bookstores and musty record stores that doubled as head shops. Businesses of all kinds thrived on the heartbeat of Denver's dark side. Oddly, the only places not opened on Colfax after midnight were the churches.

The ridealong straightened in his seat and pointed to a man and woman standing on the sidewalk. "Hey, look at that. Is that a hooker?" For the first time all evening, the man looked directly at Sam. With just a hint of a challenge, he asked, "Are you going to arrest her?"

Sam looked back at the hooker and sighed. Arresting her was the last thing he wanted to do.

Maybe it was soft glow from the corner street lights that washed the harshness of street-life off her surprisingly pretty face. Or it could have been the black leather mini skirt that accented long, bare legs. Or the sparkly blue tube top clinging to her curves and revealing a view of generous cleavage. Or possibly, it was the audacity of a hooker hanging out less than a block from Tom's. Whatever, even before the ridealong had pointed her out, Sam had already noticed the stunning blonde standing near the curb in front of a boarded-up building.

Yes, prostitution was illegal, but on a scale of one to ten, on Colfax it was about a two. Unless there was a sting or a fight or a complaint, most cops usually looked the other way. There were bigger dragons to slay. But the ridealong created a dilemma of sorts. The good citizens of Denver had certain expectations, and with the spotlight on Sam, he had to, at least, put up a show of lawful compliance.

He angled the patrol car to the curb and stopped so that his headlights bathed the woman in light. Sam had no intention of running her in, but it wouldn't hurt at least talk to her to keep up the department's image…and to find out what the hell someone who looked like that was doing in a place like this.

Sam put on his hat and adjusted his utility belt as he stepped out of the patrol car.

"Can I get out?" The ridealong's eyes were bright with excitement.

Sam shrugged. "Sure, just don't get in the way." He took a step up onto the curb and started to walk toward the hooker. "Good evening, miss. Can I see your identification?"

"She ain't doing nothin' wrong." A young black man standing in the deep shadows behind her took a step forward into the pool of light. Dressed in the street uniform of baggy, low hung jeans and sleeveless Nuggets jersey, the man's sudden appearance was as disturbing as his aggressive attitude.

"I didn't say she was." Sam's hand automatically moved up to his holster and unsnapped the strap as he forced his attention from the dazzling display of warm female flesh to focus on the man who was obviously her pimp. "I just wanted to ask her a few questions."

"She don't talk to no cops."

Sam looked back at the woman, searching for any signs from her that she needed help or wanted to say something about her situation. Instead, her steady gaze met his, and he noticed an amused twinkle in her wide turquoise colored eyes. "Are you okay, miss?" he asked.

She shrugged one pale bare shoulder suggestively. "Don't I look okay?" She tilted her head and her long blonde hair spilled provocatively down over the generous curve of her breast.

Better than okay. But Sam suspected that even if he was so inclined, he couldn't afford her. He glanced back at the ridealong who had gotten out of the patrol car but hung back behind the protection of its open door, watching the scene with interest. A car door slammed, and Sam noticed another patrol car had parked nearby. He smiled and nodded at the police officer who had just exited his cruiser and was walking toward them.

"Need any help?" What Officer Larry Resnick lacked in height, he made up for in width. Short, stocky and all muscle, he'd been on the force for almost thirty years, most on the night shift by choice. He hooked his thumbs on his gun belt and rocked back and forth on his heels as he observed the confrontation with wry humor.

"Nah, let's go." Sam turned to leave, but he couldn't resist a last glance back at the woman. She smiled at him and winked. Sam's steps faltered, and he was tempted to arrest her...just to get her off the streets and away from someone else's dick. He shook his head and would have stepped away, but a movement jerked his attention back to the young man at her side.

The pimp's dark eyes had narrowed to piercing slits, his gaze focused on Larry with a fierceness that was palpable.

The air crackled with a sudden surge of tension as powerful as a bolt of lightning. A large pistol appeared in the pimp's hand while his other arm snaked around the hooker's waist and jerked her against him. "Fuck you, Pig," the young man growled at Larry. The woman's startled screams mingled with the blast from the semi-automatic's barrel.

As if in slow motion, Sam yelled, "No!" even as he helplessly watched the bullet imbed itself in his friend's throat, just a fraction of an inch above the protection of Larry's Kevlar vest. The old cop gasped as blood spurted simultaneously from the wound and from his open mouth. His eyes widened, then glazed as his body crumpled to the ground.

Too shocked to think, Sam reacted instinctively. "Drop the gun, Asshole! Let her go!" he shouted, trying to distract the young man while inching closer. Sam had automatically drawn his gun and steadied it in both hands but couldn't get a clear shot at the pimp who was using her as a shield. Her smile had been replaced by a slack-jawed look of shock and horror. She clung to the man's arm as if it was the only thing holding her upright.

The pimp whirled and turned his gun on Sam. Careful to keep the woman between them, he fired again. The first shot pounded into Sam's vest with the force of a 300 lb. linebacker, knocking him back a couple steps. Sam steadied his stance and kept his gun leveled and his gaze locked with the killer's. For a split second, they froze, each looking down the barrel of the other's gun. A slow vicious smile curled one corner of the pimp's lips. He knew the young cop wouldn't risk hitting the woman, and he also knew there were a lot of vital areas on Sam's body not protected by Kevlar. With cold, deadly intent, the pimp squeezed the trigger.

"Fuck you, too," he said with cold blooded hatred.

Anticipating the shot, Sam dodged. There was no pain as the bullet pierced his right shoulder, only a sort of electric shock jolting along his nerve endings...then nothing. Sam didn't even feel the gush of blood that poured down his arm. His fingers relaxed, no longer able to hold the gun that clattered to the concrete and slid under the patrol car.

The woman took advantage of the distraction to land a sharp elbow into the pimp's ribs. Caught by surprise, and no longer needing the shield, the young man released his hold long enough for her to twist away. Instead of running for freedom, she grabbed his arm.

"Stop! Are you crazy?" she shouted. She watched, horrified, as her pimp kept the gun aimed at Sam.

"They're all the same." The pimp shook her off, his focus never leaving the wounded cop.

Sam's own gaze never wavered as he stared into the crazed eyes of the last man he'd probably ever see. His left hand closed around the baton still attached to his belt, and he yanked it out. But before he could take a swing, the pimp stepped closer, his arm extended, the heavy black gun held steady in his hand by a fierce hatred.

Sam didn't even have time to brace for the impact. There was a sparkly blue blur as the hooker lunged forward, followed by a deafening explosion as the gun belched fire and lead. Sam staggered backward, aware of a blinding explosion of pain and a fresh flow of thick, hot liquid pouring down the side of his head. There was a muffled pounding in his ears as the garish lights of Colfax spun around him. He struggled to focus, but his knees buckled beneath him. The concrete came up much too fast and hard. He tried to push himself up, but the dizziness dragged him back down.

All the things that should have been going through his mind, the whole "life flashing before you" thing and thoughts about how upset his mother would be at his death weren't as prominent as his own disappointment that he hadn't seen this coming. Stupid, stupid, stupid…he'd let his guard down and ignored all his training. Now his old friend already lay dead, and within seconds, Sam had no doubt he would be joining him. Precinct Shit had claimed two more victims…three if the girl didn't get away.

His senses foggy, he thought he heard another shot. His eyes were almost closed as a bright red stain spread across the Nuggets jersey. In disbelief, the young black man looked down at the gaping wound in his chest, then melted to the ground.

Sam felt soft, trembling fingers touch his cheek. He forced his eyes open and looked up into the face of an angel. His foggy senses cleared long enough for him to recognize the wide blue-green eyes of the hooker.

"I'm sorry. I'm so sorry," she whispered over and over.

Sam fought the waves of unconsciousness that tugged at him. He managed to lift his head enough to look around at the bloody scene. Both Larry and the pimp lay dead, only inches away from each other on the sidewalk, their blood oozing out and meeting to form a shiny dark red puddle. The ridealong was crouched behind the open door of the patrol car with his arms braced on the sill of the open window, Sam's pistol grasped between both of his hands.

In the shocked silence, Sam became aware of the sound of sirens approaching. He blinked through the veil of blood that was flowing into his eyes and looked back at the woman. But she had vanished. Had he only imagined her gentle touch and soft voice?

A half dozen patrol cars slid to a stop, their flashing red, white and blue lights joining the dizzying whirl, then everything went black as Sam lost his precarious hold on consciousness and slid into darkness.

Kate leaned against the closed door of her apartment, then whirled around and scrambled to lock all three locks. Her fingers were trembling so violently, it took several seconds to get the safety chain into its small round hole. Her first impulse was to crawl into bed, pull the covers over her head, curl into a ball and not move for at least a week. If she was lucky, this would all be an awful nightmare, and at any moment, she would wake up and everything would be just as it had been several hours ago. Back to the worries about coming up with the rent, getting a good long-term job, having enough extra money to get the brakes on her car fixed and maybe even being able to afford a new pair of shoes.

But tonight Kate wasn't so lucky.

She glanced down at her hands and realized they were splattered with dried brownish-red spots. Blood. She pressed her lips together and struggled to swallow the rush of bile that suddenly filled her throat. With increasing panic, she saw there were more dark red splotches all over the front of her tube top and skirt and even on the bare skin of her shoulders and chest.

Oh God, she had to get them off. Frantically, she clawed at the fastener of the skirt and yanked it off. She peeled off the tube top and dropped it on top of the skirt and added her shoes to the pile. Finally, she pulled off the long blonde wig and tossed it on a chair.

Wearing only black bikini panties and a black strapless bra, she hugged herself, trying to stop the shivering that had wracked her ever since the first shots were fired. Her jaws ached from being clenched for so long. She needed a shower…a long, hot shower to wash away the blood and the horror and the death…

Kate crossed the room that served as a combination living/dining room with a kitchenette blocked off in one corner by a folding screen. Small, run-down, yet barely affordable, she had, nevertheless, looked on it as a cozy hideaway…until now. Even with all the blinds closed, drapes pulled and the door locked, she still felt vulnerable and alone. At any second there could be a knock on the door and the police . . . She wasn't ready. Not yet.

Kate knew she shouldn't have run away. It wasn't even a conscious thought as much as an instinctive reaction to flee. When she heard the sirens, she knew help was near, and there was nothing she could do for any of the men lying on the sidewalk. She melted into the growing ring of curious bystanders and watched the emergency activity. As more and more people arrived, she had slid farther into the background until she just stepped away and disappeared into the night. Sooner or later she would have to talk to the police. Later, seemed to be the better plan.

She entered the bathroom and turned on the shower. It would take at least five minutes for the hot water to reach her second floor pipes, so she finished undressing while it ran. Her fingers fumbled as she took off her left earring, than reached for the right one. Touching the empty lobe of her ear, she sighed. Damn! The sparkling crystal hoops had been her favorite pair. She sighed and stepped out of her panties, then unhooked her bra. As she tossed it on the bed, a hundred dollar bill fluttered to the floor.

She blinked and stared at the crumpled bill for a few seconds without moving. Jameel had given it to her earlier in the evening, and because she hadn't brought a purse, she'd tucked it into the cup of her bra. In all the excitement, she'd completely forgotten about it. Stepping over it as if it was a poisonous snake, she entered the shower and pulled the curtain closed behind her.

As expected, the water was barely lukewarm, but it still felt good, pouring over her, washing away all the physical reminders of the night. She scrubbed her face and body with a soapy washcloth until her skin felt raw. Even after the water ran cold, she lingered in the protective cell of the tiled shower until she started shivering again. Reluctantly, she turned off the faucets and picked up a towel.

She made a half-hearted attempt to blow dry her hair, then wrapped a fluffy robe around her naked body. Suddenly overwhelmed by a debilitating exhaustion, she succumbed to her earlier instinct and crawled into bed. With all her lights blazing and her ruined clothes littering the floor, she closed her eyes and willed herself to sleep. As much as she hated to think about it, she knew nothing would change before morning. Sooner or later, she'd have to deal with it all . . . but for the few hours left until dawn, she would try to find peace in the depths of sleep.

It was almost 4 a.m. when he reached the newsroom. In spite of the early hour, there were already a couple other reporters at their desks, working desperately on their latest tip, trying to develop it into a story that would make it to press.

Brian smiled as his fingers closed around the cell phone in his pocket. Let them scramble. Yesterday, he'd been one of them. But this morning, everything had changed. What might have been a back page filler had suddenly become a front page headline.

Somewhere between the shootings and the arrival of the coroner, he'd called his editor who had promised him two inches on the front page in today's edition, plus a half page in tomorrow's and a full spread on the website. All with his by-line.

For eight years he'd been working at this paper, doing every crap job there was just to stay on the payroll. Denver was a great city if you liked football or skiing. Brian liked neither. His pallor was well earned spending hours inside homes or bars or malls or whatever crazy location might produce an interesting story. He couldn't get the big assignments until he'd proven himself. But he couldn't prove himself until he found a big story. That vicious cycle had generated such fascinating assignments such as the man who had painted his house, lawn and even the dog Bronco orange and blue or the woman who trimmed one of her hedges in the image of Obama during the Democratic Convention.

No matter how small and unimportant each story was, he'd struggled to keep it fresh and give it his whole heart, knowing that one day, he'd get his shot at the big time. One day someone would notice the beautiful prose and the brilliant insight that he put into each and every piece.

And that one day was today. He'd already called in the brief report that barely made it into the morning edition. He had all day to write the more detailed story that would appear in tomorrow's edition. He wasn't scheduled to be in the office until noon, but he was too energized to sleep. He could still remember the weight of the cop's Glock in his hand and the kick when he pulled the trigger. Even hours later, the rancid smell of gun powder and blood still filled his nostrils. The adrenalin continued to pump through his veins, making his heart pound wildly in his chest.

Brian's fingers danced across the keyboard as the words detailed the events of the night. This story was big enough and had a high enough profile to break him through that ink-stained barrier. And best of all, this story was all his.

BION (Believe It Or Not)

CHAPTER ONE

MONDAY, JUNE 10, 2013
FORT MYERS BEACH, FLORIDA

A wispy fog hung in the air, humid and heavy. From somewhere came the eerie whinny of a horse. The countryside was bleak, devastated by years of battles fought on its soil. The dirt was fallow, beaten down by thousands of hooves and heavy wheels, and tainted by gallons of blood and sweat.

The big bay stallion galloped through the mist, dodging the barriers and avoiding the artillery craters and the ditches that had once protected soldiers.

Kelly crawled across the barren landscape. She could feel the earth vibrating under the pounding of the horse's hooves as he came closer, closer. Every time she lifted her head to look, a bullet whistled past, narrowly missing her.

Would he run right past her? Would he leave her behind? Oh God, no, don't let them shoot him.

The air swirled as the horse reared. His hot breath heaved from his nostrils like a dragon and foamy lather dripped from his shoulders. Kelly knew this was her only chance. She jumped to her feet and tried to grab his reins.

Short staccato blasts pierced the air. Kelly felt one of the bullets rip through her left leg just as she tangled her fingers in the stallion's thick mane. The sound of the gunshots made him shy away, but she clung to him, grimacing with pain as her body bounced against him as he galloped. She felt her grip slipping. If she fell, she knew she would be trampled under his sharp hooves. He wouldn't mean to, but he was terrified and running for his life.

Bang . . . bang . . . bang . . .

Three more shots . . .

"Kelly, are you awake?" a voice broke into her dream as a door opened, spilling light into the room.

The mists blew away and the horse vanished. Kelly blinked her eyes and looked around, completely disoriented.

"We've got to leave in an hour . . . no later. The curtain waits for no one." Aunt Jane switched on the overhead light, then closed the door. Her aunt's footsteps quickly moved down the hall to the stairs.

Kelly sat up and swung her legs over the side of the bed. The dream still clung to her. It had seemed so real. She had even felt the pain of the bullet piercing her flesh. She tried to stand and almost collapsed. Her left leg ached and throbbed. It hadn't all been a dream.

Gingerly, she pulled back the bandage she had taped over the wound and looked at the bright red streak that had, indeed, been made by a bullet . . . just not in a war. Actually, she had been shot after spending what was supposed to be a relaxing one-day trip to a deserted beach off the southeast coast of Florida. Unfortunately, it had been inhabited by a lovely family of Cuban refugees and their guests . . . and a crazy man who wanted to kill them all, including Kelly and her friends.

They had barely escaped with their lives, although she had gotten nicked by a bullet on the way out. Definitely, not something she could tell her aunt. Even with an urge to confess the time traveling to her aunt, Kelly knew the gunshot wound would send her aunt over the edge. The bullet had just grazed her leg, luckily, because she definitely didn't want to go to the doctor for treatment. That would create more questions than she was willing and able to answer.

Kelly was excited because her aunt was taking her to see the play *War Horse* in Tampa for an early birthday present which was probably why her dream had been a morphed version of the movie and her own experiences. Kelly loved all things equine. She had grown up on a small ranch in Texas and had had her own horse since she was six years old. Leaving Scarlett with a friend had been heartbreaking but necessary since her aunt's house was on a small lot and couldn't accommodate any animal larger than a dog.

Her aunt was trying to keep the adjustment from being too difficult, and this play tonight was her way of helping Kelly get her horse-fix.

Actually, it had all started two weeks ago when her parents had been in a fatal car accident and Kelly had been packed up and shipped off to live with her aunt Jane in Fort Myers Beach, Florida. Overwhelmed with grief and shock, Kelly had been terrified that she would be miserable. But on the first day in her new home, she had met Scott, the boy next door and, together, they had worked to clean out her aunt's garage and organize a garage sale.

The discovery of a box containing a forgotten invention that Thomas Edison had given to her great-great-grandfather had been interesting. It wasn't until they had read the note from Edison, himself, that they realized they had found his legendary *"Telephone to the Dead"*. Even more amazing was that it had worked, and they were able to listen to voices that were carrying on conversations . . . from beyond the grave.

One voice had come through more clearly than the others, crying out for help. Using the microphone, Kelly had been able to talk with the girl and discovered that she had died in 1966 from an apparent suicide. Scott, who in Kelly's opinion, was a freaking genius had designed an app for their cell phones that would take them back in time so they could help keep the girl alive. Scott's best friend, Austin, who lived two houses over from Aunt Jane's joined Kelly and Scott as they prepared for their trip. Accidentally, a fourth traveler had joined them. At first, Zoey, a popular cheerleader had been very unhappy and uncooperative. But gradually, she had come around. That trip had been so successful that they had decided to again try out the *Telephone to the Dead*, or *Spirit Radio* as they had nicknamed it, which had led them to their last adventure to Crystal Key and their confrontation with a man with a gun.

Jane was a respected assistant district attorney who had lived alone, quite happily, for several years after her divorce. She took her job very seriously and Kelly knew that the fact that she had been shot wouldn't be something her aunt would ignore.

That meant Kelly would have to take care of it herself and make sure it didn't get infected. Carefully, she eased to her feet, taking it much slower than before. The wound was still raw and open, making her leg stiff and not easy to bend. She had already used some Neosporin and bandages from the medicine cabinet in her bathroom, but now that she had bled through her bandage, she knew she would have to redo it. It took a couple of minutes to make it across the room. Once in the bathroom, she studied her body in the mirror and was startled at her image. The shells and rocks from Crystal Key had left scratches and cuts all over her skin where it had not been covered by clothing or shoes.

Kelly didn't normally wear makeup other than a little mascara around her greenish-brown eyes and lip gloss for special occasions. But tonight she was going to have to put on a layer of concealer or something to make herself presentable. She had to hurry because being late would just complicate her conversation with her aunt. And she wanted to make sure the time and the mood was right.

As she doctored her wounds and dressed, she ran through the confession scenarios in her head. She could just blurt it all out . . . the whole story about the trips to the past, talking to dead people and saving people's lives. But then she would probably be sent for drug tests first and then to a court-appointed shrink. At a minimum, she'd lose communications with her new friends Scott, Austin and Zoey. Maybe they would all have to go to drug treatment or electro-shock therapy together. Not exactly a way to make friends and fit in in a new place.

A simpler topic to entrust to her aunt's thinking would be to get some input about her recently discovered feelings for Austin even though the only date she had ever gone on in her entire life was a couple of days ago and it was with Scott. Kelly sighed. That sounded as confused as her own feelings about the situation, and she was doubtful that Aunt Jane would be able to help clarify it. Aunt Jane didn't strike her as a romantic. She was too left-brained, dealing on a daily basis with criminals on a case-by-case, question-by-question basis. She dealt with facts, interrogating and prosecuting people. She hated compromise and probably wouldn't understand that Kelly was already developing feelings for both boys. It wasn't logical, and Aunt Jane was, above all things, logical.

Kelly decided to start with the fact that her brand new cell phone had been ruined by the water. That wasn't a lie. It *had* been water. It just wasn't the water in the Gulf of Mexico which was only a few blocks from Aunt Jane's house. It was a bigger issue that it had been in the Atlantic Ocean off the Florida Keys, and it hadn't been yesterday, but back in 1980. But it was still salt water. Maybe that would ease her aunt into the conversation about the *Spirit Radio*. Yeah…that was a plan. It wouldn't be wise to start down either the time travel road or her dating concerns right off the bat.

She thought about the downsides. After all, she wouldn't even be sixteen years old until Thursday, so she really should get her learner's permit first then worry about lifetime commitments…or maybe who to date next weekend. She frowned and shook her head quickly as she tried to not be so dramatic when it came to guys.

Kelly was finally satisfied that her face was presentable and the bandage on her leg wouldn't bleed through. She combed out her bangs and let her long dark brown hair fall straight and shiny around her shoulders, then hurried, as fast as she was able, to her closet to pick out an outfit. Something her aunt bought her at the mall would be respectful and in fashion. And it would be quick. Several minutes later as she looked in the full-length mirror, she thought that her new skinny jeans, a black sweater for night-time elegance and the seashell necklace Austin had given her made a pretty classy ensemble, although it had hurt like crazy to pull those jeans on over her wound. With a deep, steadying breath, she walked out of her bedroom and down the steps to find her aunt with car keys in hand, ready to open the door into the garage.

"That outfit looks really nice on you," her aunt said with an appreciative nod. "Ready?"

Kelly's smile was genuine. "I'm so excited. And Aunt Jane . . ."

"Yes?"

"Thank you . . . for everything. The jeans, the play tonight . . . letting me live here. You've been really good to me." Kelly blinked back the tears that suddenly welled up in her eyes.

"I'm looking forward to tonight. This will be fun."

They walked through the kitchen, into the garage and got into Jane's Mercedes. Kelly pressed the garage door opener that was on the visor and then buckled her seatbelt. "It's only 2:28! We made it!" Kelly exclaimed with a smile.

Her aunt backed carefully out and into the street as Kelly closed the garage door for her. Within minutes they had crossed the bridge to the mainland, wove their way through Fort Myers and then merged onto I-75 north toward Tampa.

"You need to pay attention to the roads we're going to take today," her aunt told her. "You're probably going to want to get your license soon, and you'll need to know how to get around the area without getting lost. Although I don't think you'll be driving this far out of town for quite awhile."

"I've been to a few places in Fort Myers with the guys. That's about it. I figure they know where they're going." Kelly smiled as she glanced over at her aunt.

"Well, that's all going to change after Thursday, isn't it?"

"Thursday? Oh yeah . . . my birthday. Mom and Dad said I could get my learner's permit when I turned fifteen, but we never got around to it. Florida's license age is sixteen, I guess?"

"Yes, with private driver's ed classes. You can take them this summer or through the school in the fall. But we can talk about all that later." Jane reached over and squeezed Kelly's left knee.

Kelly winced and bit her lip to keep from crying out. Her aunt had managed to hit the exact spot of her gunshot wound. She turned her head away and stared outside while she waited for the pain to subside.

Luckily, her aunt didn't notice as she continued, "Today's the day to have some together time . . . just you and me. So what did you want to talk about?"

Kelly wasn't ready to start that conversation just yet. She noticed the scenery was passing by at what appeared to be a high rate of speed and glanced over at the speedometer. The last speed limit sign she had seen had been 70 mph and decided it would be a good delaying tactic to change the subject. "So do you pull the prosecutor card when they catch you doing eighty-three in a seventy zone?" she teased.

"Oh I see. This is the *don't do as I do, do as I say* moment of parenthood I've heard so much about," Jane said with a guilty grin.

"Don't worry. Dad taught me how to drive on country roads and empty parking lots. He said I drove like an old lady. I guess I'm a little cautious."

Jane depressed the set-speed button on the wheel of her Mercedes until the speed dropped to seventy-eight. "There, compromise. We still have to get there on time."

They continued up I-75. As they passed the Sarasota exit, Kelly noticed several billboards advertising the Ringling Museum. "Is there a circus hall of fame here?" she asked.

"No, I think it's somewhere in Indiana. Several of the circuses wintered in Sarasota and the hall of fame was here until about thirty-five years ago. It probably should be here, but there was some kind of controversy, and they were going to split it up. That city in Indiana scraped together the money and moved it, lock, stock and circus wagon there," her aunt explained. "But the Ringling Brother's Museum is here, and I've heard it's incredible. I've never taken time to go through it, but they say it has a lot of circus memorabilia and some sort of a hand-crafted miniature circus. And one of the brothers, John, I think, lived on the property in a fabulous mansion filled with art that is open to the public. They get a ton of visitors every year. I hear it's pretty gaudy and colorful, like the circus itself. Why do you ask?"

"I just saw a sign back there. I love circuses. All those beautiful animals. I always wanted to try to ride Roman style."

"Roman style? Is that anything like Gangnam Style?" her aunt teased.

Kelly laughed. "It sort of is except you dance on the bare back of a horse instead of a dance floor. Actually, it's when a rider stands on two galloping horses with one foot on each horse's back, then jumps off and on and does all sorts of acrobatics. It's amazing."

"You sound like your great-aunt Charlotte…she was in the circus. Actually, I think it was Ringling Brothers and Barnum & Bailey."

"No kidding?" Kelly was totally fascinated at the thought of having a circus performer as a relative. "Is she still alive? No one ever mentioned her!"

"Oh no, she died years ago. She was kind of the black sheep of the family. No one knew why, but she just ran away to the circus one day. That was back in the late thirties or early forties. After she retired, she moved to a home for circus people somewhere around here."

"And she rode horses?" Kelly asked excitedly.

"No . . . she used to swing from a rope and hang by her teeth. It was a lot more dangerous back then because they didn't have to use safety nets."

Kelly was less excited after hearing her great-aunt hadn't been involved with the horses, but it was still an interesting fact about her heritage that she'd never heard before. "Well, that's pretty cool. I'll see if I can look her up on the internet."

"We used to have some old circus books in the garage. I think my great-grandma went to see her sister perform."

Kelly remembered going through some boxes of books in the garage, but she hadn't really noticed what they were about. She hoped her aunt hadn't given them to the Salvation Army along with the leftover clothes and furniture. As they got closer to the city, she observed how her aunt maneuvered in and out of the traffic as the road widened to three, then four lanes and the congestion increased as they neared the interstate loop that went on both sides of Tampa Bay.

"I made reservations for us at the best restaurant in the area. It's called Bern's Steak House and it's on South Howard. I think we have to get off on 618 and head west," Jane said as she reached down and picked up a map and a sheet of directions she had printed from the internet. She handed them to Kelly.

"What's this?"

"You're the navigator. I've never bothered to figure out how to use my GPS in this car."

"I'll get Scott to help you."

"Great, lessons from a sixteen year old about how to operate my vehicle," her aunt joked.

"He knows a lot about GPS." That was certainly an understatement. Kelly studied the directions for a moment. "You're right. You need to get off on 618, the Selmon Expressway. It's a toll road."

They followed the map through the streets after exiting the expressway and finally down to the 1200 block of South Howard Avenue. Jane turned left into the parking lot of a large warehouse-type building that looked nothing like a famous restaurant. Two valets opened the doors of the Mercedes, one on her aunt's side and one on Kelly's side. The valet held his hand out to help her exit the car which made her feel awkward, but also special. Kelly smiled, thanked the young man and followed her aunt into the lobby of the restaurant.

"Wow, this place is huge . . . and the colors, the furniture. Are you sure this isn't the Ringling Museum?"

"It's pretty eclectic," her aunt agreed. "But the food and the service are exceptional."

The hostess led the way past the butcher room where they stopped and observed steaks being cut and prepared to order. She saw how interested Kelly was, so she took them past the large, floor-to-ceiling tanks in the kitchen, each with a different type of fish. The hostess explained that when a customer ordered fish, the prep crew would select the specific type from one of the tanks, dip it out and prepare it as requested. When it arrived at the table, no one could deny that the fish was as fresh as physically possible.

They wound through several small dining rooms until they arrived at their table and were seated. The hostess carefully set down a large bound book next to Jane. "I will have our sommelier recommend a wine for your dinner when you've decided on your main course, Ma'am. Your server today will be Eric, and he will be here momentarily. Enjoy your meal ladies." Before turning away, she looked directly at Kelly. "You're going to really enjoy *War Horse,* Kelly and by the way, happy early birthday wishes." She nodded, smiled and walked away.

Kelly's jaw dropped open and she glanced at her aunt. "How did she know my name and that we were going to the play . . . and about my birthday?"

Her aunt smiled. "I must have let it slip when I was making the reservation."

Kelly had never felt so honored. She opened her menu that was about ten times thicker than any menu she'd ever seen and began to read. Her eyes opened wider. "Everything sounds delicious. I'm going to need some help choosing."

Jane was buried in the wine menu. "Thousands of wines. Too bad you don't already have your license. I'm always up for trying a new wine . . . or several."

Kelly laughed. "Everything is so expensive, Aunt Jane!"

Jane raised her right hand and index finger and wagged it side to side. "This is your birthday gift from me. I have a busy week coming up, so this is my time to say happy sweet 16! You only have one of those."

It was the most delicious meal Kelly had ever eaten. Actually, it was the overall experience that made it so incredible, all the way down to the ice cream dessert that they ate in a special area upstairs from the dining area.

Within minutes after the valets had helped them back into Jane's car, they had completed the drive to Carol Morsani Hall where *War Horse* was playing. After a quick bathroom break, they took their center seats in zone B, row A.

"These are amazing seats," Kelly said, looking around with excitement and trying not to act like this was her first play, when, in fact, it was. "It looks like the theater is sold out."

"This is what a college education can do for you, along with working in a place where colleagues sometimes have to change their plans at the last minute." Jane smiled.

"What?"

"One of the prosecutors I work with had the bad luck to have Judge Canella get their case, and the judge decided to hold court this weekend. It's a murder trial and the jury has been sequestered for a month already, so I got the tickets for face value. I was about to buy some on-line for $100 more . . . each . . . when my colleague offered me his."

Just then the lights dimmed and an off-stage voice announced, "Ladies and Gentlemen, welcome to Carol Morsani Hall. No photography of any kind is allowed. Please take this opportunity to turn off your cell phones and silence your pagers. And now, enjoy tonight's performance of *War Horse.*"

Kelly didn't move a muscle the entire first act. The staging was amazing and the incredible design and manipulation of the life-sized horse puppets were so real that she almost forgot that they were being operated by people who managed to bring the animals to life. From the moment the foal Joey came on-stage, then grew into an adult who was raised by the English farm boy, Billy, until he was sold and shipped off as a cavalry mount, Kelly was transfixed. She had read the book and seen the movie, both of which had influenced her weird dream. The play was just icing on the cake.

Far too soon for her tastes, the second act finished with Joey and Billy being reunited and returning home to the farm. She jumped to her feet, applauding loudly with the rest of the audience to give the cast and complexity of the show a well-deserved standing ovation. Her aunt bought her a t-shirt and a program that she hugged to her chest as they made their way through the crowds to Jane's car.

They inched their way out of the garage and when the car had finally merged in to the traffic on I-75 headed southbound toward Fort Myers Beach, Jane asked, "You haven't said a word since we left. Didn't you enjoy it?"

"Are you kidding?" Kelly's widened eyes sparkled. "I loved it. It was the most amazing thing I've ever seen. I can't believe they could make those puppets look and act just like horses. They even made their muscles move and it looked like they were breathing. I knew none of it was real, but it was so lifelike. Oh, Aunt Jane, I enjoyed it so much. I'll never forget this . . . any of this. Thank you."

For several miles Kelly was completely lost in her memories of the performance. When her aunt started talking again, she actually jumped.

"So how are you adjusting to Florida?" her aunt asked.

"Uh . . . great."

"Not bored?"

Kelly shook her head. "Not at all. I've been so busy."

"Busy? Doing what?"

Uh oh. She had to choose her words carefully or reveal too much too soon. "Oh, you know. Unpacking. Getting settled. The garage sale. Making friends."

"Enjoy your summer. When school starts you'll be really busy, and I expect that your grades will earn you a full ride at a good college."

"I expect that too. Mom set the bar way ahead of the mandated curriculum." Kelly had been homeschooled and her mother had done a great job, taking her far beyond required levels. Now Kelly was looking forward to being around other kids and learning from new teachers. "We had even talked about me maybe taking a college course or two my senior year. But I think I just want to enjoy my friends and a real school."

"Your friends seem like nice kids. And I like their parents. I'm kind of ashamed that before our barbecue I hadn't taken time to meet my neighbors since I moved in five years ago."

"You were busy redecorating the house," Kelly reminded her. The house had originally been built by her great-great grandfather in the early 1900s and had been passed down to her great grandmother, then her grandmother and eventually to Aunt Jane. As with all old houses, it had required a lot of maintenance and updating. It had stood strong and proud through the years, weathering numerous hurricanes and the commercialization of what had once been a sparsely populated island. The house had originally stood on several acres of land which had gradually been sold off until the house was now in the middle of a neighborhood. After Kelly's grandmother died, the house had gone to Jane and Kelly's mother, Jessica. However, Jessica was happy with her life in Texas and she let Jane buy out her interest. It was ironic that Kelly was now living in that house.

"We've got to get started on your room soon," Jane promised. "I really appreciated you and your friends cleaning out my garage. It was so full of stuff that I had hauled out of the house that I couldn't park my car inside."

"It was fun going through all those old things." *And finding the Spirit Radio,* Kelly thought, but didn't speak it out loud. She had told her aunt about finding the old invention, but she didn't want her aunt to ask too many questions about it. "Scott is really great. He was so much help with the garage. He's really smart and a little geeky, but in a good way."

"And then there's Austin," her aunt prompted.

Kelly hand automatically went to the beautiful shell necklace around her neck that Austin had so casually given her on the beach. *Yes, there was Austin,* Kelly thought. Tall, hunky and really cute with dark hair and blue eyes that made her heart flutter every time he looked at her. She desperately wanted to talk about her mixed-up feelings about Austin and Scott, but she just couldn't bring herself to confide in her aunt. Not just yet. It was all too fresh and strange. So she said what her aunt probably already suspected. "Austin's really popular. He's been nice to me, but I think he's probably nice to everyone. His dad and his football coach keep him pretty well in line, I think."

"What about Zoey? She seems different than Scott and Austin . . . and you for that matter."

"I'm still trying to figure Zoey out. She's not like her public persona, know what I mean? I think she's a little insecure at times, but she's brave. And she says whatever is on her mind. That's probably not always a good thing, is it?"

"No. We all need a filter to stop us from saying the wrong thing at the wrong time or in front of the wrong people. We'd have to drive all the way to Key West before I'd finish telling you all the mistakes I've made. I'm getting better . . . I think."

"I'm sure it will all change once we're in school. I'm kind of nervous about that . . . but pretty excited, too."

"I'm sure you'll do just fine." Her aunt adjusted the air conditioner settings, then glanced over at Kelly. "What did you want to talk about anyway?"

Kelly drew in a deep breath and sat up straighter in her seat. She reached out and redirected the airflow vent toward her face as she got her nerve up. She had never lied to her parents, and she was uncomfortable lying to her aunt. Well, she wasn't lying exactly. She just wasn't telling her the whole truth about what was going on, and that omission was making her feel guilty. She and all her friends had promised not to tell anyone about their time traveling adventures, but Kelly really wanted to come clean.

She just wasn't sure how her aunt would take it. She decided to start with the cell phone and see how that went. She glanced at her aunt who was focused on the dark road ahead.

"My cell phone got wet at the beach today. I'm sorry, but I can use the money from the garage sale you paid me to replace it."

"Your brand new cell phone that you've had for just a little more than a week?"

"Yes, but . . ."

"I admit that I'm surprised. I expected you'd be more responsible than that."

"I am, but . . ."

"How could you go swimming with your cell phone?"

"I wasn't expecting to get wet." *We were supposed to land on the beach, but instead ended up dropping into the Atlantic Ocean, fully dressed.*

"Why didn't you leave it in your bag?"

"Uh, I lost my bag." *To a psycho killer who stole it,* but she didn't think her aunt would take that information very well either. "I'm sorry, I'll replace that, too. It was stupid," she added aloud.

"This isn't about the money, Kelly. This is about making good decisions and acting responsibly. I can't be there for you every time you have to make a decision. I'm really disappointed in you."

Kelly felt bad. She hated to disappoint anyone, but she was a little surprised by her aunt's over-the-top reaction about a wet cell phone. Of course, her aunt was right. But if she was this upset about the phone, how crazed would she be if she knew about the gunshot wound or the serial killer coach they had stopped or the fact that she and her friends had passed through the time-space continuum and back again . . . twice? It definitely validated Scott's insistence that no one else should ever find out about their experiences.

"Well?" her aunt broke the silence. "What do you have to say for yourself?"

"Uh . . . I understand that it was a stupid thing to do, and I will work really hard not to bother you in the future about this kind of stuff."

"Hmmm, that's not exactly the reaction I was hoping to hear from you. Every day I see criminals stand in front of the judge and they all say they are sorry and that they will *try* to do better when they get out. Do you know what I ask the judge to do?"

Clearly her aunt's answer was going to be far better than anything she could come up with, so Kelly didn't try to guess. But did a wet cell phone and a lost bag make her a criminal? This was probably not the right time to argue that point either, she thought. "No, what do you ask the judge to do?"

"I tell the judge, *Your Honor, the State wants to know exactly what Mr. or Mrs. So and So is going to do in his or her life to actually do better.*"

"That's a great question."

"So?"

"So . . . what am I going to do?"

"Yes!" Her aunt glanced over at her with what Kelly imagined was her best prosecuting attorney's scowl.

"Leave my phone in the car?" Halfway through Kelly felt the confidence fade from her voice.

"At the very least." Her aunt's fingers tightened on the steering wheel, and she frowned. "I think I need to make sure this is a learning experience for you. I'll tell you what. On Wednesday night, be prepared to tell me exactly how you're going to make better decisions on things like this in the future."

"That sounds fair."

"And you're grounded until Thursday morning."

"Grounded?"

"Yes . . . you know, no leaving the house or yard . . . no visitors."

"Can I have e-visitors?" Kelly caught a slight twitch of a smile on her aunt's right cheek, but chose not to point it out. She really didn't know her aunt that well, so she tried to remain emotionless while awaiting the final judgment.

"E-visitors?" Jane repeated. "Listen, I'm not trying to be mean. This being a parent is new to me. I'm just overly cautious. I want to do this right, and I think this is an appropriate punishment."

Kelly sat quietly as she awaited the final decision about the e-visitor question. Another exit for North Fort Myers sped past.

"I'm okay with e-visitors," her aunt finally responded. "Assuming you're talking about your on-line game and emails. But no Skyping. Okay?"

"Okay."

The remainder of the ride home was silent and awkward. Kelly felt bad that such a wonderful evening had ended so badly, but she had learned a valuable lesson. The travelers' secret was safe with her. It was clear that her aunt . . . or any other adult, for that matter, was not ready to hear about their trips.

After another thank you to her aunt when they got home, Kelly tried not to limp as she climbed the stairs to her room. Once inside, she quickly brushed her teeth, re-medicated and bandaged her wound, changed into her sleep shorts and her new t-shirt and slipped under the sheet. With the music from the play still dancing in her head, she closed her eyes.

CHAPTER TWO

TUESDAY, JUNE 11, 2013

Being grounded sucked!

Kelly's hand trailed in the tepid water as she floated on a raft in her aunt's pool. Since this was the first time she'd ever been grounded, she didn't have anything to compare it with, but she was both embarrassed and impatient. And she was sure that her social life was going to suffer irreparable damage.

But of course, it was her own fault that she was on house arrest. And she did have a pool and access to her computer, so it could have been a lot more uncomfortable. None of those things made it any easier to swallow her punishment.

Nico, the scarlet macaw that loved to perch in the Queen palm tree outside her bedroom window had awakened her with his ear-splitting squawks at 7 a.m. Unfortunately, he didn't have a snooze button.

She had tried to ignore him and go back to sleep, but he was loud and persistent. She considered throwing something at him, but he was probably an endangered species or something. Besides, he had sort of been her first friend in Fort Myers Beach, so she couldn't just blow him off.

As she had done almost every day since she had moved to Florida, Kelly climbed out of bed, knelt down on the tile floor in front of window and rolled the valances open so she could talk to him. Each morning they had these one-sided conversations with Kelly doing all the talking and Nico listening intently, twisting his brilliantly colored head almost upside down as he kept at least one shiny black eye focused on her at all times. When he had had enough, he would repeat several notes of a whistle she'd taught him, fluff out his gaudy feathers and fly away.

Kelly and her aunt hadn't gotten home until around two this morning and five hours of sleep was definitely not enough. She thought about going back to bed, but she knew it would be hopeless. Thinking she should take advantage of her exile to start an exercise program and lose some of her puppy fat, she limped to the bathroom and changed into her swimsuit.

She had done twenty sets of her self-designed swimming program with sets consisting of a lap each of freestyle, breast stroke, back stroke and dog paddle. She realized Ryan Lochte wouldn't be too impressed with her adding a dog paddle to her set, but it exercised different muscles than the rest. However, now that that was out of the way, the day loomed long and boring. She swished her hand through the water and watched it trickle off her fingers, each drop sparkling in the sunlight. Her skin was beginning to prickle from the heat, so she slid off the rubber mat like a sea lion off a rock and glided through the water. She made it the entire length of the pool with one breath, and when she surfaced at the shallow end she shook her head to clear the water out of her ears and get the hair out of her eyes.

"Hey, mermaid. Want me to throw you a fish?" a male voice asked.

Kelly looked up and saw Scott's blond head peering over the six-foot cedar fence. "No thanks. But you could bake me a cake with a file in it so I can break out of this prison."

"What's wrong with your gate?"

"Nothing except for the fact that I can't use it until Thursday. I'm grounded." Kelly walked out of the pool and wrapped a towel around her body, still a little self-conscious about having her friend see her in a swimsuit. She picked up a lawn chair and carried it to the fence so she could stand on it and talk to Scott face-to-face.

"*Grounded?* Who does that anymore?"

"Aunt Jane, apparently. She didn't take me ruining my new cell phone too well."

"That's lame."

"My thoughts exactly."

"So, I guess you can't go to the beach with us later?"

"I'm on house arrest until Wednesday night, and then I have to come up with a plan on how I'm going to be more responsible. Until then, no beach, no movies, no *Spirit Radio*, no anything." Just saying it all out loud made her feel even more depressed. "But on Thursday, I'll need to go to the mall and get a new cell phone and a backpack. Do you want to come?"

Scott's face lit up. "Sure, we could take the bus."

Kelly's shoulders slumped. "Or we could get Austin to take us."

Another head popped up next to Scott. This one had dark shaggy hair, bright blue eyes and a crooked grin that made Kelly wish she wasn't looking like a drowned rat.

"Take who, where?" Austin asked. He had apparently found a lawn chair so he could join the conversation.

"The mall." Kelly and Scott answered simultaneously.

"I've got a college scout meeting this afternoon, but we can go tomorrow."

"She's grounded," Scott offered. "Her sentence is over Thursday."

"Really? Grounded? The last time I was grounded I was twelve," Austin teased.

"I was just hoping I could talk you into taking us to the mall so I can replace my phone. Until then, I'm kinda out of the loop."

"That's days from now. Ask me again on Wednesday." Austin looked over at Scott. "So, when are you getting your license?"

"I've got the book. I'm not in any hurry," Scott answered. "What school today?"

"FSU. It's just the scout. If it goes well, I'll see the head coach after next season."

"Good luck," she told him with a smile.

"Thanks." He flashed her that grin that made her knees almost buckle. "Can you play *Out Of Time*?"

"Yeah the warden is allowing e-visitors so *OOT* is on," Kelly answered.

"I'm off at ten tonight. How about ten-thirty?" Austin proposed.

"Sounds good. I'll be ready."

"So how are you guys doing after our island trip?" Scott asked.

"My bullet wound is fine," Kelly said. "But I thought I was going to scream when my aunt squeezed my leg last night. How about you guys?"

"I've got three layers of skin burned off from the sun," Scott said. "I thought my mom would freak, but she said I looked good with a little color. Funny thing, she didn't say anything about my black eye."

"Your mom's probably glad you're finally out there horsing around like a normal kid instead of staying indoors getting paper cuts and looking like a ghost," Austin told him.

"How are your ribs?" Kelly asked.

"They're a weird shade of yellow now, but they still feel awful and my shoulder is really sore. I'm glad I don't have to throw the ball for that scout. I'm a wreck," Austin reported. "Anyone talk to Zoey?"

"She sent me a text," Scott mentioned casually. "She has the same bruises and cuts we all got on her face, arms and legs and rope burns around her wrists . . . *AGAIN*. She capitalized and italicized that. She said her friends thought she was involved with fifty shades or something . . . whatever that means."

"Oh? She texted you? I see how it is," Austin teased.

"Yeah, so?" Scott's pink cheeks flushed an even darker red.

It occurred to Kelly that she should feel hurt that Scott seemed so happy to have been contacted by Zoey. But she was glad that Zoey had reached out to him. Kelly could live with that.

"What do you think about that Kelly?" Austin tried to egg her on.

Kelly responded dispassionately. "At least she has a phone."

"If we had landed on the beach instead of in the ocean, your phone would have survived," Austin pointed out as he gave Scott an accusatory look.

"Next time I'm going to make sure we have time to do all the research we need before we go," Scott promised. "We were lucky we got out of there alive. The cell phone was collateral damage."

"I agree. But I'm afraid I'm going to have to dip into the garage sale fund to repair that collateral damage," Kelly said.

"Sounds fair," Austin agreed.

"I'm okay with that," Scott added. "Zoey wanted to make sure she would be here the next time we make our plans. Her brother is home, but she said she can get away any time."

"I didn't know Zoey had a brother." Kelly thought back to all the conversations she and Zoey had shared and couldn't remember her ever mentioning it.

Scott answered, "Neither did I, but apparently, he's just finished his freshman year at the University of Colorado."

"Just exactly how long was this conversation, Scott?" Austin asked, his blue eyes twinkling.

"Only about . . . hey, what's it to you?"

"You boys can fight over Zoey all you want. But right now, I've got to go eat something," Kelly said as she stepped off her lawn chair, waved good-bye and returned the chair to the patio.

Scott and Austin disappeared back behind the fence, and Kelly instantly felt all alone again and just a little put out that both boys were fighting over Zoey. That was not at all how Kelly had wanted it to go.

She took a long, cool shower that felt good against her healing skin. Even her leg was feeling better. She examined it closely and satisfied that there was no sign of infection, she slathered a generous amount of Neosporin on it and stuck three bandage strips across it. After dressing in shorts and a tank top, she quickly made her bed and gathered all her dirty clothes. She sorted them and started a load in the washing machine before finally going to the kitchen and getting a bowl of cereal for breakfast.

Hours later, she was sprawled on the couch watching a Robin Williams DVD. She had cleaned the kitchen, re-organized the pantry and made a grocery list of all the things that were missing. It was a long list. Her aunt had admitted that before Kelly moved in, she had rarely eaten at home. And what she did cook, she had bought fresh, which meant there were almost no processed foods in the pantry. Kelly knew that was probably a healthy choice, but it wasn't exactly teenage-friendly. Next, Kelly had finished a book she had started a couple of days ago and was dismayed to discover that she didn't have anything that she hadn't already read. A quick glance at her aunt's bookcase had confirmed that her aunt wasn't a big fan of fiction. She had moved next to the shelves that held Aunt Jane's DVD collection, which was surprisingly mainstream.

Kelly tried to select a DVD to watch, but had ended up alphabetizing them all first. She had seen the Robin Williams movie before, but it always made her laugh. *Almost* always. Today, she just wasn't in the mood to laugh. When the DVD ended, she returned it to its appropriate space on the shelf and was about to start dinner when her aunt called and told her she would be home late and not to wait for her.

With a sigh, Kelly put a pot of water on to boil and took out some spaghetti. It wasn't worth the trouble to make sauce, so she just added a little butter and tried not to feel guilty about the calories. For dessert, she had an apple which she hoped would balance the scales.

By eight o'clock, she was at her computer in her room, killing time until Scott and Austin joined her on-line for their game. On a whim, she typed in the name Manuel Castillo and Crystal Key. Dozens of articles came up and she soon became mesmerized by his story. A few more searches revealed even more information about the family she and her friends had met on Crystal Key. She was so caught up that she barely noticed when her aunt came home and popped into Kelly's room just to say "hi" and that she was exhausted and turning in. Kelly told her goodnight and tried not to appear impatient to get back to the stories on the screen.

As soon as her aunt shut the door behind her, Kelly had jumped back to the internet updates on Manuel, Juanita and Luisa. It was ten-forty when she realized it was past time to log in to the game with the boys, so she quickly minimized her search screen and signed on to *Out of Time*, a time travel MMO game that she and the boys played with people from around the world on the internet.

Kelly logged in and connected to a private chat room with Austin and Scott. She adjusted the volume so she would be able to hear both of them clearly without using earphones.

"You're late," Scott reprimanded. He appreciated punctuality.

"Sorry. I was on the internet and lost track of the time. You won't believe what I found out about Manny and Luisa."

"Yeah, I was checking them out today, too," Scott said. "Did you see the article about the day we left?"

"Yes, I did," Kelly said.

"What? What?" Austin prompted. "Tell me what you found out."

"Just that Manny and everyone else made it to the mainland and to the hospital in time to save him," Kelly explained.

"Did they send the police or the coast guard or someone to pick up that crazy guy?" Austin asked.

"The coast guard went out the next day and found the guy drowned on the beach," Scott explained. "Apparently, he tried to get away in one of those beat-up old boats, but it wasn't seaworthy."

"I can't say I was sorry to find that out," Kelly admitted. "He would have killed us along with all those kids."

"He punched me and he shot you, Kelly," Scott reminded them. "It said he had been released from the criminally insane unit of the prison in Cuba and somehow got hired on to a fishing boat. At some point they were caught in that tropical storm while it was out at sea and the boat sank. He managed to hang on to some of the wreckage and floated ashore on Crystal Key. And you know the rest."

"Holy crap!" Austin exclaimed. "I wondered where he came from."

"But the good news is that Manny recovered and went on to sponsor more families," Kelly told him. "There were several articles about humanitarian awards he has been given, and he recently got a lifetime achievement award from the Cuban American Chamber of Commerce."

"He's still alive?" Austin was amazed.

"Yeah, he's in his seventies," Scott said.

"Any news on Luisa?" Austin asked.

Kelly jumped in to answer him because she had been truly excited to find out that Luisa had not only survived, but thrived. "She was just elected to the Florida State House . . . a real up-and-comer, they said. She's married and has two kids." Kelly shivered. "It gave me goose bumps knowing she would have died if we hadn't succeeded."

"It was touch and go. Next time, we're going to wait until we can plan it better," Scott promised. He didn't like surprises.

"But if we hadn't gone, they would all be dead," Kelly reminded him.

They were silent for a moment, a little shaken at the thought of how great that responsibility was and how close they had come to not making it home.

"Uh . . . are we playing tonight?" Austin broke the silence first, more because he didn't want to dwell on their brush with death than because he was eager to play *OOT*.

"I wonder if we can find those dudes in Dallas again. They were tough, but I like good competition," Scott said.

"Let's do this." Austin was clearly pumped for the competition.

The game continued into the early morning hours before the Dallas team was beat a second time.

LIFE'S WHAT HAPPENS

Prologue
"Try To Remember [The Kind Of September]" –
The Sandpipers

Kent State University – September, 2012

It was an early September weekday afternoon as Don
Williams drove his rented candy-apple red Ford Mustang
convertible along the narrow, uneven streets of Kent State
University. He kept to the old sections of the campus along
the north and west sides where evidence surely still existed of
his having been there over four decades ago. He could feel
the warm sun on his balding head and the air turning cooler
as it curved over the windshield and into the Mustang's
cockpit-like front seat. Incredibly young-looking kids walked
between the buildings or sat under the huge old trees. He
could remember being out there, his arms filled with books,
his head full of dreams. But God, had he ever looked that
young?

He looked around with interest as he toured the
campus streets and gradually worked his way toward his old
fraternity house. He hadn't set eyes on it since May, 1970
when he and 20,000 others were rushed off campus under
Martial Law because of the student killings.

He shook his head to clear those thoughts away and
double checked the dashboard clock to be sure he wasn't

going to be late for a meeting for which he had no clue why he had even been invited. Jennifer Kist, the attorney he had been emailing back and forth with, was neither detailed in her explanation nor very responsive to any of his questions.

The Mustang handled smoothly. It had always been the car of choice back in the day when he had driven these streets. Not that he had had a Mustang or any other car back then. He was glad he had splurged when he picked it up from the rental agency. After all, what better car could carry him into his meeting with the past?

Like almost every small town kid who went away to college, Don's time at Kent was very different than his early years in Canton, Ohio, even if his hometown was only a few miles away. It was where he had learned about life, love and brotherhood.

Today, he thought as he drove along, the girls walking the campus were probably glancing his way only because they admired the Mustang. They were looking at him with age-filtered lenses, not even seeing the middle-aged man at the wheel. But he had had his day.

A quick check of the Mustang's dash clock and he realized that his appointment, set for 2 p.m. at his old Phi Psi Kappa house on West Main Street, was but a few minutes away. He left campus and headed through the middle of the small city of Kent. Along the way, he mourned the loss of so many of the places from his past. Gone was the Robin Hood, or the Hood as everyone had known it, The Black Squirrel Grill and many of the old fraternity houses. The old Kent Hotel still resided on the South side of Main Street and had been notorious because the lounge had provided adult entertainment complete with go-go girls and a more sophisticated crowd if you were twenty-one. Less than a block west at Franklin Avenue, just before the railroad tracks still stood The Loft bar. No go-go girls. No hard stuff. Not even a band. The 3.2 beer had been the only beverage on hand.

A left turn south on South Water Street had always gotten him a complimentary 3.2 beer from the Fifth Quarter's owner when he was with his fraternity brother Cliff who had taken some amazing photos of the campus, but more importantly, art shots of hundreds of willing female students. He had even earned the nickname Hef for his ability to make even the most ordinary young woman look beautiful. The Fifth Quarter had been large enough to hold hundreds on a weekend night and had been an ideal place to display Cliff's photography. His photos of now-famous bands had built his portfolio, including Joe Walsh, who had played lead guitar with the Measles, a Kent State student band, before he moved on to the James Gang and finally to the Eagles. And Cliff was more than happy to include his brothers in his photo events. He always needed someone to carry his equipment, and free beer, hot chicks and a good band were powerful incentives.

Sadly, as student tastes changed, the Fifth Quarter had become a dive named Filthy McNasty's, and then a Honda motorcycle dealer. Even that was now gone, replaced by non-descript storefronts with neither interesting names nor pasts.

Don shook his head as he wondered how many times he had walked the two and one-half miles back and forth between the house and the campus. As he approached the tracks, he remembered, as if it were yesterday, how the train would stop around 10 p.m. each night for a crew change-out which would hold him up for an additional fifteen minutes. Of course, that had only happened in really cold or wet weather. He smiled, remembering that in that part of Ohio, that had been every night. That was typical Kent, where forty days and forty nights of continual rain in his sophomore year had created floods of Biblical proportions and contributed to supporting a several-hundred student three-day mud fight. That war of the dorms and sexes had caused the complete drainage of the campus water tower and the elimination of shitting, showering and shaving on campus for four whole days.

As if on cue, the flashing railroad lights and the sound of the bell scared him back to reality and he hit the brakes, stopping just inches from the lowered arm. The freight train rolled past and gradually picked up speed, heading south and eventually clearing the crossing. The gates rose and the lights turned off and the bells were silenced. He passed over the railroad tracks and the bridge that crossed over a river whose name he had never known. He was struck by how small the hill leading from town to the fraternity house really was. Back then, powered by his feet and fueled by an ample supply of 3.2 beer, it had seemed much larger.

He felt a rush of excitement, knowing that just over the horizon was his old fraternity house. The building was over a hundred years old and had been a funeral home in its past life. A very generous, successful and Don remembered, quirky benefactor, Brendan Harrigan, former Phi Psi Kappa fraternity brother at Kent State had bought the building and turned it into a fraternity house. Brendan had been in his early thirties when he would drop by the house every quarter with his hand out, seeking to get paid his mortgage payment. Of course, since he hadn't been wealthy when he was in college, he had to know that it was unlikely that the mortgage payment would ever be made on time or in full. But that never stopped Brendan from showing up on a regular, if not always timely basis which had led to several frantic money-raising events by the brothers.

Don laughed out loud as he thought about how, in spite of his wealth, Brendan had always worn a crumpled, but clean pharmacist's smock and drove a partially rusted powder-blue fifteen year old Ford station wagon. There were better looking beggars on the street. For a licensed pharmacist, it also seemed pretty odd that Brendan had never been without a mostly smoked but never lit cigar. The color of the dried out wrapper of the cigar had blended into the color of the sides of his index and middle fingers of his left hand, stained by a long history of togetherness.

Which brought him back to why he had returned to Kent today. Apparently, Brendan had died recently and had named several of the fraternity brothers in his will. No one could have been more surprised than Don. He couldn't imagine why the old man would have even remembered him, much less left him something. His dealings with Brendan had been minimal and unremarkable. Maybe it was some kind of joke after all those late checks and the residual damage to the building the school year always left behind. Jennifer hadn't offered any answers in her emails but after he had agreed to come, he had received airfare and ample expense money to attend the reading of Brother Brendan's last will and testament.

Don squirmed in his bucket seat and peered out over the hump in the hood that housed the oversized Mustang motor, as the house came into view on the right. He noticed that the grass still needed cut, tree branches still needed cleared, and the house still needed a fresh coat of white paint.

By force of habit, he took the single-lane driveway as fast as possible. As his car hit the gravel at the end of the drive the Mustang skidded slightly right and around the corner at the rear of the house, then slid to a stop in front of the coach house next to the large maple tree. There were already a couple cars in the lot, and he didn't know if they belonged to the new brothers or the older ones. He unbuckled his seat belt, opened the door and stepped from the car.

It had always been part of its colorful history that the coach house started life as a garage for the two horse-drawn hearses on the right side and four stalls on the left for the horses. Tradition held in the fraternity that the two most senior actives parked their cars inside the garage side for protection from the elements. The implementation of this tradition had a few rough spots depending on the most senior brothers' cars because the width of a fancy hearse from the early part of the twentieth century was about the same as an MG or VW bug in the 1960s. Any larger cars presented a problem, as well as larger actives because his waist size was almost as important as his car size as he would have to be able to slip between the frame of the coach house and the car in the narrow confines.

Don took a moment to look at the old house. It was easy to imagine pallbearers and caskets, followed by grieving friends and relatives leaving through the double front doors of the funeral home as those had been the guests of the day. The front door when he had lived there was still reserved for live guests to come and go as need be. But it was the rear door where the brothers and their girlfriends had entered and exited. Both entrances had covered porches. About 15' x 40', the front porch was large enough for ten large wicker rockers. The two large oak doors with beveled glass windows led to the foyer that not only opened wide enough for caskets but on occasion for small cars, practical jokes being the specialty of all fraternities since time began. Don was still amazed at how few young men it took to carry an entire VW bug into the house or to carry an occupied wood-framed bed outside to the lawn.

The main floor rooms were large enough for either multiple viewings on a busy night eighty years before Don's time or they worked well for parties or studying alone or with dates. The back porch was about half the size of the front porch. Its door opened directly into the commercially retrofitted kitchen. Don knew this route well as he had never missed a meal. There had been an ever-changing cast of cooks who, no doubt, hadn't been appreciated or paid enough for their trouble.

No one had wanted to think about what had gone on in the basement in the far past, but when Don lived there, it had been a place for more intimate parties and storage.

As Don walked around the back of his car and headed toward the rear porch, a very muscular man, head shaved and in his early twenties bounded down the steps heading directly toward Don. He looked like he had jumped off the cover of a romance novel. He extended his right hand and said to Don as he glanced at the Mustang, "Hey, nice ride, dude! Can I help you?"

Don attempted to return the handshake but soon realized the student was either not a modern Phi Psi Kappa fraternity brother who knew the same secret handshake Don knew or the student was not expecting Don to be one. Fumbling briefly as he withdrew his right hand, Don answered. "Yes you can. I'm Don Williams. I have a meeting with Jennifer Kist here today. Your name is?"

"Josh, Josh Miller. Jennifer Kist? I don't think I know her. Does she date one of my brothers?"

Don realized his added knowledge would not make Josh any better informed as Jennifer had specifically instructed him to not go into details about Brendan, his will or any plans, not that he knew anything anyway. "No, I doubt it. She's an attorney. She asked me to meet her here at 2 p.m. today."

Josh studied Don from head to foot and glanced again at the Mustang in an effort to unravel the mystery a little. Finally, he commented. "Attorney? Interesting. Is anyone else coming?"

Don smiled and shrugged. "I don't know."

They both turned to look as a black Mercedes E350 sedan flowed around the corner of the house and headed toward the backyard parking lot. The raven-haired driver carefully maneuvered the car around the pot holes and away from other cars and shut it off. The driver's door opened and two long shapely legs exited and planted their expensive 4" heels on the ground. A tall thirty-something woman stood. Her clothes and the confidence she exuded perfectly matched the current model year $60,000 car. She turned and walked directly toward Don. With a smile, she extended her hand to him, "Mr. Williams, I'm Jennifer Kist. Sorry I'm a few minutes late."

Don nodded and was horrified to hear his voice crack as if he was back in college. "No worries. I just got here, myself. It's a pleasure to meet you."

Turning to Josh, Jennifer extended her hand. Her gaze swept his shoes, pants and broad shoulders before stopping at his eyes. "And you are?"

Josh, cleared his throat, suddenly looking less cool than earlier when he had been dealing with Don. "Josh Miller. I am actually the President of the fraternity or what was the fraternity." Josh glanced at the ground and shook his head. "I heard we're losing our house."

"That sucks," Don added. "Brendan did a lot for hundreds of guys. He was a pain in the ass twice a quarter, but overall, he was very generous."

Jennifer asked, "Josh, is there a place where we can get some privacy? I'm expecting a few more people, and I have some things to go over with them."

Josh motioned toward the coach house. "Sure, upstairs in the coach house on the right is a large meeting room. No one should bother you there. Most of the guys are on campus right now."

"Thanks Josh." Jennifer smiled and walked toward the coach house door that opened to the staircase to the second floor. About fifteen feet across the uneven, partly graveled parking lot she glanced back and called back to Josh, "If anyone is looking for Jennifer Kist or maybe asking for Brendan Harrigan's attorney, send them upstairs, would you please?" Don followed her, leaving Josh standing alone and confused in the parking lot.

From the outside, the coach house appeared to have undergone more renovations than the exterior of the fraternity house itself. Don pulled open the door and allowed Jennifer to enter the building and climb the single set of narrow wooden stairs. A wave of aroma from years of beer-soaked boards flowed down the stairs and hit them as they entered the building. As Don walked up the fifteen steps, he automatically counted them. The exact number had been a pledge test on oddities and trivia about the fraternity property. He also recalled the number of windows in the house, the steps leading to the front porch and how many trees were in the backyard. All critical knowledge needed to be recalled at times of duress like hell week and was, even after all this time, still stuck in his memory.

The stairs entered the second level through the center of the floor. The old basketball half court remained on the left side and the right side had been carpeted since he had been here forty years earlier. There were folding tables arranged in a giant rectangle shape for meetings. The far wall was covered floor to ceiling with the signatures of all the seniors who had ever graduated Kent State as a Phi Psi brother. Jennifer and Don gravitated toward it, drawn by all the voices from the past.

Together, they stared at the signatures written with scores of ball point pens, felt tip markers, colored pencil and even quill pens that had been the weapon of choice by those who had graduated from the very demanding architecture school.

"What's this all about?" she asked as she walked along the wall.

"It was a tradition that all seniors had to come up here on graduation day and sign the wall. As you could guess, there are hundreds more now than when I left."

Don slowly shuffled his way along the wall, carefully touching the inked signatures with his fingertips.

"You're looking at those names like you're at the Vietnam memorial in DC."

Don turned to Jennifer and blinked against the tears that welled up in his eyes. "You really get to know someone when you go through college, growing up with them. Being with them as they met and lost girlfriends, pass and fail classes and especially the hell we all went through our senior year. They were always there for me. But we've lost touch."

"Did Mr. Harrigan sign it?" she asked.

"Sure. He's way over to the left and toward the top," Don said as he pointed her in that direction. "He was in one of the first classes to live in this house. I guess he bought it after he graduated and got rich."

"Whose is this?" Jennifer pointed to a mostly illegible autograph that included a rough drawing of the iconic *Playboy* bunny logo. "What's with the rabbit?"

"That was Cliff Baker. His nickname was Hef."

"Ahh, I see. After Hugh Hefner, right?"

"Yeah. Cliff used to be a photographer."

One perfectly waxed eyebrow arched with the unasked question that would naturally follow such a confession.

"They were art shots," he defended his brother without apology. "Remember, it was the Sixties. It was all about freedom and beauty and love."

"Where's yours?"

Don pointed to a spot about five feet off the floor and left of the window overlooking the parking lot. "Right there."

"The one with the little rocket?"

"Yeah, that's it." He smiled at the memory that invoked. He hadn't thought about that in years.

"You're living in Texas now, aren't you?"

"Yes, for the last few years. My wife grew up in Austin. She had to stay behind with our daughter who's expecting our first grandchild any minute."

"That must be nice." Jennifer glanced at her watch, clearly moving her focus back to the meeting. "Do you know who is planning on making it?"

Don shook his head and shrugged. "I have no idea. I never even heard who was invited."

Jennifer walked over to the meeting tables, and laid her briefcase on one of them. "I didn't send you the list? My assistant must have forgotten to put that into your package," she told him as she shuffled through her briefcase.

"I guess we'll both know soon enough," Don commented.

"I left my phone in the car. I'm going to run down and call the office and make sure the food I arranged for is on the way," she told him. "I'll be back in a few minutes."

Don turned back to the wall. He moved slowly, looking for familiar names and stopping to touch the inked signatures with his fingertips. With each one he recognized, he'd stop, smile and sometimes nod as he recalled his experiences with every brother whose name he found.

Larry Reed with a small baseball drawn over his name. Stanley Freeman. Jeff Tallmadge accented by the faces of comedy and tragedy. Frank Pucci. Ted McCoy. Barry Smith next to a drawing of two sticks that no one but the class of 1970 would understand. Ira Schwartz. Rick Rogers. Alfonso Garcia and a paw print of a monkey with the name Carlos, inked above it. Someone, probably Jeff, must have added the tiny paw print after Alfonso signed because Alfonso and the monkey's hatred for each other had been legendary. There was Kevin Nash and Mike Anderson with an airplane drawn near his name.

Those guys had been his best friends, and yet he hadn't heard from any of them for years, not since the day they closed the campus. He was overcome with all the memories that flooded back. It was as fresh as if it was.

Suddenly he heard the sound of a basketball bouncing, then something hit him in the back of his knees so hard his legs almost buckled.

"Hey," Don yelled as he whirled around to see who else was there. "Watch what you're doing." He hadn't heard anyone come up the stairs.

From the dimly lit basketball court about fifty feet away he heard someone yell "Come on, Don! A little help here. We want to finish our game before registration."

Chapter One

"It's Your Thing" – The Isley Brothers

Kent State University – September, 1969

"Ball, Don! You're holding us up."

Don picked up the ball and dribbled forward and made a shot. The ball swooshed through the bare hoop and his team cheered. The ball hit a warped board on the old wooden floor and rolled toward the tables on the other end of the room.

"Hey, Hef, throw it back."

Cliff Baker looked down at the basketball and reluctantly picked it up. Not being coordinated enough to dribble and walk at the same time, he tossed the ball toward the group of young men waiting on the basketball court. It took an errant bounce, then shot out the open window.

All the guys who had been playing basketball rushed to the window and peered out. "Shit!" Frank Pucci grumbled. "Bet you couldn't do that again."

Cliff didn't doubt that. He had enough trouble getting it through the hoop. Bouncing it out the window was a feat he could never replicate.

Frank, at five foot eight inches tall, shouldn't have been much competition on a basketball court either. But growing up in a large, male-dominated Italian family had made him a force to be reckoned with. He tried harder, played longer and yelled louder than anyone else. "Hey Stan," he shouted out the window. "Can you toss the ball back up here?"

Stanley Freeman, an English major and self-acclaimed book nerd looked up at Frank and then across the potholes that were several feet wide to where the basketball was lying in the middle of the deepest one. He knew he didn't have the strength or accuracy to throw the ball back through the window. Nor was he inclined to walk through the puddle to retrieve it.

"I'm on my way to the Hill," Stan called back. Everyone called the campus the Hill because the first dozen or so buildings built since the early part of the twentieth century were on a higher piece of ground compared to the rest of the town of Kent.

"Just throw me the ball," Frank persisted.

Stan sighed and carefully inched his way between the small lakes to get the ball. He turned and yelled up, "I'll toss it up the stairs."

Frank waited at the top of the stairs, and it wasn't until the third throw that the muddy ball made it all the way to the second floor. "Thanks Stan."

"We need another load of gravel dumped back here. It's a mess." Stan waved to Frank and then got into his car and left.

"Come on Frank, Let's go. It's your out," Fred called.

Nothing defined lake effect like the weather at Kent State, located about 30 miles south of the city of Cleveland which was on the south shore of Lake Erie. A typical fall northeastern Ohio day could be hot, cold, sunny, rainy, snowy or even pelted with hail. Today rain poured down from the heavy, dark gray sky where clouds bumped against other clouds, rolling around in different directions. After a few minutes the rains always created a large muddy mess in the parking lot between the Phi Psi Kappa coach house and the main fraternity house. There was never enough gravel to avoid walking through mud.

The basketball game continued and the noise could be heard well out into the yard. Men's voices combined with an occasional female scream and a variety of profanity rolled through the open windows. The north end windows had been broken out by any number of games or other events over the years. The south end windows remained intact as that was the party room and where weekly chapter meetings were held. The volume of the meetings often exceeded that of any basketball game. On more than one occasion the Kent city police had walked up the stairs on a Monday night to quiet the lively discourse. That was also the area used by the brothers who needed table space for large projects ranging from architecture to aerospace to photography.

Cliff was taking advantage of the space now as he worked on his final junior class project of a photo layout, trying to ignore the noise and the girlfriends, pin mates and fiancées of his brothers who wandered over after dropping out of the game. The girls rarely lasted long in the games because the guys played for blood, and it took only a broken fingernail or a knock to the floor to discourage all but the most determined young woman. Besides, the girls found Cliff's photos more interesting.

The basketball again bounced his way and rolled under the table on which he had carefully placed his photos.

"Throw it back!" The plea came across the floor from one of the players. "And keep it in the building."

Cliff yelled back, "This is my last time guys. I have to get this done today. Its 40% of last spring's course grade that I got an incomplete on." Cliff picked up the ball and quickly carried it over to the other side and tossed it back yelling "I'm not officially a senior until I get it turned in. And they're going to draft my ass if I don't get a passing grade this week." He knew journalism wasn't exactly one of the anointed protected degrees and career choices like teaching and engineering, so keeping his class credits above minimum was critical.

Soon the yelling, dribbling and clapping died down and the players ran down the steps. First out the door to run through the rain and mud to the rear porch was Ted McCoy, a tall muscular blond-haired man with a very bloody nose. "I think you broke my fucking nose, Pucci," he yelled. "My dad's law firm is taking pictures next weekend. He's going to kill me."

"Pictures?" Frank couldn't imagine such a stupid reason to be concerned. He still had the remnants of a black eye he had gotten when his brother had cold cocked him last week. He kept pace with Ted as they walked briskly across the parking lot in the cold rain.

"Senior year all the partner's sons who are graduating get their picture taken for the wall of shame," Ted answered somewhat unenthusiastically.

Frank had to ask, "What happens if you don't get your law degree? Hell, Kent doesn't even offer a law school."

They reached the dryness of the back porch where they paused for a moment to drain off before entering the kitchen.

"Haven't you heard? I'm the fifth generation and my father is the senior partner. He's still pissed I didn't go to Penn State on a football scholarship. I don't have a choice but to become a lawyer and join his firm."

Frank considered Ted's plight for a moment. He always thought Ted was an interesting study in 1960s' materialism. Locked into his parents' view of his future to join the family law practice, Ted also had what was one the prettiest girlfriends back home in Pittsburg. Country club-raised, Elaine was, unfortunately, only sixteen. But she had the blessings of both sets of parents who were determined to co-mingle their families. So Ted was forced to miss college social life by driving home almost every weekend and all holidays.

Next to cross the growing mud lake was Ben Martin and Fred Thomas. They bolted up the steps and stopped next to Frank and Ted who was still trying to staunch the flow of blood from his nose.

Fred studied Ted and chuckled. "Now your nose looks sort of like mine." Fred knew he wasn't a pretty boy, but it hadn't affected his self-confidence. Back home in Aurora, he had had the distinction of being both smart and popular.

"Not funny," Ted muttered. "I'm going to go to Pill Hill and get this looked at." Pill Hill being the on-campus infirmary, it was the place to go for free medical help.

"You'll probably catch a terminal disease in there," Frank quipped. "Last quarter Pill Hill was under investigation by the health department."

Kevin Nash and his girlfriend Donna sloshed up onto the porch as the rain had grown even heavier. "Christ Ted, what the hell happened to you face?" Kevin wrinkled his nose and stepped back as if Ted's sudden ugliness was contagious.

"Kevin, why don't you re-break Ted's nose and get it straightened up?" Frank suggested.

"Kevin?" scoffed Ted.

"Why not? He's studying to be a chiropractor. What difference does it make? How different could it be? Adjust a back, a shoulder . . . a nose?" It made perfect sense to Frank.

"I wouldn't do that no matter how polluted I was," insisted Ted. "Anyone raiding the house refrigerator has seen what Kevin does to his lab partners."

"You're just jealous because I get to cut things up," answered Kevin. "And besides, I flunked out of cat anatomy, so I have to retake it this year. Plus I get to tear apart a rat next quarter."

Frank moved his hands to sweep across the sky as if reading a newspaper headline. "Dr. Kevin Nash leads the way in the development of a rat chiropractor program at Kent State. Rats with back problems all over the world are rejoicing. Members of The Weathermen rush to protest this new breakthrough discovery."

Everyone laughed except Ted who was still pinching his nose to stop the blood. The comment was even funnier because The Weathermen were a small group of leftist college student radicals that had gained a foothold on the Kent Campus known for their daily protests about any and everything, but particularly the Vietnam War.

"I'll drive you there," Donna volunteered. "I've got to go anyway. I've got a volleyball game tonight." She turned to Kevin. "You coming?"

Kevin shook his head. "Nah, I'm staying in tonight."

Donna didn't try to hide her look of disappointment. She was majoring in physical education and was a good match for Kevin except that Kevin had fallen two years behind in his classes. This and other evidences of what she perceived was his lack of initiative had, over the two years of their on-again/off-again relationship been the source of several of Donna's attempts to break up. She felt that Kevin never treated her like he loved her except when he was lonely. And he was so moody. His emotions spiked up or plummeted, depending on how things went at the house or at home or the weather or the way his hair looked or a hundred other variables. But whenever they broke up, he had always managed to talk her into coming back to him.

Don was one of the last out of the coach house along with Sam Douglas and Susie Parks, Barry Smith and his girlfriend, Carolyn, and Mike Anderson. Their trip across the thirty yards from coach house was less hurried as the downpour had slowed to a drizzle.

"It's good to have you playing ball again with us, Sam," Don said.

"I figured Mom was out at one of her afternoon teas, so the coast was clear."

Everyone still remembered Sam's run-in with the house mother, Mabel Brown two years earlier.

The third floor, at the time, had been used as one large dorm room. It wasn't heated and the practice had been to use electric blankets. When the electric blankets had become worn, electric sparks could be seen flashing in the dark of night whenever the bed's occupant would roll over. That one quarter saw more sparks coming from Sam's bed than a small town Fourth of July fireworks show.

None of the brothers really minded that Susie had sneaked in and slept in that third floor dorm room with Sam . . . and twenty five other men. It was only for one cold winter quarter when she had lost her lease for making too much noise. But when Mom found out, all hell broke loose.

There was a long list of behaviors that violated the house, college and fraternity rules. Alcohol and girls sleeping over were the most frequently challenged, but seldom broken. And while Mom never shared the information, she had never quite forgiven Sam for the position he had put her in.

"Yeah Mom is really big on the answers to her questions being truthful more than the acts themselves," Frank said and everyone nodded in agreement.

Sam knew he should have owned up to it as soon as she found out. The consequences were that he was now sharing a trailer in a lot across from the campus with Susie. He was missed at the house, but their trailer had become the location of some wild parties and as a hang-out spot between classes.

The last couple to arrive, Barry and Carolyn, was sort of the accidental couple of the fraternity. She was considerably taller than Barry and inch-for-inch more serious. If there was a negative point of view, Carolyn had it and could bring any party to a screeching halt. Barry, on the other hand, was the life of the party and would grab his guitar and lead a sing along or parody of a popular tune that he made up as he went along. From week to week no one knew if they were still together or not, and with Barry sharing a room with Kevin, few guys hung out there if they didn't have to. Since neither of them had anything positive to say about the females in their lives, it was pretty painful to listen to them bitch and moan.

Frank stomped the excess water off his shoes. "We're going to be late to our registration." That reminder sent most of the brothers charging into the house through the kitchen door while Sam and Susie headed toward Sam's VW bus.

"Come on Ted," Donna said.

"Can you drop me off on campus?" Carolyn asked. "I don't want to wait for Barry."

Donna agreed and they all ran through the increased downpour to Donna's Dodge Dart.

The traffic on Main Street heading east toward the campus was unusually heavy as hundreds of students were still moving into both the on-campus and off-campus housing. Donna kept adjusting the mirrors as they left the house. Kevin had borrowed her car that morning, and he had reset them all to fit him. The drive that should have taken fifteen minutes took closer to thirty minutes. The criminal justice and law enforcement majors standing at each intersection, stopping every car and giving directions wasn't that helpful if you already knew where you were going.

"So how are things with Kevin? Carolyn asked as she glanced over at Donna. The two girls seemed to have forgotten Ted was in the back seat.

"Fine. Why do you ask?"

"No reason really."

Donna slowly crept along the street.

"I was surprised to hear Kevin has to do his cat anatomy class over again," Carolyn continued. "Didn't he have a tough time with it last spring?"

"No shit, he did. And to make it worse, the head of the biology department is teaching it this quarter."

"Weren't you ready to break up with him last spring? Over his grades or his classes?"

Donna thought for a minute and readjusted the mirror on the windshield. "I wish he would get out of my blind spot." Donna hit the brakes and then resumed speed as the car on her right passed. "Ready? I did break it off. We didn't see each other over the summer except once."

"Why did you go back?"

"Kevin has a way of whining and hanging around and it just . . . well, wore me down I guess. Why do you ask? Do you want to take him off my hands?" she smiled and glanced over half seeking a reaction.

"Hey, I'm back here. I probably shouldn't be hearing this," Ted spoke from the back seat.

The girls continued as if they hadn't heard him.

"God knows I have enough trouble with Barry," Carolyn complained.

"Every time I go through this, and it happens too often, I'm torn between wanting him back and kicking him in the balls. How are you and Barry doing now that you're back from summer break?" Donna asked.

Carolyn turned toward Donna as if to reinforce the seriousness of what she was going to say. "I don't get how people wake up one day and all their feelings for someone are suddenly gone."

"With Barry?"

"Still back here," Ted called more loudly.

Donna gave him a dismissive wave, then said to Carolyn. "Yes, I do. Do you ever have that awkward realization that you have nothing in common with the person you sometimes love and sometimes hate?"

"Fuck!" Carolyn yelled and pounded her fist on her knee.

"What happened?"

"I think that you and I are in the same spot but for different reasons. I can't get a serious minute out of Barry. When we're talking and his guitar is there, he picks it up and starts singing…"

"…and badly too", Donna offers.

"*Very* badly. He just doesn't take life or us . . . or me seriously. How do you deal with Kevin putting off his classes and taking five years to graduate? What are you going to do when they draft him because he hasn't earned his degree after all this time?"

"He'll start his 6th year in January. I think he has become a professional student." Donna shrugged. "I don't know about him, but I'm graduating in the spring, and then I'm moving on . . . with or without him."

"This Vietnam thing worries me. Three years of investing myself with Barry, and I may have nothing to show for it," Carolyn lamented as she stared out the window at the students and parents carrying boxes and suitcases and pulling luggage carts into the dorms.

"Look, just drop me off here," Ted interrupted, almost frantic to escape the car and the conversation. "I'll walk the rest of the way."

"Sit tight. We're almost there."

Donna's Dart finally pulled onto the campus and headed to Pill Hill. Ted gratefully fled into the infirmary, and Donna continued the two blocks to Prentice Hall.

Prentice Hall was one of many women's dorms on campus. It wasn't one of the older dorms, nor was it new, and there were only two girls to a room. The baby boomers had put a definite crimp on the campus facility planning process. The only closer women's dorm to where most of Donna's physical education classes were held used to be a men's dorm. It was nearly forty years older and lacked a lot of the creature comforts like enough showers needed for that many girls to wash their hair on a Friday or Saturday night, the peak days of female fix-up. To compensate for the lack of full showers, the University took the time and expense to install hand sprayers on top of the old urinals in the bathrooms on every floor. Donna had spent her first two years in that dorm, but this year she had been able to get into the much preferred Prentice Hall.

"This is where I stop," Donna said as she looked solemnly at Carolyn. "I don't have the answers . . . wish I did. Barry's a decent guy, but then I used to think that about Kevin, too. Listen, you got my number if you need to talk."

Carolyn leaned over and hugged Donna tightly. "I'll tell you this much, the next time I follow my heart, I'm taking my brain with me." Her eyes welled with tears as she reached over and opened the door to leave.

CPSIA information can be obtained at www.ICGtesting.com
Printed in the USA
LVOW01s1722070414

380671LV00015B/1063/P

9 781492 876670